The Quira Chronicles Book One

KISMET

The fated are destined to take on the darkness.

KAREN DUBOSE
KATIE HOLLAND

Copyright

Kismet is a work of fiction. All names, characters, locations, and incidents are the products of the author's imagination or are used fictitiously. Any resemblance to actual events, locales, or persons, living or dead, is entirely coincidental.

KISMET: A NOVEL

Copyright © 2020 by Karen DuBose & Katie Holland
All rights reserved.

Editing by KP Editing
Cover Design by KP Designs
- www.kpdesignshop.com
Published by Kingston Publishing Company
- www.kingstonpublishing.com

The uploading, scanning, and distribution of this book in any form or by any means — including but not limited to electronic, mechanical, photocopying, recording, or otherwise — without the permission of the copyright holder is illegal and punishable by law. Please purchase only authorized editions of this work, and do not participate in or encourage electronic piracy of copyrighted materials. Your support of the author's rights is appreciated.

Table of Contents

Copyright 3
Table of Contents 5
Dedications 9
Chapter One 11
Chapter Two 14
Chapter Three 17
Chapter Four 20
Chapter Five 24
Chapter Six 28
Chapter Seven 32
Chapter Eight 35
Chapter Nine 39
Chapter Ten 43
Chapter Eleven 46
Chapter Twelve 50
Chapter Thirteen 53
Chapter Fourteen 58
Chapter Fifteen 62
Chapter Sixteen 66
Chapter Seventeen 69
Chapter Eighteen 73
Chapter Nineteen 77
Chapter Twenty 81
Chapter Twenty-One 84
Chapter Twenty-Two 88

Chapter Twenty-Three 92
Chapter Twenty-Four 96
Chapter Twenty-Five 100
Chapter Twenty-Six 104
Chapter Twenty-Seven 107
Chapter Twenty-Eight 112
Chapter Twenty-Nine 116
Chapter Thirty 120
Chapter Thirty-One 125
Chapter Thirty-Two 129
Chapter Thirty-Three 133
Chapter Thirty-Four 137
Chapter Thirty-Five 141
Chapter Thirty-Six 146
Chapter Thirty-Seven 150
Chapter Thirty-Eight 153
Chapter Thirty-Nine 157
Chapter Forty 161
Chapter Forty-One 164
Chapter Forty-Two 168
Chapter Forty-Three 171
Chapter Forty-Four 175
Chapter Forty-Five 179
Chapter Forty-Six 183
Chapter Forty-Seven 187
Chapter Forty-Eight 191
Chapter Forty-Nine 195

Chapter Fifty	199
Chapter Fifty-One	202
Chapter Fifty-Two	206
Chapter Fifty-Three	209
Chapter Fifty-Four	213
Chapter Fifty-Five	216
Chapter Fifty-Six	221
Chapter Fifty-Seven	225
Chapter Fifty-Eight	229
Chapter Fifty-Nine	233
Chapter Sixty	237
Chapter Sixty-One	241
Chapter Sixty-Two	246
Chapter Sixty-Three	250
Chapter Sixty-Four	254
Chapter Sixty-Five	258
Chapter Sixty-Six	262
Author's Note	268
About the Author	269
About the Author	272
About the Publisher	275

Dedications

We want to thank our families and friends for joining and supporting us on our crazy journey. Without you guys none of this would happen. Thank you from the bottom of our hearts.

We also want to thank our beta readers for taking a ride on this journey as well and helping us keep this baby on track.

Suzanne Cobb
Pat Labrie
Maggie Montgomery
Tara Bradley
Eryka Exum Cook
Kara Kieffer

Chapter One

VIOLET

"Violet, you've been out there forever. Are you ever going to come in?" Amy yelled from inside our apartment.

"In a minute," I yelled back.

I was watching the sunset. Dusk was my favorite time of day; it had been since I was a little girl. To me, there was something magical about the bright sun fading into the oranges, pinks, and yellows until it was totally gone. I'd always felt anything was possible at this time of day. Once I could no longer see any light left, I left the balcony and went back into the apartment.

"It's about time," Amy said, when I closed the sliding glass door. "We have to leave in like an hour."

I laughed. I could be ready to do anything in ten minutes. She needed at least two hours when we were going out to a club, which was what we were doing tonight.

"I'll be ready in plenty of time," I told her. "Are Becky and Lana meeting us there or are they coming here?"

"They're meeting us at the club."

"Okay, I'll be ready soon."

I closed the door to my room and went to my closet. Sliding the hangers over, I looked for what I wanted to wear. I wasn't a skirt kinda girl, so I picked out my favorite light blue halter top and paired it with some dark skinny jeans. As usual, my makeup was minimal, just mascara, lip gloss, and a small amount of blush. I decided to leave my hair down tonight. It was dark brown, straight as could be, and never took a curl. Finally, I slipped on a pair of silver strappy heels and I was ready.

Looking at the time I saw it wasn't even seven thirty, so I got out my phone and opened Instagram. The first three pictures were of Amy getting ready, no wonder it took her so long. I took a selfie, posted it, and then scrolled through the rest of my feed until Amy emerged from her room.

We left the apartment and got in the Uber she'd called. Ten minutes later, we were walking past the very long line and straight into the club. As usual, we were getting a lot of dirty looks from everyone in line.

"Good evening ladies," the bouncer said. "You look lovely tonight."

"Thank you, Bruce," Amy said with a wink.

Did I mention that Amy's dad owned the place? It was great. We never had to wait, drinks were always free, and we had our own reserved table every Friday and Saturday night.

Becky and Lana were already at our table when we got there. As soon as we sat down, we each had a drink delivered to us. Even though I was twenty-two, I wasn't a huge drinker and I always drank the same thing, a Cool Breeze. It was something my super cool aunt had made up. Malibu with Sprite and a hint of lime. And since she was the coolest person, I knew I stuck to her drink of choice.

Three Cool Breezes later I was ready to dance. I pulled Lana to the dance floor with me and we moved to the music. Most of the music they played here was fast and loud. Slow songs were almost nonexistent unless Amy wanted to hear one. She had her dad and all the staff wrapped around her finger.

Several songs later, I was parched and needed a drink. I motioned to Lana that I was going back to the table. She spotted a cute guy and latched onto him. I grinned and went back to our table.

Becky and Amy were both absent, but a new drink was waiting for me. I downed it and signaled for another. While I was waiting, I looked around the club. I loved people watching and this was a great place to do that.

As I was scanning the room, someone caught my attention. He was tall, at least six-three, had dark hair, and was hot as hell. But it was his eyes that I noticed first. Even across the dark club, I could tell they were the most gorgeous eyes I'd ever seen, and I couldn't even tell what color they were.

When our waitress delivered my drink, she stepped in front of my view of him. I thanked her and she left. I looked for the guy with the eyes, but he was gone. I even went so far as to leave the table and search for him, but there was no sign of him.

Something about him made me want to know more. Who was he? What was his name? Did he have a girlfriend? I laughed at myself, it must have been the several drinks I'd already had that night that had me curious. Guys rarely interested me. Most of them were so self-absorbed, I couldn't stand to be around them. But for some reason, this guy seemed different. I had no idea why since for all I knew he could be a serial killer.

Finishing my drink, I decided it was time to hit the dance floor again. It didn't matter to me if I had to dance alone, dancing made me feel free. I loved feeling the beat of the music and the way my body moved to it.

It didn't take long for someone to join me. He was cute enough, but not for me. I ignored him and soon he was replaced by another hottie, then another. Some people called me a bitch, but I liked to call myself picky. If there wasn't an initial spark with a guy, I knew he wasn't worth my time.

I saw Amy dancing with a cute blond guy, if what they were doing was called dancing. They were so close to each other you couldn't even get a piece of paper between them. I grinned at her. It looked like I'd be going back to the apartment by myself tonight.

Eventually, I was done for the night. Even though I'd had at least ten drinks I wasn't drunk, but that was normal for me. I figured it was all the dancing. I called an Uber to take me home.

Just as I was leaving, I thought I saw the guy with the eyes, but when I blinked, he was gone. Must have been my imagination.

Chapter Two

Waking up after dancing all night long you would think I would be sore. But I never was. I felt more energized and alive. Thankfully, today was my day off. I planned to be lazy today, but there were things I needed to take care of. Like visiting my favorite aunt Milana before she started to worry.

I jumped out of bed and headed straight to my bathroom to start the shower. I needed to get the smell of the club out of my hair. I could smell the cologne of all the guys that danced with me on my skin. That was the only bad thing about the clubs. Once the water was at the perfect temperature, almost burning my skin off hot, I jumped in and sighed. This was heaven.

Twenty minutes later, I was dressed and ready to go. I went and looked for Amy. She may not even be here if she got lucky last night, and from what I saw, she was having a great time with that blonde. I knocked on her door and listened for her response. When I didn't get any, I cracked open the door to see if she was here. Her bed was still a mess from last night. That gave me my answer. I left her a note on the counter before I headed out.

Getting into my car, I cranked up the music and backed out of the parking spot. As I headed for the freeway, I sped down the side roads. I loved to drive fast. The faster the better. Dancing in my seat, I couldn't help but think about the guy with those amazing eyes. I wished he would have come over to me last night. I hadn't gotten him out of my head since.

Hitting the on-ramp to the freeway, I punched it. My aunt lived over an hour away in Tupelo, Mississippi. I made it there in thirty-five minutes tops, every time. I couldn't wait to see her. It's been three weeks and we used to see each other every week until I moved away for work. Now, both of our schedules were jammed with work and other things. My Aunt Milana loved yoga. So much so, she now taught two classes every day except on Saturdays. She tried to leave that open for me.

I reached my exit and took it. I look down at the clock on the radio. Twenty-nine minutes. I'd beat my record. She lived two minutes off the freeway. Taking the last turn, I saw her house come into view. I slowed down and pulled into the driveaway. All the memories from living here invade me as I smiled. This will always be home to me. It didn't matter how old I got, this place was where my heart would always be.

The front door opened with a bang and my aunt came running towards me. "Violet!" she squealed. She wrapped her arms around me and squeezed me tight. "I was just starting to wonder if I was going to see you today. Let me see you." She moved me to arm's length. "By the gods, you look amazing. I'm kind of jealous," she said with a smile. I knew she was kidding.

"And you look just as amazing. Look at that body. Yoga is doing wonders there auntie." I loved to tease her about yoga. She'd been trying for years to get me to join a class. I just didn't want to. I'd been blessed to have a toned body. It didn't matter what I ate, I wouldn't gain a pound. I found this out when the man I loved broke my heart and I went on an eating binge. I didn't gain anything.

"What do you want to do today?" Aunt Milana asks.

"I was hoping we could go to the garden in the back. I need some therapy today."

She nodded her head and we walked around back. Most of the backyard was a garden with flowers, fruits, veggies, and herbs. The gazebo was covered with ivy we planted three years ago. This place was magic, and the aroma filled me with peace.

"This place amazes me every time I come here. I swear, it comes alive as soon as I walk into it."

She giggled. "I've always thought the same thing. I swear to you, it's like it's in a depressed mood when you're away. I got new carnations to plant. You want to do it?"

I twirled in her direction and smiled at her. "You know I do. Where are they?"

She laughed at me and took my hand. We walked to the shed on the outskirts of the garden. I looked at the mounds of plants. There had to be at least fifty new carnation babies. All I did was smile and got to work doing one of my favorite things, planting with my aunt and relaxing in a small heaven.

Five hours later, I heard both of our stomachs growl at the same time. We both looked at each other and laughed. "I take it you haven't eaten today?" she asked.

I shook my head at her. "Food was the last thing on my mind. I was too excited to come see you. You want to go to Kathy's for some soup and sandwiches? They don't have the good stuff in Southaven." After I graduated, a company there wanted to hire me. I couldn't turn it down when they told me how much I would make a year.

"That sounds amazing. Let's get cleaned up and we can go."

I jumped up and down with excitement as I followed her. It didn't take much to make me happy.

Chapter Three

The best thing about Kathy's were the desserts. The first thing you saw when you walked in was a huge glass case filled with cakes, pies, and pastries. I was definitely going to get a box or two to take home with me.

I ordered a bowl of broccoli cheddar soup and a club sandwich. It was good, but it was just a sandwich. When I was finished, I started wiggling in my seat.

"Go on," my aunt said smiling at me. "Go pick out what you want."

I practically ran over to the glass case. The lady behind the counter smiled at me.

"Violet, I haven't seen you in a while," she said. "How many boxes today?"

I grinned. "Just two."

She raised her eyebrows. "Cutting back?"

"Okay, three. You talked me into it."

My aunt and I had been coming to Kathy's for as long as I could remember. And that whole time Carol had been working there. She knew by now how much I loved a good pastry.

I watched as she filled three large pasty boxes with a variety of goodies from the case. She handed me the boxes and I handed her my credit card. By the time I finished paying, my aunt was ready to go.

We went back to the house and I brought in one of the boxes. I started with a brownie and then moved on to a slice of apple pie.

"I don't know where you put all that," my aunt said. "I've never seen anyone who could eat like you and stay so slim."

"I guess I was blessed with a super-fast metabolism."

My friends hated that I could eat anything I wanted and never gain a pound.

I spent the rest of the afternoon with my aunt. It was nice catching up and I promised I'd be back sooner rather than later.

There was more traffic on my way back to Southaven, so it took me forty minutes instead of the twenty-nine to get there. I grinned when I walked into our apartment and heard Amy singing. That meant she was in a good mood.

"Hey," I said.

She jumped. "You scared the shit out of me, Violet. You need to wear a bell or something. How the hell are you so quiet all the time?"

"I wasn't quiet," I said. "You were singing so loud, I heard you outside."

"Whatever," she said, but she was smiling.

"Did you have fun with Aunt Milana?"

"Always."

"I see you brought some of those famous pastries back, too."

"Of course. Help yourself," I told her.

"God, you know I can only eat like one of those right? Not everyone can eat a whole cake and look like you."

I shrugged. I was used to comments like that. In high school, most of the other girls hated me because of the way I looked. It used to bother me, but I was old enough now that I really didn't care what anyone thought of me.

"What time are we leaving tonight?" I asked her.

"Nine. You know everything gets started later on a Saturday."

"Okay. Did you eat today?"

Amy was always on some kind of diet and I worried that some days she was starving herself.

"Yes mom," she said sarcastically. "I had oatmeal for breakfast and a grilled chicken salad for lunch."

"What do you want to do for dinner?" I asked, ignoring her tone.

"Chinese?"

"Sounds good to me. I'll place the order," I told her.

"Something with lots of veggies for me," she said.

"No problem."

Neither one of us cooked, so we either ate frozen food, ordered take out, or made something super easy that we couldn't mess up, like toast or instant oatmeal.

The club was busy when we got there. As usual, we got the stares as we walked right in the door. It made me laugh every time.

I drank my first drink quickly and started scanning the crowd. I'll admit, I was looking for the guy with the eyes from last night.

A couple of hours and several drinks later, I saw him. This time I wasn't waiting around. I made my way through the crowd to where I saw him last. When I got there, he was gone. Frustrated, I went back to the table.

"What's wrong with you?" Amy asked, when I sat down.

"I saw this guy here last night. Then I saw him again just a few minutes ago, but I lost him in the crowd."

"Was he hot?"

Grinning at her I said, "Totally fucking hot."

"Don't give up," she said. "I'm sure he's still here."

I nodded. I intended to find him. Two drinks later, I was back on the dance floor with Becky.

"*Violet,*" I heard someone say.

"What?" I yelled to Becky. She gave me a funny look. "You said my name."

"No, I didn't," she told me.

I was sure I'd heard my name. I looked around to see if anyone was trying to get my attention, but no one was. I went back to dancing, but I had a strange feeling.

A couple of songs later, Becky had found a guy to dance with and I went back to the table. That's when I heard it again. It was the same voice from the dance floor, but there was no one around me. I looked up and saw the guy. This time he was looking directly at me from across the club.

I immediately left the table and went straight in his direction. Once again, he was gone when I got there. Who the fuck was this guy?

Chapter Four

Sunday mornings were the worst. Today was even worse than normal. I couldn't get that guy out of my head, or the voice. I knew I wasn't hearing things; it had been loud and clear like someone close by was calling my name. I didn't get much sleep last night because of it. That strange feeling followed me back home and I still couldn't get rid of it.

Jumping out of bed, I headed to the kitchen. I knew Amy wasn't up yet. She liked to sleep in on Sundays. She said it was to help with her beauty. She was already drop-dead gorgeous. Grabbing a bowl for cereal, something I couldn't mess up, I got the box and poured some in as I walked to the fridge and took out the milk.

I sat at the island and stared out the sliding glass door. What was up with that guy and why couldn't I just forget him? It was obvious he didn't want anything to do with me. If he did, then he wouldn't keep disappearing when he knew I was coming towards him. And what was up with the voice? Maybe I do need to go see a shrink or something.

"Good morning," Amy said, with a yawn.

I looked up at the clock and it wasn't even eight am. She normally didn't get up until after ten.

I turned to look at her with a puzzled look. "Are you feeling okay?"

She shrugged her shoulders. "Nothing like a nightmare to wake you up."

That piqued my interest and hopefully would take my mind off of mystery guy for a while. "What was it about?"

She plopped down in the next seat with her own bowl and poured herself some cereal. "This guy with red eyes was chasing me and kept asking where you were."

I scrunched up my face. "Me? Why would your nightmare guy ask about me?"

She looked at me sideways, giving me a 'like, I know' look. "Maybe he wanted to date you. How am I supposed to know? All I know is he messed up my beauty sleep. Now I'm going to look like hell tomorrow." She started to pout over her bowl of cereal as she took a bite.

I looked over at her. "I've told you before, you don't need beauty sleep. That's for people in their forties. We are far from it."

I'd try anything to get a smile out of her. But this time it didn't work. I guess that nightmare really got to her. I tried to remember what my aunt used to do when I had a nightmare. It always seemed to work. Maybe we should have a shopping day and get her out of the apartment for a while.

"I need some shopping therapy. What do you say we go hit up the mall and see what we can't find on sale?"

That got her to smile. "I'll be ready in thirty minutes."

She took off towards her bedroom and I did the same. Surely, this would take both our minds off of our troubles. If not, nothing would.

I was ready way before she was and decided to get some fresh air on the balcony. The view was perfect. You could see most of Southaven from here. I picked this apartment because I could watch the sun sink down into the city. It was amazing.

"Violet! I'm ready! Where are you?"

I slid into the kitchen and yelled. "I'm in here."

Just as I was locking the sliding glass door she appeared. "You love it out there way too much. I don't see how you can stand being out there all the time."

I shook my head at her. "How can you not love the view?"

She shrugged her shoulders. "It's nothing I haven't seen a thousand times. Are you ready? Let's get this therapy going. I hear Vera Bradley has a huge sale going on. I need a new purse."

I laughed at her. "I'm ready, too. Let's hit the mall and shop until we drop."

Twenty minutes later we were parked and walking up to the mall entrance when I got that unsettled feeling again, but worse. I looked around and didn't see anyone staring our way. I tried to ignore it. I linked my arm with Amy's and walked a little faster.

"Girl, if you don't slow down, I will drop before we even get to the first store. You know I'm a lot shorter than you."

It's true; her five foot nothing compared to my five foot ten was a big difference. I slowed down now that we were inside the mall where there were a lot of people to witness something if someone was following us. I didn't want to scare her.

"I'm just excited to be shopping. I need new work clothes and a new pair of boots." I really didn't , but I didn't want to seem off to her.

"Let's hit up that new store. I think they have boots there."

"Sounds good to me."

We shopped for hours. We went into almost every store on the bottom floor and we hadn't even made it to the second level yet.

"I don't know about you, but I'm starving. Want to hit up the food court or go somewhere else to eat?" I asked her.

"I was just about to say that. Food court. I'm not done shopping yet."

One thing I'd learned about Amy was that if you really didn't want to shop, don't ask her to go.

"Okay, let's go before my stomach eats itself."

She laughed as she dragged me to go eat. The smell of all that food made my stomach growl loudly. Next came the hunger cramps. I hated it when that happened. Entering the food court, I went to the first place I saw. It was a Chinese place and the best part was that it wasn't busy. Amy took off to the pizza joint. Her and pizza I swear, she could eat it every day if I let her.

I ordered my food and found an available spot for us to sit. As soon as I sat down, I got the feeling I was being watched. I slowly glanced around me, but didn't see anyone. This was getting out of hand. Either I was losing it, or they were really good at hiding.

Amy sat down along with Becky and Lana. "Look who I found."

I gave them a smile. "Well, well, well. Trying to sneak in a shopping spree without us?"

Lana looked at me like I was crazy... "You guys are shopping without us."

We all laughed. "I guess we're all guilty. What did you get?"

I really wasn't paying attention as they told us what they got. I was scanning the area to see if I could spot the reason I kept having that feeling. Just when I was about to give up, I saw him. The guy with the eyes. I stood up from my chair and marched over to him. There weren't a bunch of people for him to hide from me this time.

I was only ten feet away when he just vanished into thin air. I spun around to find him, but he was just gone. Now I knew I was losing my mind.

Chapter Five

"What was that all about?" Amy asked me, when I got back to the table.

"I thought I saw someone from work, but it wasn't them," I lied. There was no way I could tell them I just saw some guy disappear right in front of me.

The girls went back to talking about clothes, but I couldn't focus on the conversation. What the hell had just happened? People don't just disappear. Either something really strange was happening, or I was going crazy. Maybe I was more stressed out than I realized.

"Hello, earth to Violet," Amy said.

"Huh?"

"I said, are you ready to get back to shopping?"

"Oh, yeah, sure," I said. After whatever just happened, I really didn't feel like spending the rest of the day at the mall, but this was my idea, so I had to at least act normal.

A few hours later, we were finally leaving the mall. I'd kept my eye out for the disappearing guy the rest of the time we'd been there, but there was no sign of him and the feeling of being watched was no longer there.

Amy and I picked up Thai for dinner and hauled our numerous bags up to our apartment. I'd spent more than I'd planned, but I did get some really cute things for work.

With dinner finished it was Amy's turn to pick what we watched on TV. Since I had a lot on my mind, I really didn't care what she decided on.

When I noticed the time, I went out to the balcony for my nightly routine of watching the sunset. Sitting in my chair with a glass of wine, I relaxed for the first time in hours. Being outside always made me feel better and the colors of the setting sun had a calming effect on me. By the time it was dark, I felt a whole lot better.

As usual, Amy shook her head at me when I came in. She didn't understand my need to be out there every chance I got, but that was just fine with me. There were a lot of things she did that I didn't get either.

Eventually, I got bored with her stupid reality show and went to my room. I picked out my outfit for work the next day, then grabbed my tablet off my nightstand. One of the girls at work had suggested I read a series of books called Shady Oaks about a paranormal town in Kentucky. I was always up for a good paranormal read, so I downloaded the first book and read for the next hour or so.

I wasn't tired, but six am came early so I made myself put down my tablet and got ready for bed.

****

I was standing on a dark street. None of the stores were open and I was under the only streetlight that was on. Even though I couldn't see anyone, I knew I wasn't alone.

"Hello?" I called out. "Who's there?"

Silence.

"I know someone is out there. Show yourself," I yelled.

I heard a sound behind me and whirled around. It was the guy from the club.

"Who are you?" I asked.

He just looked at me and didn't say a word.

"What do you want with me?"

He took a step closer to me. Even though I was alone on a dark street with a complete stranger, I didn't feel like I was in danger.

Once again, he moved closer to me. I could reach out and touch him now if I wanted to. I almost did, but I forced my hand to stay at my side.

I wanted to say something else, but all I could do was stare at his face. It was perfect, more like a statue than a person. He was the most beautiful man I'd ever seen. His dark hair was artfully messy, his lips were slightly pouty and definitely kissable. But it was his eyes that had me completely transfixed.

They were a cross between green and blue and seemed to shine under the streetlight.

"You can't be real," I whispered.

"I'm most definitely real, Violet."

It was the same voice I heard at the club.

"Who are you?" I said again, but he was suddenly gone.

****

BEEP ... BEEP ... BEEP, my alarm blared. I finally found the snooze button and made the sound stop. I struggled to wake up. The dream I'd been having was stuck in my head. Something wasn't right, but I had no idea what. I laid there until my alarm went off again and finally got up. I put on my workout clothes and headed downstairs for my run.

As my feet pounded on the sidewalk, I couldn't get that strange dream off my mind, so I decided to think about this logically. First, at the club, it was entirely possible that he didn't actually see me looking at him or head in his direction. It was dark and crowded in the club, he could have been looking at me without really seeing me.

Second, maybe at the food court yesterday someone walked in front of me and the guy just got up and left. Third, last night it was just a dream about a guy I thought was hot. I wasn't going crazy and seeing or hearing things. Everything had a logical explanation. I kept telling myself that for my whole thirty-minute run.

Once I got back to the apartment, I showered and got ready for work. Amy was already gone, but she had a longer drive than I did. I pulled into my parking spot and made my way to my office.

"Morning, Violet," my assistant said. "Don't forget you have that meeting with Mr. Edington at nine."

"Thanks, Sue, it's on my calendar."

Peter Edington was the President of Edington Advertising and the only person I reported directly to. After graduating top of my class,

Edington snapped me up as fast as they could, and I was more than happy to take the position.

Sue brought me my first cup of coffee of the day and I made sure I was prepared for my meeting. We were trying to lure a new client to us and away from the current advertising firm they were using.

The day flew by and before I knew it, Sue was telling me she was leaving. I wanted to finish what I was working on. The next time I looked up from my computer, I realized I was the last one at the office and it was after six.

I grabbed my purse and went to the elevator. While I waited for it, I got that feeling again, like I was being watched. I started getting antsy and pressed the button a few more times. I knew that wasn't going to make the elevator go faster but it was helping my nerves.

I heard a ding and the door opened. Moving quickly, I got in and pressed the button to close the door. Just as the two parts of the door were almost shut, I thought I saw the blue-green eyes from my dream. I shook my head to clear it.

"You're not crazy, just hungry and tired," I said to myself. "Just get to your car and get home."

The elevator door opened on the parking garage level. I peeked out and looked around. Thankfully no one was there. I ran to my car and got in as fast as I could. Starting the engine, I roared out of there. Being in the car made me feel instantly better. I drove as fast as I could the entire way back to the apartment.

I walked in and went straight to the balcony. I sat in my chair and let the feel of the wind and the sunset relax me. I felt almost normal again when I went inside. Now, I just needed to get those eyes out of my head everything would be perfect.

Chapter Six

Almost a week had gone by and there had been no sign of the guy with the eyes. Maybe I just needed to get laid and be done with it. It was probably my mind telling me I needed to get some. It was the only logical thing I could think of. I couldn't be going crazy.

Amy was already getting ready for Friday night at the club. Maybe I just needed to be more open-minded about one night stands. I mean, what could it hurt? It wasn't like I was going to fall in love with the person. Right? I think that was the problem. I couldn't have sex with someone I had no spark or feelings for.

"Why does it look like you're thinking too hard?" Amy asked, as she walked out of her bedroom.

I looked up at her and smiled. "Just a project I'm working on at work," I lied again. I hadn't told her, or anyone for that matter about the guy with the eyes. They would all think I was nuts.

She gave me a 'yeah okay' look before she said. "Are you ready for tonight? Didn't you say Sue was coming tonight?"

I stood up and started to head for the sliding glass door. I didn't want to play twenty-one questions right now. I might end up blurting out everything and I wasn't ready for that. "I invited her. She said she would think about it and if she was coming, she would meet us there."

"You're acting strange. What's going on?"

Damn it. "Nothing. I want some fresh air is all."

She took a step towards me. "Are you sure? You can tell me anything."

This was one thing I couldn't tell her. Maybe when this all blew over then I could, but until then, it was staying locked up tight.

"Thank you and I know I can. It's just work. We have a huge client that's throwing everything we present to her back at us. If we lose her, we're screwed." That wasn't a lie. We do have a bitch we were dealing with.

"Okay, if you need to vent let me know. Alright?"

I nodded my head. "You'll be the first person I come to. Now go finish getting ready. We only have three more hours before we have to leave. I'll order us a pizza soon."

She jumped with excitement. "This night just got better."

I watched her run to her room and shut the door. That was a close one. I needed to get my shit together around her.

I ordered the pizza and made my way out the sliding glass door to my favorite spot and watched as the sun slowly dipped down behind the city. How could anyone not want to watch this every night? All of my stress slowly went with the sun. Just as the sun disappeared, the doorbell rang. I got up to go get the pizza.

When I opened the door, a very distraught Sue was standing there. It took me a minute to realize I was staring at her. I moved to the side to let her. "What's wrong, Sue?"

Her mascara stained face looked up at me. "I didn't know where else to go. I was on my way out the door when I got robbed. He took everything. My wallet, keys, money. Everything!" she sobbed.

I took her into my arms and tried to calm her down. "Let's call the police. You can stay here until we can figure something out."

Amy came racing into the living room and stopped. "What's going on?"

I told her what happened. She called the police while I held on to Sue. I couldn't even imagine what she was going through right now. I would be scared to even go to my apartment if I knew someone had the key to it.

I rubbed her back and asked, "Do you remember what he looked like?"

She nodded her head. "He was over six feet tall and fat. He smelled of whiskey and like he hadn't bathed in a really long time. His beard was scraggly looking. Black hair and those black eyes. I swear to you they were black."

"It's okay. If that's what you saw, then that's what you saw. Is there anything else you can remember? What was he wearing maybe?"

She sat up and stared at nothing. She was trying to remember what else she could think of. "He had on a baby blue shirt with holes and black jeans with holes in them, too. I didn't see what kind of shoes he was wearing."

With that much detail, I'm surprised she was even alive to tell us. He must really have wanted the money and didn't care about anything else.

There was another knock on the door. This time Amy answered it. I brought my attention back to Sue. "Do you want anything to drink? I can get you water, soda, or even something stronger if you prefer."

She gasped. "Oh no, I ruined your night. I can leave and go somewhere else. I don't want you to have to sit with me and miss out on your club night. I'm so sorry… I shouldn't have come here." She started to stand up to leave. I grabbed her arm and gently pulled her back down.

"You are not going anywhere. You did the right thing by coming to me. If you didn't show up, I would have been worried and especially if you didn't answer your phone since he has it. We'll get you a new phone tomorrow and we will also go get your stuff," I told her.

Sue let out another sob. "Are you sure? I don't want to be a bother."

I patted her shoulder. "I'm sure."

Amy walked in with three plates full of pizza. "You need to eat something before the cops come. They'll be here for hours getting your statement. We can't let great pizza go to waste." She handed each of us a plate and plopped down on the floor in front of us.

"Thank you. Both of you," Sue said. "I really had no other place to go. My family lives in Washington state. I moved here to get away from an abusive ex. That guy brought back all those memories. All I did was stand there and cower down like some child. All those self-defense classes didn't do anything."

I grabbed her hand. "It's okay. Those classes don't work for everyone. PTSD is nothing to be ashamed of. You did the right thing. Come on, let's eat before it gets cold."

Fifteen minutes later, the cops finally arrived. I decided to go outside and let her have some privacy. Amy went to the club after I told her it was fine and to go have fun. I really wasn't in the mood to be there anyway. Sue needed me more than drinking and dancing, or worse, running into the guy with the eyes. If he was even real, that is. At this point, I was starting to think I needed to seek out some help or I was going to lose my mind altogether.

Chapter Seven

It seemed to take forever for them to take Sue's statement. As she recounted what happened, I could see she was still shaken up. It was after ten by the time the cops left.

It turned out that Sue wasn't this guy's first victim, but with her description, they told her there was a good chance they could find him.

There was no way I was letting Sue leave our apartment, so I gave her something to sleep in and made her take a shower to help her relax. I told her to use my bedroom. I could tell she was exhausted and needed to sleep. Tomorrow we were supposed to call the police when she was ready to go home. They wanted to make sure the guy wasn't there and that nothing had been taken.

When I knew she was asleep, I stepped out onto the balcony. It had been a stressful night and I wasn't even the one who got mugged. I took a few deep breaths and let the gentle wind calm me down.

I stayed out there for about an hour. When I came in, I picked up my tablet instead of turning on the TV. I went back to that book I started. I really wanted to see what happened next.

I guess at some point, I fell asleep because the next thing I knew my tablet fell off the couch and woke me up. It took me a minute to realize I was on the couch in the living room.

"Violet," a voice said.

I was instantly awake. It was the same mystery voice. I sat up and looked around the dark room. There was a strange current in the air.

"Who's there?" I said weakly.

"Violet," it said again.

I started to say something when I felt something brush my hand. That made me jump up off the couch and run to the kitchen. I grabbed a knife and held it out in front of me.

"Who's there?" I said, trying to sound like I wasn't totally freaked out.

"We'll meet soon enough," the voice said.

Suddenly, the strange feeling in the air was gone and I knew I was alone again. I turned on the lamp and sat back down on the couch, the knife still in my hand. I set it on the coffee table and pulled my feet up. I hugged my knees to my chest and thought about what just happened.

It wasn't a dream; I knew that for a fact. I was positive there was a ... well, a ... something talking to me, that they'd been in the living room with me, but I couldn't see them. Wow, that sounded super crazy.

There was no way I was going back to sleep after that so I turned on the TV and waited until Sue was up.

When she woke up, we met the police at Sue's place. There was no sign anyone had been in there, so that made her feel a little better. I took her to get a new lock and it took the two of us an hour to replace it. We ended up laughing more than working. Let's face it; neither one of us was a handyman. I spent the rest of the day with Sue and only left when I felt she would be okay alone.

Saturday night we went to the club. The only reason I was there was to see if the guy with the eyes was there. After spending a few hours looking for him, I left and went home. It was like there was something inside me driving me to find this guy. I didn't understand it but I couldn't get rid of the feeling.

The rest of the weekend was uneventful. I checked on Sue a few times and she was doing okay. She was one tough cookie if you asked me. I think I still would have been terrified.

By Sunday afternoon, I was bored out of my mind and actually looking forward to going to work Monday morning.

My alarm went off the next morning and I didn't even hit snooze. I got ready and headed to work. It wasn't a surprise that I was the first one there, it happened at least three times a week. I checked my email and saw one from my boss that he'd sent late Friday. We had a meeting with a new client first thing this morning. He wanted me to do some quick research on their company. I pulled up the internet and typed in Selgan Inc.

After twenty minutes of reading, I was really impressed with this company. They built low cost, high-end housing for people in need. A percentage of profits were donated to women's shelters, inner-city rec centers, and to helping the homeless. I decided I was going to really like this client.

"Mr. Edington is ready for you," Sue said, popping her head in my office.

"Great, Sue. Thank you."

I grabbed my notepad and pen off my desk and went down the hallway to the conference room.

"Violet," Mr. Edington said with a smile. "I'd like you to meet Aviel Mann, owner of Selgan Inc."

When the dark-haired man turned around, I stopped in my tracks. It was him, the guy from the club with the eyes.

"It's a pleasure to meet you, Violet," Aviel said.

I couldn't move. Not only was he the guy with the eyes, but that was also the same voice I'd heard from the person I couldn't ever see. Something was very seriously wrong here.

Chapter Eight

I gathered my courage and tried to speak normally. "It's nice to meet you, Aviel." I know he could see right through me at how freaked out I was.

He walked over to me and stretched out his hand for me to shake. "I can't wait to work with you. We're going to be spending a lot of time together."

I slowly took his hand. As soon as we touched, I felt a sense of home. Why or how that was even possible was beyond me, but it felt so right and wrong at the same time. I jerked my hand away from him and looked over to my boss. "Is there anything else you need me to do before this meeting starts?"

I needed some space to wrap my head around all of this. If not, I might just say what was on my mind in front of Mr. Edington. That would make me look like an idiot.

"Can you ask Sue to bring us lunch in a few hours and to bring us coffee when she gets the chance?"

"Yes Sir, I'll be back shortly," I said, and left the room.

I'd never moved so fast in my life. I needed some fresh air. I grabbed Sue by the arm and dragged her outside with me.

"Are you okay? You look like you've seen a ghost or something."

I looked around me to make sure we were alone and told her everything. How he had been haunting me ever since the first night I saw him in the club. How he disappeared at the mall. I know I sounded crazy as fuck, but it all happened. I know it did.

"To top it all off, when we touched, I got the feeling like I was finally home. How the fuck can you explain that?"

Sue stared at me wide-eyed. She'd never seen me like this. Hell, I'd never seen me like this. What had this guy done to me?

"I believe you," she said. "I just never thought I would see the day you would freak out like this. You've always been level headed. Even when I showed up at your apartment, you had it all put together. I envy you."

I snapped my head in her direction. "Why would you envy me of all people? I'm nobody special, Sue."

She shook her head. "That's where you're wrong. You got snatched up right out of college and were hired for your dream job that most people would kill for. You have friends that would die for you if they had to. I have no one here."

I grabbed her and hugged her. "But you do have someone and that someone is me. You're not alone here. Got it. Come on. I've been gone long enough and I need you to get us lunch and when we get up there please bring us coffee and lots of it. I'm going to need it to make it through this meeting."

She smiled at me. "You got it, girl. Thank you for being there for me this weekend. It meant a lot to me."

I waved her off. "It was the least I could do."

I walked back into the meeting with a fake smile on my face. There was no way I was going to let this guy know he'd gotten under my skin. As I sat down I took one of the folders and opened it. "What did I miss?"

Aviel looked me up and down like I was his prey. I didn't give him the satisfaction of reacting to him. "Nothing. I wanted to wait until you got back. Since I'm the one who hired you to work on this project, I want you to know everything about it."

Arrogant much? "Awesome, so what is it you want out of this?"

I was asking about more than just this project, hoping he would get the message. As he stared at me with those unbelievable eyes, I couldn't help but get a little lost in them. The sense of peace and home swirled inside me. I shook my head to clear it. I needed to get a grip and soon, or something bad was going to happen.

"I want everything you can offer," he said, looking directly at me. "My business is booming and I want to keep it that way. I want something positive to show the world. There is too much negativity and not enough good. Don't you think?"

Okay, so that wasn't what I expected from him. "You're right. There is too much negativity in the world. But do you think we could change that? I'm great at my job, but to change the minds of others is something I can't do."

I needed this guy to know there was no way I could do such a thing. I wasn't a miracle worker.

"But that's where you're wrong. I've seen your work. You've changed the lives of a lot of people, even if you think you haven't. Every single person you've helped is a better person than what they used to be. I think together the two of us can do wonders."

Okay, this guy needed a dose of reality before he was too far gone. "I highly doubt that was me. Some people just want a better life. I just happened to work with them. But I will work with you the best I can and try my hardest to make this the way you want. Tell me more about your business."

We talked for hours until Sue popped in with lunch. The smell of food made my stomach growl loudly. I looked at Aviel and my boss, both of them had smiles on their faces. I ducked my head down as I got up to help her. I whisper to her, "Thank you, you're a lifesaver. I needed a break."

She gave me a smile and slightly nodded to me. "Is there anything else I can get anyone?"

"Can you get me a Propel water? Please," I asked

"Sure thing. Anyone else?"

"I would like a Propel water, too," Aviel said.

Mr. Edington piped in. "More coffee would be great please."

"I'll be back shortly," Sue said, as she ducked back out of the room. I envied her right now. The energy between me and Aviel was getting unbearable. A part of me wanted to jump his bones, and the other part wanted to run as far away from him as I could. If this is how it was going to be every time he was around me, then I needed to figure out how to deal with it, or I just might end up fucking his brains out and not regret it.

Chapter Nine

It wasn't until Mr. Edington cleared his throat that I realized I'd been staring at Aviel. I noticed the smirk on his face and quickly looked away. I normally had more control of myself, but there was something about him that was cracking my ever present control.

"How did you end up starting your company?" Mr. Edington asked Aviel.

I was grateful for the distraction.

"For as long as I could remember, I was interested in building things and I've always had this need to help people. When I got old enough, it just kind of happened. I've been very lucky."

"You seem quite young for having such a successful company," I said, without thinking.

"I'm not as young as you think I am," he said, with an intense look. "I could say the same thing about you, Violet. You're awfully young to be in the position you're in."

"I'm good at what I do," I said, defending myself.

"And, so am I."

It was like an old western standoff, only I wasn't sure what the issue was. I shook my head and took a drink of my water. I needed to get this meeting back on track, so I started asking him questions about what he saw for the future of his company.

Despite the strangeness that was going on with us, I could see he was very passionate about what he was doing. It was refreshing that it wasn't all about the money for him.

"Excuse me, Mr. Edington," Sue said from the door, "it's time for your next meeting."

"Oh yes, thank you, Sue. Tell Kristi I'll be right there. Mr. Mann, it's been a pleasure. You're in good hands with Violet."

"I'm sure I am," Aviel said, with a smile.

I watched as he left the conference room and I was left alone with Aviel. The second the door closed and it was just the two of us, it was like the air was suddenly charged with electricity.

"Who are you?" I asked, in almost a whisper.

"I'm many things, but right now, I'm just Aviel, a businessman in a meeting."

I'd never been so confused in a meeting before and it was starting to make me mad. I had to forget about all the weird feelings he was giving me and just focus on business.

I gave myself a mental shake and I was back where I needed to be. We spent the next hour talking about what he had in mind for his advertising campaign.

"I think this is going to be a great partnership," Aviel said, as we wrapped up the meeting.

"Thank you for choosing Edington Advertising," I said.

"I'll be in touch," he said, and held out his hand for me to shake it.

I was hesitant because when I did that before, I had that strange sensation of being home, but it would be rude just to leave him standing there, so I put my hand in his. This time it was just a normal handshake. I watched him walk out of the conference room.

As soon as he was gone, I went back to my office with Sue right behind me.

"I'm so over this day," I told her.

"How did the rest of the meeting go?" she asked.

"Like a normal meeting," I said. "I think I imagined the feeling I had before."

"Don't start with that," Sue said fiercely. "You're not crazy or imagining things. There are things in this world that can't be explained, but that doesn't mean they aren't real."

"What are you trying to say?"

"Maybe Aviel is different. I mean, what kind of name is that anyway, I've never heard of anyone with that name before."

Sue kept talking, but I wasn't listening. There was definitely something different about him, but I had no idea what it was.

"I need a drink," I said, interrupting her.

Sue giggled. "He really got to you, huh? Well, considering you've been trapped in the conference room for almost the entire day, I think you can take off a little early today. There's nothing on your schedule that can't wait until the morning so go home. Make yourself a drink and put your feet up."

"I think I will," I said, and turned off my computer. Five minutes later I was in my car and driving out of the parking garage.

Instead of making the right-hand turn that went to my place I turned left and headed for Tupelo. I really needed to talk to my aunt.

I didn't go as fast as I normally did on my way there as there's just too much traffic in the city, but I still make it there in under an hour. As soon as I pulled up in front of the house, I saw her coming out to greet me.

"How did you know I was coming?" I asked, as I gave her a hug.

"I always know when you need me, Violet. Now, come in and tell me what's on your mind."

There was a cup of tea waiting for me on the coffee table when I walked into the living room. I picked it up and sat down in my favorite big puffy chair.

I told her everything. First time I saw him in the club, the voice I kept hearing, the dream and finally meeting him today as a client. My aunt was what most people considered a free spirit, so I knew she'd believe me. I just had no idea what she was going to say about it.

After a few minutes, she still hadn't said anything and when I looked at her face, she looked worried.

"What's wrong?" I asked her. "Do you think I'm going crazy?"

"No honey, but what I'm about to tell you might sound crazy, but every bit of it is true. I know you don't know much about your mom since she died giving birth to you, but she and I were close. No two sisters had ever been closer and we told each other everything. So, when she came home one day and told me about this boy she kept seeing, I didn't think much of it. But then she started hearing a voice and when she finally got to meet this boy, she knew he was the one talking to her in her head. When they touched, it was like no one else existed. She told me that his touch made her feel a sense of belonging that she couldn't fully explain.

"As soon as she turned eighteen, she ran off with him. A year later, she came back very pregnant and alone. All she told me about this man was that he was called back to heaven. I assumed he died and she couldn't bring herself to actually say it.

"The day you were born your mother was as happy as I'd ever seen her. She kept telling me that she was finally going to join her love. I had no idea what she was talking about and then when the doctors couldn't save her, I understood. Somehow, she knew she wasn't going to survive the day and was going to see him again in heaven."

I sat there, not sure what to say at first. "Why didn't you ever tell me this?" I wanted to know.

"Because it made her sound crazy and I know she wasn't," my aunt said. "But something similar seems to be happening to you and it was time to tell you."

"I don't know what to think about all of this," I told her. "What was my father's name?"

"I wish I could tell you, but I don't know. The only thing she ever called him was 'my angel'. She never used his name. I'm sorry sweetheart."

"I think I need to go and think about all of this," I told her.

She gave me a hug and I felt like a little kid again, safe in her arms.

"I love you," I told her.

"I love you too honey. Be safe and let me know when you get home."

"I will." I got up and walked out the door, got in my car and started driving.

Chapter Ten

I took my time getting home. I had a lot to think about. What did this all mean? Was I going to fall madly in love like my mom and have him die on me? Why did I feel the way I do around him? There was so much I still didn't know and it was driving me bat shit crazy. On one hand, I wanted to see if he felt the same as I did, and on the other hand I just wanted him to remove himself from my life so it could be normal again. But was that what I really wanted? To be normal again?

I pulled into my parking spot and shut the engine off. Sitting there trying to figure out what it was I really wanted; I did something I hadn't done since I was a little girl. I prayed for guidance. I'd always believed there was something higher up watching us and helping us get through this life. If we just listened, it would guide you on the right path.

Hopping out of the car, I headed straight to the balcony when I got to our apartment. The sun would be setting soon, and I didn't want to miss it. Especially not tonight when I needed it the most. I needed to feel the peace and calm.

I sat there staring out at the open sky as the colors faded into darkness. The sun set a while ago, but I couldn't seem to move to go inside. It was like I was rooted in that spot for some reason.

"I know you think you're going crazy, but I assure you, you're not."

I whipped around to see Aviel standing there leaning against the brick wall with a relaxed stance. How could one man be so damn sexy, and smart?

"What the hell are you doing here and how did you get up here?"

He didn't move as he took me in with those bluish-green eyes that seemed to have purple and black specks. He watched my every move until I finally got his attention. "Hello! Earth to Aviel! Are you going to answer me or not?"

There was no way I was letting him see just how much his stare was causing my lady bits to rear their heads. He pushed off the wall. "I came by to ask if you would like to have dinner with me."

I was so shocked by his question, I forgot that he just appeared out of nowhere on my balcony.

Everything inside me was screaming yes, but a small part of me knew if I went, things might happen that couldn't be taken back. Was it really worth it? The hell with it. "Sure."

His smile stretched across his face as he walked towards me. "Shall we," he said, as he gave me his arm. As giddy as I was inside, I played it cool and took his arm.

We left the apartment and headed straight to the only expensive restaurant in town. Calbo's had a waiting list for months. I was about to tell him that before we got to the door, but a man in a uniform was waiting for us.

"Ah, Mr. Mann, how great it is to see you again." Then he turned to me. "And this must be Miss Lathan. It's a pleasure to meet you. Please follow me."

I took a look around the place. It wasn't my first time coming here, but it was my first time being here that wasn't for a meeting, or was it? Is that why he asked me here, to talk about work? I sure hoped not. We were shown to a corner table away from the rest of the crowd, which I was thankful for.

The hostess told us the specials and asked for our drink order. After she was gone, I looked at the man sitting across from me. In a way, I felt extremely lucky to be having dinner with someone like him. He cared about people and not just himself. Which, for a man in his shoes, was something unheard of. Most people, even women, forget about the small people who helped them get to where they were today and that was sad.

"I'm glad you agreed to have dinner with me. I wanted to ask you something."

I looked up from my menu and gave him my full attention. "What is it?"

"I know we just met and all, but there's a connection between us. I know you feel it, too. I was wondering if maybe we could spend time together and see where it leads." The shocked look on his face when he was done talking almost made me laugh. "I'm so sorry, I didn't mean for it to come out like that. Let's just forget I said anything and enjoy our meals."

I smiled at him and shook my head. "No, you're right. There is something between us. To tell you the truth, it scares the hell out of me. If we're being honest, a part of me wants to, but the other part is telling me to run and never look back."

There was no point in beating around the bush. He opened this conversation, and I felt the truth was the only way to go. Besides, I wanted to ignore that part of me that was telling me to run. I hadn't ever had a spark like that with a guy and I wanted to see how this turned out. Hopefully, my heart could take it if he decided this wasn't what he wanted.

His smile melted my heart a little. "I feel the same way. I really do want to get to know you better. I feel like we may have a lot in common." The rest of the evening we sat there and talked for what seemed like hours. It was a really nice change for once.

Chapter Eleven

It was late when Aviel pulled up in front of my building. I didn't want to get out of the car, but I knew I had to.

"Thank you for dinner and the company. I had a great time," I said.

"You are very welcome, Violet. I had a great time, too."

I really wanted to lean over and kiss him, but I wasn't not sure if I should. Moments later, the decision was made for me. The feel of his lips on mine was by far the best thing I'd ever felt. His kiss was like nothing I'd experienced before. I felt it in every inch of my body.

"Wow," I whispered when he pulled back.

He chuckled. "It's been a pleasure, Violet. I'll see you soon."

Slowly I got out of the car and entered my building. I turned around, but he was already gone. I thought about that kiss all the way to my apartment. It wasn't until I was in bed, that I remember him just seeming to appear on the balcony with me and that he never told me how he got into the apartment. I was definitely asking Amy about that in the morning.

Tuesday morning, I got up, went for a run, then showered. I missed Amy, which was weird because she never left early. I decided to text her when I got to work. After getting dressed and grabbing a granola bar, I got in my car and took off.

All I could think about was the kiss with Aviel last night. It was hardly more than a peck on the lips, but I could still feel his lips on mine. I blinked and had to slam on my brakes. When I finally stopped, I was only inches away from the car in front of me.

"Get it together, Violet," I told myself. The last thing I needed was to get into an accident on the way to work because I was thinking about a guy.

I arrived at work without any more incidents and when I got to my desk, I pulled out my phone to text Amy.

Me: Did you let someone into our apartment last night?

She was quick to respond.

Amy: Yes. He said he knew you. OMG, are you ok?????
Me: I'm fine and yes, I knew him. I was just surprised to suddenly see him standing on the balcony.
Amy: So, you're not mad at me?
Me: No. Is that why you left early?
Amy: Yes
Me: Next time just let me know ok?
Amy: Ok

I felt a little better now that I knew he didn't just appear out of thin air. I guess I was just too caught up in the sky to hear him come out to the balcony. Wait a minute, how did he know where I lived? There seemed to be more questions than answers when it came to Aviel. Questions that really should be concerning me, but for some reason didn't seem that important.

For the rest of the day, I was completely focused on work. I had a million emails to return, two meetings with clients, and a storyboard to complete. I was grateful I had a lot to do, so I didn't have time to think about him.

"See you tomorrow," Sue said, at the end of the day.

"Bye," I said and waved.

I quickly finished the email I was working on then left. When I got home, I knew Amy was apologizing when I saw the box of cupcakes on the kitchen counter.

"You didn't have to get me cupcakes," I yelled.

She came out of her room. "I know, but I feel bad. He was just so convincing and hot."

I smiled at her and took a seat at the island. "Yes, he is both of those things."

"But you do know him, right?"

"Yes. He's a new client, but I think I've seen him at the club a couple of times too."

"Ooooh, hot, successful, and likes to party, can I have him ... please?"

"No, you cannot. He kissed me last night."

I'd been dying to tell someone, and this was the perfect opportunity.

Amy squealed. "Is he a good kisser? I bet he's an excellent kisser." She was practically jumping up and down.

"I felt it all the way down to my toes," I admitted.

"Oh my God Violet, that's awesome. Are you seeing him again?"

"I don't have his number," I said and I realized I was disappointed.

"But you said he's a client, so maybe Sue can find it?"

"I'm not going to get his number from work. If he wants to see me again, he knows where to find me."

"God, you can be so stubborn sometimes. It's not the 1950's anymore. Women can go after what they want, even men."

"I know," I said. "But I'm still not going to have Sue find it for me. I think I need a cupcake." Yes, I was totally changing the subject.

Amy shook her head at me, but didn't say anything else about it. I ate a cupcake, okay-- I ate three cupcakes and changed out of my work clothes. I put on some yoga pants and a tank top and plopped down on the couch. It was my turn to pick what we watched, and I was in the mood for some Stranger Things.

I ordered us some dinner. An hour later, I was stuffed and quite content to spend the rest of the night on the couch. Just as I was getting into the latest episode my phone rang, it was Sue.

"Hey," I said, when I answered.

"Hey, I need a favor. The police think they caught the guy that mugged me, and I need to go to the station and see if I can identify him. I really don't want to go by myself and I was wondering if you'd go with me."

"Of course, I will."

"Good, I'm downstairs in the car."

I laughed. "I'll be right there." I put on some shoes, grabbed a hoodie, and went down to meet Sue.

Chapter Twelve

Once we got to the police station, I pulled her to the side. "You've got this. Don't be afraid to identify that asshole. He won't be able to see you."

She looked up at the station then back to me. "I don't want him to do something like that to someone else."

I wrapped my arm around hers and we headed inside. She went to the front desk and told them what she was there for. The lady officer asked her to take a seat, and they would come and get her when they were ready for her. I found us two seats that were together. For a Tuesday this place was packed. I didn't think our town had so much crime.

"You kept yourself busy today. Would that be because of a certain guy we know?" She wagged her eyebrows up and down.

I laughed at her. "Maybe." Was all she was getting out of me. We weren't here for me.

She scrunched up her nose. "There's no maybe to it. It was. Have you heard from him since the meeting?"

I nodded my head and jumped up and down in my chair. I told her everything from the night before.

"Damn Violet! You go girl. Now I really do envy you. To have a hot guy like that interested in you. Makes my own body ready, you're one lucky woman."

I gave her a sad smile. "I may be lucky, but I really don't know him all that well, yet. For all I know what I've seen isn't who he really is. Hell, he could be a killer for as much as I really know about him."

Just thinking about that sent shivers down my spine. I sure hope he wasn't a killer.

"Girl please, a man like that is not a killer. You need to stop thinking like that. Just be happy and see where it goes. If it doesn't work out, it doesn't work out. Have fun."

"You know what, you're right. I'm going to have fun." I stood up and stretched. Just as I was about to say something else, the female officer called Sue's name. "If you would follow me ma'am, I'll take you to the room."

Sue looked like she was about to flee. I gently placed my hand on her shoulder. "I'll be right here when you're done."

She gave me a weak smile. "Okay."

I watched her disappear around the corner. I took a seat and pulled my phone out. I needed to get to the bottom of Mr. Mann. There had to be something about him. There was no way he could just disappear like that. I was sure he did. I just had to prove it.

After twenty minutes of research, I didn't learn very much. I now knew he was thirty-years-old. Had no kids or wife. Lived outside of Southaven. That was about all I could find, that and how huge his business was . By the time I was done, I looked up to see Sue coming back. Her face looked relieved and I was hoping that was a good thing.

"I'm hoping that look on your face means you identified the guy?"

She nodded her head. "He was in there. They also got my wallet back. He had it on him."

"Are you serious?"

She nodded again. "Apparently, he had a few on him."

I shook my head. "Let's get out of here."

As we walked back to her car, I saw Aviel leaning against it with his arms crossed.

"What are you doing here?"

He pushed off the car and walked towards me. "I went to see you tonight and Amy said you were here with Sue. I wanted to make sure you two were okay."

My heart melted a little. "Thank you. She got the man who robbed her. The streets are a little safer."

He took my hands into his. "If it's okay with Sue, I'd like to take you home."

We both looked over at her. The smile on her face gave me the answer.

"It's totally fine by me," she said. "Have a good night. I'll see you in the morning."

Without another word, she got into her car and drove off. I looked at Aviel and smiled at him. "I guess it's just you and me. Are you ready to take me home?"

He shook his head. "Not until I get some food in you. I heard your stomach growl a few minutes ago."

I guessed my stomach was louder than I thought. Even though I ate a few hours ago I was hungry again "That sounds like a plan. Where are we going tonight?" Anytime spent with him was great in my book. I still couldn't stop thinking about that kiss and hoped to get another one tonight.

"I was hoping I could cook for you. That is, if you'd like to come over."

Shock went through me. Did I want to go over there alone? Hell yes! "Sure, I would love that."

We got into his car and arrived at his house within ten minutes. He drove just as fast as I did and I loved it. Could this man be any sexier?

Chapter Thirteen

I was expecting his place to be some great big mansion in a gated community, so I was surprised when we ended up at an old farmhouse in the country.

"This is unexpected," I said honestly.

He laughed. "I try to live like I run my company. I bought this and recently renovated it. Almost all of my work is in the city, but my heart belongs out here."

I was a city girl through and through, but I had to admit it was peaceful out here.

He opened the door and turned on the light. The house was stunning and nothing like I thought a farmhouse should be. It was light and airy in a way that was modern but still country. I didn't really know how to describe it other than welcoming.

"This is amazing," I said, as we walked into the kitchen.

"Thank you. I did everything myself."

Aviel was hot, successful, and considerate. And now I could add talented to that list. I watched as he started pulling things out of the fridge, oh yeah and he could cook too. He was almost too perfect. There had to be a catch and I wondered what it was.

"Is it okay if I take a look around?" I asked.

"Sure, the food will be ready in thirty minutes. Make yourself at home."

As I wandered around the main floor, I was continually amazed by each room. There was the same overall feeling of peacefulness in each room. I'd only been here a few minutes and I was in love with this house. If I ever decided to build a house, Aviel was definitely going to be the one to build it.

My exploring was interrupted by the wonderful smell coming from the kitchen, so I went back to see what Aviel was making.

"Whatever is in that pan smells fantastic," I told him.

"Homemade alfredo sauce," he said with a smile. "I hope you like chicken alfredo."

"Love it. Actually, I eat pretty much anything," I said.

"Bonus points for not being picky," he said, and winked at me.

"I don't ever remember being a picky eater. My aunt made a lot of different kinds of food when I was a kid and I guess I just got used to trying new things."

"Your aunt?"

"Yeah, I was raised by my Aunt Milana. My mom died giving birth to me and I just recently found out that my dad died before I was born."

"What do you mean, recently?"

"As in just yesterday. I'm going to be honest with you, Aviel. I know there's something different about you and after our meeting yesterday, I went to see my aunt. She's like my safe place where I can go no matter what. I told her some things and then she told me the real story about how my parents met and what happened."

When I looked at Aviel's face it was very serious. I wasn't sure if he was angry or really thinking about what I'd said.

"Violet," he finally said, "I have something to tell you, but I'm going to wait until after we eat. I want to give it my full attention."

"Okay, I guess," I said frustrated. One of my biggest pet peeves was when someone said something like that and didn't finish.

I guess I had a pouty look on my face because Aviel stopped what he was doing and moved to stand in front of me. He took his hand and gently lifted my chin up so I could look at him.

"Hey," he said. "What I want to talk to you about is going to take more than a few minutes and I want you to enjoy our dinner. And I promise what I have to say isn't bad."

He gave me a very quick kiss and went back to cooking. Now I was more curious than anything. A few minutes later, he had two plates in his hands, and we went to the table.

"This is really good," I told him after my first bite.

"Thanks," Aviel said with a smile.

"I can't cook anything to save my life," I admitted.

"Your aunt didn't teach you?"

"She tried, but I didn't have the patience for it." I smiled. "Who taught you?"

"I taught myself."

"Is there anything you can't do?"

"Probably, but I haven't found it yet," he said, with a grin.

I rolled my eyes, but couldn't help the smile. We finished eating and he told me to go to the living room and make myself comfortable. When he joined me, he had two glasses of wine with him.

"Here," he said, handing me one.

"I don't like wine," I said.

"Try this one, I think you'll like it."

"That's what everyone says."

"Just have a sip and if you don't like it you don't have to drink it."

"Fine," I said, taking a sip. I was surprised that I liked it.

"Okay, you win, this is good."

I had a feeling I was going to need the wine for this conversation, so I drank the entire glass and Aviel filled it back up.

"I think I'm ready now," I told him.

"You said earlier that there was something different about me. I want you to be completely honest about what you think makes me different. Even if you think it might sound crazy, I want to know."

Well, here goes nothing, I thought.

"First of all, you have these crazy, beautiful, intense eyes like I've never seen before. I've heard your voice in my head when you weren't actually near me. I had a dream about you that was too real to be a dream and finally, I think you can disappear at will."

Everything I'd just said made me sound like a lunatic, but he wanted honesty and that's what I gave him. Now I waited to see what he had to say.

"You are one hundred percent correct about everything you just said."

Okay, that was totally not what I was expecting to hear. "Huh?"

"I'll explain my eyes in a minute, but yes, I've spoken to you through our minds only. The dream in your apartment wasn't a dream, I was really there. And yes, I can disappear at will. It's a perk of being an angel."

Either I'd heard him wrong or I was officially going crazy. Then I started laughing. "Very funny Aviel. An angel, yeah right."

I continued to laugh until he suddenly vanished and reappeared across the room.

"What the fuck?" I said, and looked at my glass. "Did you put something in my wine?" I had to be seeing things, right?

"No Violet, and your eyes aren't playing tricks on you. I'm an angel sent to protect you."

I set my glass down and stood up. "Nope. No way. You're freaking insane. This isn't real. I've gone crazy." I was pacing.

"Violet, you're not crazy," I heard in my head. It was Aviel's voice and then he suddenly was right in front of me. I'm pretty sure I squealed a little.

"Violet," he said out loud. "This is real. I know this is a lot to take in, but I also know you can handle it."

Just as he said that I felt myself starting to fall. For what seemed like just a fraction of a second everything went black. When I opened my eyes, I was in my bed and it was morning.

"It was just a dream," I said, and turned over. That's when I saw an envelope with my name on it sitting on my nightstand. I opened it.

Violet,

You passed out on me last night, so I brought you home. I'm sorry I kind of sprung that on you and thinking back, I probably could have done it better. But the fact is, that I am an angel and all that entails. I was sent here to tell you the truth about who you really are and also to protect you. We need to finish that conversation so please call me when you are ready to talk.

Aviel

His number was at the bottom of the note. There's no way any of this could be real, was there?

Chapter Fourteen

I didn't call him. I couldn't bring myself to do it. Yes, I wanted answers. But what if I didn't really want to know? I mean, he said who I really was. Did he think I wouldn't know who I really was? I've lived with myself all my life.

Sue poked her head into my office. "There is a Mr. Jameson wanting to talk to you."

I scrunched up my eyebrows. I don't know a Mr. Jameson. "Does he have an appointment?"

She shook her head. "He said he is a friend of Mr. Mann's."

What did he do, send out the search party for me? He knew where I worked. I stood up from my chair. "Let him in, please." If he was going to talk about angels, he could just leave. I was not in the mood to talk about that.

A tall handsome man walked in. He had short black hair and jade green eyes with a hint of honey in them. He was built like Aviel, but yet, he seemed completely different. Like light versus dark, which sounded strange, even in my head. Why was I even comparing the two?

"How can I help you, Mr. Jameson?" I said, as I gestured for him to take a seat.

He disregarded me and said, "I'm looking for Aviel. I've been trying to track him down for over a month now."

This took me by surprise. "May I ask why you're coming here for answers?" I'm not telling this dude shit. If Aviel wanted to be found, he would have been.

"You are working with him, are you not?"

I didn't like this guy's attitude. "Just because we might be working with him, doesn't mean we know where he is. Now if you will excuse me. I have work to do." Asshole.

"I know you have his address somewhere in his files. I need it," he said, with much more force. Like that was going to make me give it to him.

"That is not for me to give out. Now, would you please leave before I call the cops."

He took a step towards me. "I'm not leaving until you give me his address."

Just as I was about to say something back, Aviel appeared in the doorway. "What the hell are you doing here, Kylen?"

Kylen turned around and sneered at Aviel. "You know what I'm doing here. Unless you want this human to die, I advise you to go with me before she does."

Aviel looked torn between leaving me and protecting me. I gave him a slight nod, telling him it was okay.

"Let's go," was all Aviel said, before they were both gone in a blink of an eye.

I dropped down into my seat. What the actual fuck was that all about? Now I have to worry about a psycho angel? Just great! I couldn't even be at work today. So, I decided to work from home. At least there it would be quiet, and I wouldn't have to worry about answering questions I didn't have the answer to.

"Sue, I'm going to work from home today. I'm not feeling well. Transfer all my calls to my cell," I said, as I was dashing out the door. I didn't want to explain to her how both men were no longer in the building.

Once I got into my car, I broke down. This was too much for me to handle. I needed to get away from all of this so I could think straight. There was only one place that I wanted to be right now. I threw the car in drive and sped towards my aunt's house. She'd help me figure this out somehow.

Twenty minutes later, I was sitting in front of my aunt's house, debating if I wanted to drag her into all of this. Is this what my mom felt like at first? Confused. Is this why she never told my aunt the real story? Was she trying to protect her from all of this? If so, why? Is there more to all of this that I'm not seeing? So many questions and no answers. I decide not to tell my aunt until I can figure everything out and make sure she would be safe. I couldn't lose her.

I jumped out of the car and ran up the steps. Entering the house, I could hear her inspirational music going. That only meant one thing: she was in the middle of either teaching a yoga class or her personal yoga time. Instead of interrupting her, I went to the kitchen, grabbed a drink, and went to the garden. Maybe it would help me figure out what to do.

I picked up a tiller and started weeding around the flower beds. Not like they needed it, but it helped me take my mind off of things.

"I wasn't expecting to see you during the week. Is everything okay?"

I wiped my hands on my pants as I stood up. I rushed over to my aunt and hugged her. Just being in her arms had calmed my nerves a little. "Yeah, I'm just having one of my off days and needed one of your hugs." I hate lying to her, but for now, it was for her own good.

She hugged me a little tighter. "I'm glad they still work. Want something to eat?"

I looked at my watch and saw that I'd been outside for an hour already. "I would like that, thank you."

We went back into the kitchen and I sat at the table, while my aunt made us lunch. I looked at my phone and I hadn't received any calls, which was really weird. I texted Sue and asked if she transferred my calls.

Her answer was quick.

Sue: No, Mr. Edington said he would take care of the calls today and said if you call or text to tell you to take the day off.

Well that was nice of him, but I didn't want the day off.

Me: I'll text him. Thank you.

While I waited for Mr. Edington to text me back, I asked my aunt a question. "Do you know how long my parents were together?"

She looked at me over her shoulder. "About six months. Why?"

I shook my head. I didn't even know where I was going with this. "Just want to know more about them is all."

She stopped what she was doing and turned the burner off. Turning around, she leaned on the stove. "I've known you your whole life. I know when there is something on your mind. Spill it."

As much as I wish I could, I just couldn't. Not yet, anyway. "I've been thinking about what you told me already and I'm just trying to piece everything together." At least, that part wasn't a lie.

She made our plates and brought them to the table. "I don't know much about your father, other than what I've already told you. I wish I knew more."

We ate in silence after that. I was lost in thought and who knew what my aunt was thinking.

Chapter Fifteen

As we were cleaning up after lunch, I had a thought. "Do you have any pictures of mom that I've never seen?" I asked my aunt.

"You know what; I think there might be a box of her stuff still in the attic. Let's go have a look and see what's in there."

As most attics were, this one was dark, dusty, and full of old boxes. I started at one end while my aunt went to the other. She said it should be labeled with mom's name, so that's what I was looking for.

I think I must have moved fifty boxes but none of that mattered when I saw "ROSE" written in big letters.

"I found it," I yelled to my aunt.

"Good, bring it downstairs so we can get out of all this dust."

It wasn't a huge box, but it was still awkward to carry down the steep attic ladder. We went to the living room and opened it.

There were some of her medals from dancing and a couple of old t-shirts, but what really interested me was the shoebox. I had a feeling it was holding at least one answer I was looking for.

I opened it and found letters. I started to read one and I realized they were love letters between her and my father. The first one I opened was to my mom. I quickly scanned it, but my eyes were drawn to the bottom. It said *Love Always, Remiel.*

"Auntie," I practically yelled, and she was sitting right across from me. "Look, I think my father's name was Remiel." I handed her the letter.

While she looked at it, I kept going through the box. What I really wanted was a picture, so when I found one, I got really excited. I recognized my mom from other pictures I'd seen, but I had no idea who the guy was that was with her.

"Do you know who this is?" I asked, and handed her the picture.

She took a really good look at it. "No, I don't know who this is, but I can guess that is your father." She handed the picture back to me.

I was feeling a range of emotions, but I think the prominent one was curiosity.

"He was hot," I said and laughed.

"He certainly was," my aunt said and smiled. "I can see why Rose fell so quickly for him."

"I kind of look like him," I said, studying the picture.

"Yes, you do. How are you feeling right now?"

"I'm not quite sure. Maybe a little overwhelmed. I mean, this is the first time I actually know anything about my father. Even though it's only a picture and a name, it's more than we've known for twenty-two years. Crazy, huh."

"Crazy is one word for it," she said.

"I wonder if I can find out more about him with just this," I said.

"It's worth a try," my aunt said. An alarm went off on her phone. "My next yoga class is soon. Are you going to join me?"

"I don't think so," I said, with a smile. "I should be getting home anyway. Thank you. You're the best aunt in the world."

"And you're the best niece in the world."

I got another one of her famous hugs, grabbed the shoebox, and went to my car. Driving as fast as I could to get home, I found that Amy wasn't at the apartment, so I decided to look through the shoebox to see what else was in there.

About ten minutes later, I looked up from the box and screamed. Aviel was standing in my living room like he belonged there.

"What the fuck, Aviel?" I yelled.

"Sorry, Violet. I needed to see if you were okay."

"Ever heard of a cell phone?" I was pissed.

"I needed to see you in person."

"As you can see, I'm fine."

"Did you get my note this morning?" he asked.

"Yes."

"You didn't call."

"No shit."

"Why?"

"Why, you want to know why I didn't call you after you tell me you're an angel? Maybe because this is crazy."

He moved closer and sat down beside me. "I'm going to touch your arm. Tell me what you feel."

I rolled my eyes. "Whatever."

Aviel put one finger on my arm. I just felt his finger, but then a few seconds later, there was this warm sensation that started on my forearm and quickly spread throughout my entire body.

"What the hell?" I muttered.

"What do you feel, Violet?"

"It's like the sun is inside my body. It feels relaxing and peaceful."

He took his hand away and the feeling went with it.

"How did you do that?" I asked.

"I'll tell you in a minute, but first I have to tell you something that you're probably going to have a hard time with." He stopped and took a deep breath. "You are half-angel."

I started laughing. "It sounded like you said I was half-angel."

"I did."

When I saw the look on his face, I could tell he wasn't joking.

"No, no, no, no, no." I stood up and started pacing. "Angels aren't real. People don't just appear and disappear. Your touch made me feel like that because I think you're hot."

Aviel was suddenly in front of me and held me by my arms. "Violet, I'm going to say a few things and you're going to tell me yes or no."

"What?"

"Can you eat anything you want and never gain weight?"

"Yes."

"You have the perfect body, but never have to work for it."

"Yes."

"You have an uncanny ability to read people."

"Yes."

"You're extremely intelligent, but never had to study."

"Yes. How could you possibly know that?" I was super confused and a little amazed at the same time. It seemed like every time I was around him, I was a ball of conflicting emotions.

"I know that because I know what you really are. Your mom was human, and your dad is an angel named Remiel."

My knees felt weak. "What did you just say?"

"Your father is an angel named Remiel."

"Is? Like he's alive?"

"Yes."

"I need to sit down. This is too much. Just an hour ago, I found out his name. Saw him for the first time in a picture. Then you come here with all this talk of angels. Know things you shouldn't." I know I was rambling, but I couldn't help it.

"This isn't the way I wanted to tell you all of this but with Kylen showing up today I didn't have a choice."

"I don't understand any of this," I said. "I feel like I got dropped in the middle of a movie or something."

"I understand that this is a lot to process in a short amount of time."

I snorted. "That's an understatement. So, let me get this straight. You're an angel sent here to protect me, from what, I don't know. My father was also an angel and that makes me half-angel. And some guy named Kylen shows up looking for you and threatens me. Do I have that right?"

"Yes, that's the stripped-down version of events."

"This is insane. I need a fucking drink."

Chapter Sixteen

I was starting to think one drink wasn't going to be enough. I grabbed the bottle of vodka and took it into the living room with me. If I was going to listen to any more of this crazy talk, I might as well get drunk. At least then it might all make sense. I doubted it, but it was worth a shot. I poured myself a shot and downed it in less than a second. I was about to pour another one when Aviel slowly took the bottle away from me.

"I would rather you be of sound mind when I tell you the rest. After that, you can drink until your heart's content."

I was about to argue, but what was the point? Everything he had said so far was true. I gestured for him to continue as I took a seat on the couch.

"There is a war that is about to come to Earth. A war only you can save this world from..."

I stopped him right there. "I am nobody. There is no way you have the right person."

He rubbed his face with the palm of his hands and muttered something under his breath. "You are the key to all of this, Violet. Your father knew if he had a child, that child would save this world. He didn't expect to fall in love with your mother. He didn't know God gave him the gift of a true soulmate."

I stared off into space just so I could figure all of this out. "Why me? What makes me so special?"

He sat next to me and took my hands into his. I let him because I really needed something real to hold on to. "Because only a half-angel can take on the Dark Angels and live through it. I'm not saying this is going to be easy and you could get seriously hurt, but you can't die by an angel. Not like we can."

I stood up and started to pace. "How many other half-angels are there?"

He didn't stop me as he answered. "Twelve total."

I stopped dead in my tracks. "You expect twelve of us to stop millions of Dark Angels? Are you fucking insane?"

This time, he came to me and brought me into his arms. I was too shocked to care. "Yes. We just have to find the others. You're the first one I've found, only because of your mother. She knew her sister wouldn't move away. I just had to wait and be patient."

"Is that why you kept disappearing on me?"

His laugh rumbled through my body causing it to come alive. "No, the reason I kept running from you is because you are my true soulmate and I didn't know how to process that information."

I pulled away from him and took a step back. "What did you just say?"

He looked at me with heated eyes. "You are my soulmate, Violet."

My knees grew weak as I took a seat, no longer able to stand. "That's what I thought you said. How is this even possible?"

He walked over slowly like I was fixing to bolt. If my legs would work properly, I probably would have. "Ask God when you see him."

I snapped my neck in his direction. "Excuse me? How can I do that, unless I die? I'm not ready to die."

He placed his hand on my shoulder and did what he did earlier, and it calmed me. "You are half-angel, which means, you can go to Heaven. Just not for long periods of time. Heaven will reject you after a while, knowing you are part human."

Again, why me? I tried to take my mind off the whole we are soulmates thing. I wasn't ready to talk about that yet. "When is this war supposed to start?"

He let out a slow breath. "It's already started in Heaven. It won't be long before it trickles down to Earth."

"Why did the war even start?"

"Lucifer had more followers than we realized. We thought we'd banished all of his followers, but that wasn't the case. Michael and the other Archangels are trying to keep the war in Heaven. We don't want it down here, because if it reaches Earth, a lot of humans are going to die. If that happens, we need all twelve of you to keep it contained in one area. That's why it's so important to find the others."

"Wow!" was all I could say. I mean, seriously what else could I even say to that. I was the only one who could save the world. But I have to find the other half-angels in a world with trillions of people. It shouldn't be that hard. Right? Right!

"Who is Kylen? Why was he looking for you?"

He placed a hand on my leg. At first, I wanted to remove it, but he was sharing that feeling again. "He is a Dark Angel. I'm glad he didn't figure you out, if he did, he didn't show it. Don't trust him. Ever."

Great, Just great. I've known I'm a half-angel all of two seconds and I've already encountered a Dark Angel. What the flying fuckity fuck? That was all I needed, for him to figure me out before I even had a chance to wrap my head around everything.

Chapter Seventeen

I grabbed the bottle of vodka to take a drink, but then I put it back down. Getting drunk right now wasn't going to help the situation. "I need to really think about what you've just told me, and I have a lot of questions. Can we go somewhere, not here? I don't want Amy to come home to me freaking out."

Aviel smiled and nodded. "How about my place?"

"I think that would be perfect. Let me change first," I said, when I realized I was still in my work clothes.

I quickly changed into some yoga pants and a baggy sweatshirt, wanting comfort over fashion. After I found my purse, I told Aviel I was ready. As I started to walk to the door, he stopped me.

"I have a faster way," he said, and walked over to me. "Put your arms around me."

I had no idea what he was up to, but I did as I was asked. The next thing I knew, we were standing in Aviel's kitchen.

"Um, what just happened?"

"I transported us to my place," he said, like this was an everyday occurrence for me.

"Angel thing?" I asked.

"Yes."

"Can I do that?"

"No. Only full angels can transport somewhere instantly."

"Well damn, that would have been a kickass trick."

Aviel grabbed a couple of bottles of water and handed me one. Then he started getting food out of the fridge. I guessed he was cooking for me again, which was totally hot by the way.

"So, are there different kinds of angels?" I asked, taking a seat at the eating bar.

"Yes, just like humans have jobs, so do angels."

"What kind are you?

"I'm a Warrior Angel."

"What was my dad?"

"Your father is a Ferrier Angel. He transports souls to Heaven. You have to remember that your father isn't dead, Violet, he's in Heaven doing his job."

"Right," I said with a sigh. "It's just that my whole world has been turned upside down today. This has been a lot to take in."

"I know, and I'm here to help you through this."

"So, did my mom meet Remiel when he was doing his soul thing?"

"Yes, he'd encountered her on one of his trips to Earth. He knew instantly she was his true soulmate, but she was only a girl at the time. He watched over her as she grew up and even went to her while she dreamed. So, when your mother was old enough Remiel appeared to her one day. On some level, your mother already knew him, so it only took her a few days to fall in love with him. She knew it seemed crazy, so she kept everything to herself."

"Did my mom know he was an angel?"

"Yes. After she found out she was pregnant with you he told her everything about him."

"How do you know so much about this?" I asked.

"Remiel and I have known each other for thousands of years. He confided in me the first time he saw your mother."

"So, why did he leave if they were soulmates?"

"It is forbidden for angels to fall in love with humans. His punishment was having to leave your mother on Earth knowing he wouldn't see her again, until he was sent to collect her soul."

"Wow, that's just ... tragic," I said. "So, my mom died giving birth to me so she could go to Heaven and be with him?"

"Yes."

"I don't know how to feel about that," I said honestly.

"Once two soulmates find each other and fall in love, it is very hard to be apart. I don't think your mother made the conscious decision to die, but she didn't fight to live when she needed to."

"Well aren't you just a ray of sunshine." The sarcasm was coming out now.

"I'm sorry, Violet. I really am. Your mother is a lovely soul and leaving you is the only regret of her mortal life."

"Wait, you know my mother? Like in Heaven?"

"Yes. Once she went to Heaven, your mother and father were allowed to be together for all eternity, so yes, I know her. And you should know that she watches over you."

That was it. "Wait, stop, just stop talking, please. I still have a million questions, but it's just too much right now. Can we do something normal like watch a movie?"

Aviel smiled at me. "We can do anything you want to, Violet. We have all night to talk about this, when you want to, of course."

"Going to work tomorrow is really going to suck."

"Actually," Aviel said, "I've arranged for you to have the rest of the week off."

"How in the hell did you do that?"

"Human minds are easily manipulated."

"What? Wait … I don't want to know, at least not right now. What are you cooking?" Yes, it was a total subject change, but I needed a mental break. The last thing I wanted to do was freak out because my brain couldn't process what I'd been told.

"Stir-fry," Aviel said. "Since cooking isn't your thing."

I gave him the evil eye. "I can't help it. I was worried about other things growing up, like my grades. But it does smell good."

"The secret is the sesame oil," he said. "Cooking can be very therapeutic."

"I didn't think angels needed therapy."

"We don't. I just like making things with my hands."

That made me think about something. "Is your company even real?"

"Yes, it is. I believe in what it stands for. An angel's main purpose is to help humans. Even though I'm a Warrior Angel I still feel the need to help, so I started Selgan, which is the word angels scrambled by the way. I don't make a thing from it, but I employ a lot of people and we help many more."

"That's really admirable. Do many angels own companies on Earth?"

"No, I'm kind of the exception to the rule."

"What makes you so special?" I asked.

"I'm really good at my job."

Since I didn't want to know exactly what a Warrior Angel did, I changed the subject again. "What movies do you have?"

"I don't have any, but we can watch anything you like?"

"How is that possible? Wait, I don't want to know. Maybe we should just turn on the TV and see what we can find."

"Like I said, it's all up to you tonight, Violet."

The look on his face said this was about more than just my questions. It was a look that made me weak at the knees and my lady bits tingle.

Chapter Eighteen

We ended up watching Buffy the Vampire Slayer. Not something I would normally watch, but it took my mind off everything for a while. Something I was thankful for. Once the last episode was over, I took a deep breath. This wasn't going to go away; I might as well start talking.

I somehow managed to rest my head on his chest. I sat up and faced him. "Alright, I'm ready to talk."

He smirked at me. "Are you sure?"

I watched his reaction before I answered. "There's no point in beating around the bush. I've postponed it long enough. Here are some of my questions. One, how are we going to find the other eleven half-angels before the war comes here? Two, why hasn't my father come to see me, if he can come here? Three, how does this soulmate thing work?" I might as well get it out there and over with.

The smile on his face melted my insides a little. Damn, he was sexy as all get out. "Do you want me to answer them in order?"

"Very funny, smart ass!"

He laughed that hearty laugh that made me want to jump him right there.

"Okay, we need to go to Heaven to find them. That's how I found you. Your soul was brighter than anyone's here. If we can find a close location, we should be able to find them all. Your father didn't want to disrupt your life. He saw how good you were doing and didn't want to make your life harder." He grabbed my arms and pulled me into his lap. "Much better." He leaned into my neck and breathed me in. "As for the soulmate part, I'm sure you can feel the connection between us. It's something that makes you want me. It's not just my looks. It's everything about me. I feel the same way, except my need to protect you is in overdrive."

I didn't think. I took his face into my hands and kissed him like I wanted to the first time I saw him. I lost myself in the kiss. Hoping he could feel everything I was feeling. When the heated kiss ended, he gently kissed my cheek.

"I've wanted to do that for so long," he said, and brushed my hair out of my face.

The only thing I could think about right now was how much I wanted his lips on mine again.

I was breathing heavily as I stared into those remarkable eyes. "Me too."

This time he took the lead and kissed me with passion, instead of greedily like I did. It was the best kiss I'd ever had, and it was making me want to rip his clothes off and have my way with him. Before things could get any further, he pulled away and placed his head on my forehead. "We need to stop before we do something we aren't ready for. I want to take this slow and really get to know each other."

"I think we're past that point. I'm going to combust if we don't do something -- soon." I was done playing it safe. It'd been months since I'd had sex, and Aviel had lit the fire that wouldn't stop until he made me his.

He chuckled and stood up with me in his arms. "Are you sure you are ready?"

"I've never been more sure."

With that, he took me to his room and laid me on the bed. He took off his shirt then his pants, and let me tell you something, I almost had an orgasm just looking at all his glory. The man was built perfectly in my eyes. I straddled him and slowly took off my shirt and bra. His callused hands were like magic to my body. Everywhere he touched me it felt like fire, in a good way. He yanked my pants off, then panties. Let's just say, I was more than ready for him. My body was screaming for him. "If you don't stop teasing me, you'll force me to take action."

He teased me a little bit more until I couldn't take it and was about to have my way with him, when he did what I wanted him to do. He entered me with ease and all I could do was hold on for dear life.

After hours, we finally came up for air. If having sex with him was going to be like that, I was I would get addicted, quickly. I'd never felt this way before. I couldn't explain the connection we shared.

I got up to go clean myself up and use the bathroom. Before I could even get all the way off the bed, strong arms brought me back against a hard chest. "Where do you think you're going?"

I pressed him even closer as I said, "I was going to go pee, but if you have other plans by all means." I loved the feeling when I was in his arms. I felt safe and protected.

He chuckled as he released me. "You go do that; I'm going to make us a snack." He kissed me on the forehead and disappeared.

"It must be nice to just be where you want to be!" I shouted.

I heard him laugh. Men, I swear. I used the restroom and walked out butt naked. If I had my way, there would be no reason to get dressed again. Once I got to the kitchen, the smell of something cinnamon and sweet filled the air.

"I hope you like cinnamon rolls."

I wanted to jump up and down, but I refrained myself. "Absolutely. They're one of my favorites. Let me guess, you figured that out while stalking me?" I had to say it. I knew he was only trying to figure me out, but it still creeped me out the way he did it.

He put the cinnamon rolls into the oven then walked over to me. He took me in his strong arms and wrapped me up. "I'm sorry I did it the way I did. I had to figure out a way to approach you without scaring you."

I laughed this time. "Hate to tell you this, but the moment I first laid eyes on you, I wanted you. I felt the pull then, but didn't know what it was."

He picked me up and placed me on the counter. I moved my legs so he could lean into me. "I realized that, and I didn't know what to do about it. But I'm here now and nothing is going to take you away from me."

I felt a warm sensation down my spine from his protective side. It was like his power traced up and down my spine. "What about the Dark Angels? Won't they try and do something to stop me?"

I could feel him grow angry in my chest. "They can try all they want. I won't let them get to you."

"How can you stop them from doing whatever they want? I'm not trying to be a smart ass; I'm being real here."

His anger was at the boiling point. "I will kill anyone who dares to try to hurt you."

Was it bad that I wanted to take him back to bed and do things to him that I'd never done before? I wrapped my legs around him to bring him closer. When I felt him grow against me, I couldn't stop what happened next.

Chapter Nineteen

Before I knew it, Aviel's head was between my legs and I was leaning back on the counter. I found out that he was good with his mouth as he was with his hands. It seemed like an eternity that he kept me just on the edge. When I finally came, I'm pretty sure I swore at him. I heard him chuckle and then some kind of beeping sound.

I wasn't able to move quite yet, but I felt him leave me and then I heard the oven door open. That got my attention. I jumped off the counter and went to inspect the fresh cinnamon rolls.

"You're going to have to wait a minute," Aviel said, as I tried to reach for one. "They're too hot and I have to put the frosting on."

I pouted, he laughed. "How long do I have to wait?"

"At least twenty minutes."

"Twenty minutes huh," I said with a grin. "I'm pretty sure I know a way to use some of those minutes. I think you should get a reward for making me one of my favorite things."

"Oh really," he said. "I think that sounds like a perfect idea."

I pushed him back until he hit the counter. Without saying a word, I dropped to my knees and took him in my mouth. His sharp intake of air made me smile. I loved having this kind of power over him, knowing I was the one causing him to make those sounds. I took my time at first, but then could sense his urgency and I picked up my pace. He came saying my name and that made me giggle, and I wasn't a giggler.

"You seem very satisfied with yourself," he said, when I stood up.

"I am."

"You should be. I could do that all day."

"Well we have all day," I said.

"Actually, I was wondering if you wanted to get your first taste of Heaven."

I opened my mouth to say something, but nothing came out. Did I want to go to Heaven?

Aviel pulled me into his arms. "I know everything is happening so quickly, Violet, and you're handling this remarkably well. I just think since you have the week off this is a good opportunity to give you a crash course in everything angel. But if you're not ready we won't go."

"Can I think about it for a few minutes?"

"Of course. Take as much time as you need."

"Can I eat one of those cinnamon rolls yet?"

He laughed. "Not yet."

"Fine. I guess I'll go take a shower."

He nodded and I left the kitchen.

Aviel had one of those showers that looked like it could hold ten people and had a rainfall showerhead. I stepped under the water and let my thoughts drift to the events of the last twenty-four hours.

It was hard to believe that this was my life, it felt more like a dream than reality. In the last few days, my life had completely turned upside down, but not all of it was bad. Aviel was, well Aviel was perfect and I felt connected to him in a way I didn't think was possible. But the fact that I was going to have to stop a war was kind of overwhelming.

After a while, my thoughts calmed, and it was time to get out of the shower. I got dressed and went to the kitchen. Aviel had two cinnamon rolls waiting for me.

I took a bite of one then devoured the entire thing. I saw him smile at me, but he didn't say a word. I was halfway through the second one when I finally spoke.

"I think I want to go to Heaven."

"Yeah?"

"Yeah. I don't see a reason for this little whirlwind of truth to stop."

"Are you sure?"

"Yes. I did lots of thinking in the shower and I want to see it."

"Okay. I'll go take a shower and get ready." He kissed me and left the kitchen.

Once I was done with the second cinnamon roll, I went to the living room. I saw my purse on the floor and realized I hadn't checked my cell in hours. There were a bunch from Amy and Sue.

Amy: Everything ok?
Amy: You weren't at work. What's up?
Amy: Where are you?
Amy: Why aren't you answering me?
Sue: Hey, I think you need to call Amy before she goes ballistic.
Sue: I hope you're ok
Amy: You'd better be in a locked room having lots of sex or I'm going to kill you
Amy: I'm calling the cops in an hour if I don't hear from you

The last one was thirty minutes ago. I hit send on my phone.

"Violet!" Amy yelled on the other end. "Talk to me."

"Hey, Amy. I'm okay. I ended up getting the rest of the week off and I'm at Aviel's place."

She squealed on the other end of the phone. "It's about time. How's the sex?"

Amy always did get right to the point. "It's off the charts good," I told her honestly.

"I knew it would be," she said, with a giggle. "When are you going to be home?"

"I don't know. I think I might stay here for a few days."

"Yes, you definitely should," Amy said. "Just check in every so often so I know you're alive, okay?"

"Yeah, okay. Bye for now."

"Have fun. Bye."

Aviel walked into the living room. "Everything okay?"

"Yeah. Amy was worried that I'd been kidnapped or something."

"Well she wasn't exactly wrong," he said, with a smile. "Are you ready?"

"I'm as ready as I'm going to be. How do we get to Heaven?"

"I transport us. Take my hand."

I took his hand and closed my eyes. I felt the same sensation as before and when it stopped, I knew we were somewhere very special, I could feel it.

"Open your eyes," Aviel whispered.

I wasn't sure what I was expecting to see, but it wasn't what I was looking at. Everything just looked perfect, I didn't know how else to describe it. People were walking on the street; buildings were standing tall, but there was just something different about it all.

"Are you okay?" he asked me.

"Yeah, it's just so ... something."

He laughed at me. "Did you think you were going to see white clouds and golden columns?"

"I don't know. This looks so ordinary, but in a perfect kind of way. I mean, there's a bakery and a dress shop next to a dog groomer and chocolate shop. I didn't think people had to work in Heaven."

"People get to do what they want when they get to Heaven. Some souls are meant for different things, but they ultimately are doing what they love, like baking or grooming dogs."

"Huh." I didn't know what else to say to that.

"Come on. Let's have a look around."

I started to get that excited feeling, after all, how many people get to see Heaven and then go back to Earth?

Chapter Twenty

As I looked around, I couldn't help but wonder if I could meet my mom and father while I was here. I wasn't even sure if that was allowed or not. Then again, was I even ready to meet them? I'd lived my whole life without them. What if they didn't want to meet me?

Aviel pulled me into him. "I know what you're thinking. They have waited so long to meet you." I gave him a confused look. "Your parents. They want to meet you."

I tried not to let him see how much my heart was twisting right now. If I only knew the truth long ago, I wouldn't be freaking out. "I don't know if I'm ready. Maybe one day, but not today."

He gave me a sad smile and nodded his head. "As you wish, my dear."

We walked around a little while longer before I could feel Heaven start to reject me. I fell to my knees from the cramps that had started. I felt strong arms around me and the next thing I know, everything stopped. The cramps, dizziness, everything. I was able to breathe normally. I took a deep breath in. "That was intense. Remind me not to stay for so long next time. I don't want to feel that again."

He didn't let me go and I was okay with that. "It was my fault. I knew you had limits and I was so excited to show you, Heaven, I lost track of time."

I raised up on my tiptoes and kissed him. He lifted me up and I wrapped my legs around him. I could kiss this angel all day long. He made me forget all my troubles, even for a few minutes. Something my brain needed sometimes.

The kiss ended way too soon for my liking and I growled in response. "I wasn't done yet."

His laughter rocked through me. "Yeah, but you need to eat. We've been up there all day."

I looked out the window and realized it was dark out. "How can that be? We were only up there for maybe an hour."

He set me down and took my hand as he led me to the kitchen. "Time works differently there. Minutes up in Heaven, are hours here on Earth."

I shook my head in disbelief. "How come I didn't see the war up there? You said there's a war going on."

He gave me a grim look. "I didn't take you to that part of Heaven. If it were up to me. You would never be in this war, but it's not. We need to start training soon as well."

I balked at this. "What do you mean training? Like in combat training or something?"

I loved hearing him chuckle, but not at this moment. I was freaking out. "Something like that. You have to learn how to fight, if not, all is lost."

Well, ain't that a bitch. Maybe I should have done yoga with my aunt growing up. I've never exercised in my life. I never had to. "Just so you know, I don't exactly exercise. Sure, I run occasionally to clear my head, but as for real exercise to get fit, never a day in my life."

He grabbed me and placed me on the counter. "I figured as much. I'll get a few angels to help out with all the training. Just so you know, we won't be going easy on any of you." I gave him a nasty look. He raised his hands in the air in surrender. "If we are, it won't benefit you in the long run."

As much as I hated to admit it, he was right. "Fine. But don't kick my ass the first day okay. At least let me have some dignity."

He laughed as he gave me a kiss on top of the head. "As you wish. Now, are you ready for me to cook?"

Hell yes! "Yep, what are you making this time?"

"I was thinking something easy. How about spaghetti?"

"A man that knows his way to my heart. I'm going to get a movie ready if that's okay."

"Sounds like a plan. I'll be in there as soon as it gets done."

I bounded into the living room to pick out a rom-com. I needed a laugh. Plus, I didn't want to bore him too much. I looked through the directory on the TV and came across Knocked Up. I pushed play then paused it.

"Hope you don't mind the movie I picked out," I hollered.

"I'm sure I will love it no matter what!" he yelled back to me.

Could he be any more perfect? While I waited, I texted Amy. Just to tell her I was alive.

Me: Hey chick, I'm still alive.
Amy: Are you getting all the sex you want?

Leave it up to her to ask that question.

Me: It's not all about the sex. There are some things I need to talk to you about. We will talk when I come home. Just don't freak out ok.
Amy: What's wrong? Is everything ok?
Me: Yes and no. It's a long story. Talk to you later. Bye
Amy: As long as you are ok. We will talk later. Bye chic.

I didn't know how she was going to react to all of this, but I wanted her to know what was about to happen, hopefully not too soon. I wanted her to know about the war that would be coming. I'd do anything to keep her safe.

The smell from his cooking made my mouth water. I got up and went into the kitchen.

"Oh my gosh! That smells so good. Is that garlic bread?"

"You can't have spaghetti without it, now can we."

The smile that spread across his face made my girly bits wet. We may not be watching that movie for long if I had my way. Especially, if he kept that up.

Chapter Twenty-One

Dinner was delicious and as we started watching the movie, my mind wandered to our trip to Heaven. Then I started thinking about the war, then training. I had questions and decided to ask them now.

"If I'm half-angel, why can't I do anything special?"

"You mean, like transport?" Aviel asked.

"Yeah."

"Your human DNA sort of blocks a lot of the angel side of you."

"Is there a way to like turn it on or something?"

"That's part of what the training is for."

"Do we have to wait to find the other half-angels before I can start training?"

He smiled. "We're supposed to wait, but I think I can teach you a little something without getting in too much trouble. Why are you so eager to get started?"

"Honestly, I'm planning to tell Amy all of this and I think I'm going to need some kind of proof so that she doesn't think I've gone crazy. And, I really want to learn how to do something cool."

"Are you sure you want to tell Amy?"

"Yes. If I'm going to be gone a lot and acting strange, she needs to know why," I told him.

"Okay," he said, and turned off the TV. "I think we can work on two things, your speed and harnessing energy. Stand up," he told me, as he got off the couch.

I stood. He held his hands out to me and I grabbed them.

"I want you to close your eyes and just feel. This will be like when I touched your arm, just on a larger scale."

Closing my eyes, I pushed everything out of my mind and waited for Aviel to do his thing. A few seconds later my entire body felt like it was humming. I was sure I could have run a marathon in minutes. I'd never felt so much energy at the same time.

"How do you feel?" he asked.

"Like I can take on the whole world right now."

Aviel chuckled. "Good. Now you're going to have to learn how to do that on your own."

"That sounds … impossible." I didn't think there was any way I was going to be able to replicate the energy I'd just felt.

"It's not going to be impossible, difficult maybe, but not impossible. You are surrounded by energy all the time; you just can't see it. The secret is tapping into it."

"Yeah, that doesn't sound hard or anything," I said sarcastically.

"You're going to need to have more of an open mind, Violet. If you think it's going to be hard it will be. Once you get the hang of it, it'll become natural. The angel side will take over and you won't even have to think about it."

"Okay, my mind is open. Now tell me how to do this."

"You know what dust looks like when it catches the light and you see it floating in the air?"

"Yeah."

"I want you to picture that, but increase the particles by a million times. The air is full of tiny bits of energy that aren't visible to the naked eye."

I tried to do what he asked but my visualization sucked. "All I can think about is billions of dust particles in the air and it makes me feel like I can't breathe."

Aviel shook his head a little but didn't make fun of me. "Try thinking of them as little fireworks that you can hold in your hand."

That sounded way better than dust, so I tried that. When I thought of itty bitty fireworks, I was sure I could start to feel something.

"Now what?" I asked.

"Try to take some of that energy into your body. Let the bits of energy move through your skin and allow them in."

That sounded really weird. "Open mind," I mumbled to myself.

Taking a deep breath, I focused on one firework only. I thought about it sitting on my hand, then watched it sink into my palm. I felt the slightest change in my body, so I tried it again. A few minutes later, I could feel my body accepting the energy. It wasn't anything like when Aviel did it, but it was a start.

"Very good, Violet. I knew you'd be a fast learner."

"Thanks. So now that I've tried that, what can I do with it?"

"Allowing the energy into your body is going to be the key to everything else. It'll allow you to be quicker and stronger than humans. You'll be able to stay in Heaven for longer periods of time. And, you'll eventually be able to use that energy as a weapon."

"Cool. But how is this going to help me prove anything to Amy? Right now, I can't actually do anything." I know I sounded disappointed.

"Violet," Aviel said seriously, "you only learned how to feel the energy a minute ago. You have to give yourself a little bit of time to figure things out."

"I've always been an overachiever, so I expect a lot from myself."

"That's the angel part of you, you can't help it. But you still had to learn to walk, read, do math, and make friends. None of those things came instantly. It's the same with this. Okay?"

"Fine." I wasn't thrilled, but he was right.

"So, try it again. I bet you can do it faster this time."

I smiled at that and it turned out he was right. I did do it faster. Then I did it again and again and again.

"Let's take a break," Aviel said after a while.

I agreed and followed him to the kitchen. He got out a tub of chocolate ice cream and made us each a big bowl, complete with whipped cream.

I grinned when he took a bite and got a little whipped cream on his lip.

"What?" he asked.

"You got a little something right here," I said.

Instead of telling him where it was, I licked it off. He growled and set his bowl down. Next, he took mine, set it on the counter and then his lips were on mine. I moaned and practically attacked him. Clothes were lost and hands were everywhere. Eventually, we made it to the bedroom. I lost count of how many times he made me come. I fell asleep in his strong arms and with a silly grin on my face.

Chapter Twenty-Two

Aviel was going to be gone the next morning so I planned on going to the apartment to grab a few things while Amy was at work. I wasn't ready to tell her anything yet without proof. I wanted to be able to show her I wasn't lying to her or that I'd gone completely mad. How Sue believed me was beyond me. I really think she was just humoring me to be honest. To calm me down that day. I really needed to check on things at work.

Me: Hey Sue, just checking in on things. How are things going?

I went to the shower while I waited for her to respond and turned it on. If I was being honest with myself, I really needed the alone time to get my head together. My phone dinged with a new text. I picked it up to read it.

Sue: Things are a lot different without you here. I think Mr. Edington is about to beg you to come back sooner. He is having a hard time with this new client and is trying everything to win him over. How is your mini-vacay?
Me: It's something I didn't know I needed until now. What is wrong with this client? Maybe I can give my opinion on it.
Sue: He wants you and only you. I don't know how you keep getting these hotties wanting only you, but you need to share. Lol.
Me: What do you mean hottie?
Sue: I'll try to take a pic the next time he comes in.
Me. Ok, well let me know if there is anything else I can do.
Sue: Will do. Talk to you later. Have fun with your hottie.

I laughed, but didn't respond back. Instead, I jumped into the shower. I let the water relax me as it hit my skin. I could be in this shower all day.

Once I was done, I got dressed and headed to the apartment. It was almost eleven, so Amy should be gone by now. Speeding down the street, I turned the corner to see two cop cars at my building with their lights on. I slowed down enough to pull into the parking lot and threw it into park. I jumped out of the car and raced to the apartment.

When I got there the door was busted wide open and Amy was on the love seat shaking so bad, it looked like she was having a seizure. I ran over to her and held her tight. At first, she fought me.

"It's okay, I'm here, Amy. It's okay," I soothed her.

She wrapped her arms around me to the point I couldn't breathe, but that was okay. She needed me to calm her and I was going to stay like this until she was. I didn't know what happened. I didn't care as long as she was okay. I would get the details later.

"Miss, who are you to this woman?"

I turned my head in the direction of the female officer standing just a few feet away.

"I'm her best friend and roommate."

She came over and kneeled down next to us. "Maybe you can get answers out of her. She hasn't said a word. Not even when she called 9-1-1. We came here and found her like this."

I looked back at Amy and smoothed her hair down. "Amy, please tell us what happened."

She started to shake her head furiously. "No, no, no. It can't be. I was seeing things. I had to be seeing things. There's no other way around what I saw. I've lost my mind."

She pulled away from me and stood up to pace the floor. I gave her her space to work everything out in her mind.

"I mean, he had wings for Christ sakes, fucking wings. Did you hear me, Violet? He had fucking wings."

My heart dropped to my toes. Oh my gods, an angel was here. I need to calm her down to get more information from her.

"I heard you Amy. He had wings. What did he want?"

She stared at me and shook her head in disbelief. "I just told you he had wings and you're going to ignore that fact?"

I stood up and walked over to her. "No, but he must have wanted something. If you say he had wings, then he had wings. We need to get to the bottom of this and find him."

"What do you think he wanted, Violet. He wanted you, it's always you!" she screamed. "I almost died because he was looking for you."

She tried to walk out of the door, but a male officer was blocking her way. My heart sank at her words. It was my fault. I should have protected her. Her words brought me back out of my thoughts and guilt.

"Get out of my way. I've done nothing wrong," she yelled at the officer.

He gave her a pitiful look. "I understand that, but you need to tell us what happened here."

"A guy smashed the door down, grabbed me by the neck and asked if I was Violet. I shook my head no and he left. That's what the fuck happened." She turned back to me. "I'll move out as soon as possible." Then she walked out of the apartment.

I raced after her. I can't lose her as a friend. "Amy, please wait. Talk to me."

I was a few inches away from her and I grabbed her shoulder. When she faced me, tears soaked her face. I didn't say anything as I held her while she broke down. After a few minutes she pulled away. "I'm so sorry, Violet. I didn't mean to say those things. I swear to you, they just came out."

I gave her a sad smile. "Yes, you did. I know you better than most. You're hurt and scared and the only way to make you feel better is to lash out. Can you please tell me everything?"

She closed her eyes and took a deep breath in. "He came to the apartment around seven a.m. He busted the door down, looked around and attacked me. Once he realized I wasn't you, he just left. He did have wings and they are fucking black. He had a tattoo of a falling star on his face."

I stood still. It couldn't be, could it? There is no way Lucifer himself came to look for me. Right?

"Violet, are you okay. You look like you just saw a ghost."

I shook my head to clear the thought that it could possibly be him. I'd have to ask Aviel about all of this. "I'm fine. I was just trying to picture it, is all. You ready to talk to the police now and get them out of here? We're moving today. I will keep you safe." Amy nodded and we went back to talk to the officers.

Chapter Twenty-Three

As soon as the police left, I told Amy to go to her room and pack whatever she needed for a week. I wasn't sure where we were going, but I was getting her out of this place today. We could come back for anything else we needed another time.

The next thing I did was call Aviel. He didn't answer so I called again. The third time he finally answered.

"Amy was attacked by an angel looking for me. And I think it was Lucifer," I said.

"What?" he said, instantly alert.

"I came to the apartment to get a few things, I borrowed one of your cars by the way. Anyway, when I got here there were two police cars outside of the building and the police were in our apartment. Amy was hysterical and saying that she was attacked by a guy with wings and a falling star tattoo on his face. I'm getting her to pack and we're leaving. I'm afraid to have her stay here." I waited for him to say something. "Aviel?"

"I'm here," he said from behind me.

I managed to stifle my scream. I didn't want to scare Amy. "What the fuck, Aviel? You can't just pop in like that."

"I needed to know you were safe. I'm sorry if I startled you."

"Give me some kind of warning next time."

"I want you to take Amy to my place. You'll both be safe there. Take my car back there, I'll make sure both of your cars get to my place."

I decided to ask the most important question. "Was I right? About Lucifer, I mean."

"I'm afraid you were. It's highly unusual for him to come to Earth. He usually has his followers do his bidding. This is bad, Violet. I knew you were the key, but I didn't think Lucifer knew."

"So, what the fuck do I do now?"

"You get to my house with Amy. I'll be waiting. I also need to talk to a few angels about this situation."

I was officially worried now. "How do I know I'll get there safely? What if he comes back?"

"You won't be alone. You'll have protection that you won't be able to see."

Aviel was suddenly gone. I assumed he was talking about some kind of angels protecting us. I felt better knowing I had backup. As quickly as I could, I packed everything I thought I might need.

"Violet," Amy called, "Are you ready to leave?"

I could hear the near panic in her voice.

"Yes," I said, as I walked out of my bedroom. "Let's go."

We left the apartment, broken door and all. The police had told me that they were getting the landlord to replace it in a couple of hours, but that was the least of my concerns right now.

I led Amy to the parking lot where I'd parked Aviel's car. She was looking around the whole time. I hated that she was scared because of me. Shoving the suitcases in the trunk we got in and took off.

My normally fast driving came in handy. I weaved in and out of traffic until we got to the highway that led to Aviel's.

"Where are we going?" Amy finally asked.

"Aviel's house. It's in the country."

"Why are we going there?"

"It's the safest place for us to be right now. I can explain everything when we get there."

She didn't say anything else the rest of the way there. When I pulled up in front of the house, Aviel came out and came straight to the car. He helped Amy out and we all went inside to the living room.

"Amy," Aviel said, "I want you to know that you're safe here. Nothing will get you while you're on this property. I need you to tell me exactly what happened this morning. No matter how crazy you think it sounds. Can you do that?" His voice was soft and soothing.

She nodded. "I was getting ready for work when I heard a huge crash. I went to see what it was, and I saw a man standing in the living room. I screamed and started to run back to my room when he was just suddenly in front of me and put his hand around my neck. He asked me if I was Violet. I shook my head. The first thing I noticed was the tattoo on his face, it looked like a falling star. Then I noticed he had huge black wings coming out of his back. I tried to scream, but he squeezed harder. He threw me down on the floor and started looking around the apartment. I was too scared to move, so I just watched him. Then he said, 'Tell Violet I'll find her.' And then he was just gone. Am I going crazy?"

"No Amy," Aviel said, "everything you saw was real. This probably isn't the time to tell you but it's important that you know. Angels are real and you just had an encounter with Lucifer."

I watched as Amy's face got even whiter. Then she got mad.

"You think this is funny?" she yelled. "Making fun of me after what I just told you. I need to get out of here."

Amy got up and started for the door. Aviel was suddenly in front of her. She screamed and turned to me.

"Aviel is an angel Amy, but a good one."

"Are you fucking insane?" she asked me.

"No. I know this is a lot to process, but you have to believe me. Please sit down Amy, you're going to have to trust me on this."

At first, I thought she was going to try to run out the door again, but she slowly walked over to a chair and sat down.

My phone dinged and I ignored it. I had more important things to worry about right now. But then it rang, and I checked it. The only person who usually called me was Sue.

"Hello?"

"Did you get the picture?"

"No, I didn't have a chance to check it. Why?"

"It's the hottie I told you about. The new client that only wants to deal with you."

"Hang on, let me check." I looked at the picture but didn't recognize him. "I don't know who he is. Tell Mr. Edington that I'll be back on Monday to deal with him."

"Will do. Enjoy the rest of your time off."

"What was that all about?" Aviel asked ,when I hung up.

"Apparently, there's a new client who's been in the office several times over the past couple of days asking for me. He said he'll only work with me. Sue sent me a picture to see if I knew him. I don't."

"Can I see the picture?" he asked.

I handed him my phone. He looked concerned when he saw the picture. Then he took my phone over to Amy. "Is this the man who attacked you this morning?"

Her face went white again. "Yeah, but without the tattoo."

Aviel started to pace the living room. "This has just gotten more serious. He's taking human form to look for you."

"Why does …" Amy paused. "Why does Lucifer want Violet?"

"Because she's the key to saving the world."

Chapter Twenty-Four

Amy hadn't said a thing in a very long time. I was starting to wonder if she was in shock.

"Amy, Are you okay?" I asked

Aviel brought me into his arms as we waited for her to answer. He leaned in and whispered into my ear, "I think she is in shock."

"I'm not in shock. I'm trying to wrap my head around this and not call you both liars."

I took a step towards her. "I swear to you everything he has said was true. We can prove it." I turned to Aviel and reached for him. He took my hand and stood next to me. "Show her." I'd never seen his wings, but I knew he had them. I'd seen that the angels in Heaven had different colors. I just didn't know what they meant yet.

He took a few steps away from us and let his wings out. I couldn't help but admire the color. His massive white wings with black tips made me want to caress them. Amy, on the other hand, looked like she was about to pass out. I rushed over to her. "Amy, Amy, are you okay."

She had her hand over her mouth and her eyes were about to bug out of their sockets. "OH MY GODS!!" she yelled. "What the hell! Are you fucking kidding me right now!"

I grabbed her and held her. "It's okay. He is a good angel."

She whipped around to face me. "I'm not freaking out about that. I knew there were real angels among us. I'm freaking out because how could you keep something like this from me?"

I was more confused than anything. "You're not freaking out with Aviel, but with Lucifer you freaked out? How are you okay with Aviel?"

She started to laugh. "I'm not okay, but I'm not scared of him like I was with Lucifer. How are you the key to saving the world? You're human. Right?"

I squirmed under her stare. "About that, I just found out I'm a half-angel."

"WHAT!" she screamed.

I had to cover my ears before she blew my eardrums out. "Can we bring the screaming down to a lower level. I don't think my ears can handle much more."

Amy crossed her arms and tapped her foot on the floor. "I'm sorry, my excitement is bothering you."

I took my hands away from my ears. "I'm confused as to how you're excited. I freaked out when I found out. Matter of fact I kind of still am."

Aviel had been quiet this whole time. He came over to me with his wings tucked away. "Why didn't you tell me you were still freaked out?"

I gave him a sad smile. "Because I'm trying to be okay with this. But being the key to stopping a war is more than I want on my plate. I don't even know if I can learn everything there is to learn. Now that the Morning Star is after me, I doubt I will be able to find the others without him on my ass."

He brought me into his arms, making me feel safe. "I will never let him near you."

I placed my hand on his chest and looked up at him. "You can't promise me that. I will have to face him one day. Now he knows where I work, he won't stop, and I won't let him make me live in fear. You said I can't die, but I can get hurt. Right?"

"Not happening. You are not facing him until you can master everything. He plays dirty and will break your will to live. That's his ploy and always will be."

I laid my cheek on his chest and shivered. "I knew he was awful; I didn't think he was that bad."

"Hello! I'm still here," Amy said, clearly a little pissed off.

"What's wrong? I thought you would be happy for me."

"Oh, I'm happy for you, but I don't want any PDA. We need some rules if I'm staying here."

I giggled at her. "Then you might want to find a room on the other side of the house."

She shook her head. "That's my cue to leave. Call me when we have food. I'm starving."

We watched her walk down the hallway and out of sight. I looked up at my sexy angel and kissed him. I needed his touch to chase away the fear and doubt. There was nothing better than being in his embrace.

He growled against my lips and I moaned. "If you want me to make lunch, I'd advise you to stop while we are ahead."

It was my turn to growl. "You are mine after lunch. No ifs, ands, or buts about it." I reluctantly let him go. "Can I help you with something that doesn't involve the stove?"

He pulled away grabbing my hand in the process and dragged me into the kitchen. "I'm going to teach you how to cook if it's the last thing I do. Everyone needs to at least know the basics."

I laughed at him. "I'll try, but I warn you, I get bored easily when it comes to cooking."

He chuckled at me. "I'll make it interesting for you. For everything you learn you get to choose when and where we have sex."

Now this got my attention. "Anywhere and anyway?"

He nodded. "Yes, ma'am."

"When do we get started?" I said, as I moved him a little faster.

His laugh vibrated through the kitchen and I couldn't help but smile at him. "If I knew that was the key to get you to learn something. I would have done that when we were trying yesterday."

I hopped onto the counter next to the stove. "Well, you know the secret now. So, let's get started."

He took some stuff out of the fridge and placed it on the counter. He went to the cabinet, taking out a bowl. He came back over to me. "We're going to make something simple and easy. Grilled chicken sandwiches and homemade fries. Grab those potatoes and cut them longways. I'll get the chicken into a Hawaiian marinade."

When we were finished, I leaned over and whispered into his ear. "When we're done, meet me in the shower." I turned away from him and yelled for Amy. "Lunch is ready!"

Chapter Twenty-Five

While we're eating, Amy asked me to tell her everything from the last few days. Starting with finding the picture of my father at Aunt Milana's, to learning how to gather energy into my body.

"Wow," she said, when I was done. "I always knew there was something special about you, I just never would have guessed you were half-angel. I have the coolest best friend in the world."

I couldn't help but laugh at that, but I was glad she seemed to be okay with everything.

"So," she started, "can I ask questions now?"

"Sure, but I have one for you first," I said. "You said earlier that you knew angels were real. Did you mean because of Lucifer or something else?"

Amy took a deep breath and got a far off look on her face. "When I was a little girl, I was in the hospital room when my granny died. I saw a man with wings talk to her while she was in the bed. Then I saw her get up, but she was transparent now. The man with the wings took her hand and I watched as they faded until I couldn't see them anymore. I thought it was a dream, until today. Now I know it was real."

I looked at Aviel. "How could she have seen that?"

"Children are open-minded, they see things no one else does."

Then I had a thought. "I'll be right back." I went to my purse and got the picture of my mom with my father. "Amy, is this the man you saw?"

She grinned when she looked at the picture. "Yes, I'll never forget him."

"That's my father."

"No freaking way. Wow. What a strange coincidence."

"Not really," Aviel said. "Your encounter with Remiel changed you, even though you didn't know it. Deep down you knew about angels and that drew you to Violet."

Amy smiled at that. "Cool, now it's my turn. How are you going to find the other eleven half-angels?"

Aviel took that question. "I'll have to go to Heaven for that. The Room of Souls shows every living person on Earth. When a soul is about to leave Earth, it starts to flicker. That's when Ferrier Angels know to go to that soul. When a soul needs help it turns blue and a Protection Angel goes to help that soul. A half-angel has a soul that is brighter than the rest. But they can be really hard to find, as they only show up a fraction of the time."

"How many different types of angels are there?" Amy asked.

"There are quite a few, but the most common are Warrior Angels like me, Ferrier Angels like Violet's father, Protection Angels, Messenger Angels, and of course the Archangels."

"Will I get to meet any more angels?"

"If you're going to be sticking around here then that's very likely," Aviel told her.

"Yay!" Amy started clapping her hands together like a kid. At least she was entertaining. "I have one more question for now. Can you do anything cool Violet?"

"Not yet," I said. "But I'm going to have training to help me."

"I can't wait for that," Amy said and yawned. "I think I need a nap. Today has been, well, fucking crazy. I'll see you two in a while."

I watched as she left the kitchen. "That went better than I expected. I was sure she was going to go postal when she found out I was a half-angel."

Aviel cocked his eyebrow. "That's what you were most worried about?"

"Yeah. Amy hates to be left out of secrets, like she really hates it."

"She's a little strange."

"I know, but I love her anyway. I think it was the way she was raised. She was very spoiled as a kid, hell, she still is. She only works because she gets bored. Her dad owns the club we always go to so money isn't an issue."

He didn't say anything to that and just walked out of the kitchen.

I followed him. "Where are you going?"

He looked over his shoulder and winked. "I think you promised me a shower." Then he just disappeared.

"That's so not fair," I said to the empty room.

By the time I got to the master bathroom, Aviel was already in the shower. I got undressed in record time and joined him. I barely had a chance to step in when he was on me. I sucked in a breath at the cold tile as my back was pushed up against it. But as soon as his mouth found my nipple my whole body was on fire and I forgot all about the cold.

With his hand between my legs and his mouth alternating from nipple to nipple, it didn't take me long to come. I tried to be quiet since Amy was here, but I'm positive I wasn't successful.

"I need inside you now," he growled.

I moved my legs apart because I needed him inside me too. He entered me in one quick thrust and we both moaned. Nothing had ever been as good as it was with Aviel. I didn't know if it was because he was an angel or my soulmate, but it was like I could never get enough of him.

By the time we got out of the shower the water was getting cold. He dried me off and carried me to the bed.

"I'm not tired," I told him. "I think I need to do more training."

"We will. But right now, I just want to feel you against me. I have a feeling that things are about to get a lot crazier."

"You mean Lucifer?"

"Yes. It's still hard to believe he's on Earth."

"How can I stop him from getting me? I mean, I know nothing about being an angel or fighting. And I assume he's like the ultimate super bad guy."

"He is. You just have to remember he can't kill you."

"Why is that? I would have thought that being only half-angel would make me easier to kill."

"You would think it would make you easier to kill, but no angel, fallen or otherwise, can kill a human, or half-human. What I mean by that is, it's physically impossible for us to do that. I guess you could say it's in our DNA or something. He may want to but he won't be able to. He can hurt you, or send humans after you, but he or his followers can't end your life."

"That's not exactly reassuring."

"I know and I'm sorry. Just know that whenever you leave this place, you'll have an army of Protection Angels with you at all times, Amy, too. You'll be safe until you're trained. Then you can take care of yourself."

I liked the idea of that. I was always independent and never liked it when someone had to do something for me. But right now, until I can be a badass half-angel, I'll take all the help I can get.

Chapter Twenty-Six

Friday night was club night and I wasn't going to let anyone, or any angel stop me from living my life. I found the perfect place to watch the sunset before I got ready for the night. The balcony outside the room Aviel and I shared looked out at the perfect spot.

"I guess even half-angels are summoned to the sunset."

I looked over my shoulder to find Aviel leaning against the door frame with his arms crossed, staring at me. I turned fully in his direction. "It calls to me. The peace that washes over me is addicting."

He pushed off the frame and stalked over to me with that hungry look in his eyes. I hadn't gotten dressed yet and all I was wearing was a towel. His look made me wet and my woman parts begged for him. I dropped the towel and jumped on him as soon as he was in front of me. Wrapping my legs and arms around him, I kissed him with all the passion inside me.

I didn't know when or how he got his pants off, but when I felt him slide into me with one stroke, I couldn't help the moan that filled the room. Having him inside me was like nothing I'd ever felt. The pleasure and connection we had were more than anything I could ever explain.

The harder he went the louder I got; I couldn't help the orgasm that rocked through me. I held on for dear life while I rode it out. When I felt him pulse inside me, I knew he was finished. I looked deep into his eyes. This man right in front of me was the only man that could make me come just by looking at him.

"Is it a soulmate thing? Why do I feel the way I do when we are together."

He walked us to the bathroom to clean up. "Yes. We are connected on a different level than others."

"I've never thought having sex was so addicting. I didn't really care about it before."

He set me on the counter as he chuckled. "I'm glad I satisfy you. It makes me happy to know. But if there's anything you don't like; I want you to tell me."

I leaned forward and gently kissed his plump lips. "You'll be the first to know."

"You better get dressed before Amy barges in here and drags you out of here, naked and all."

I laughed because he wasn't lying. "You know her so well. When do I get to meet my bodyguards?"

He got serious. "You'll meet them in a few minutes. They'll be with us tonight in the background."

"Do you think he will show up tonight?"

He helped clean me up which only made me want him again. When he was finished, he looked me in the eyes. "If he's after you, he'll find you."

A shiver ran down my spine. "Let's just hope he doesn't show up. I'm not going to live my life in fear. I can't. If I do then all hope is lost."

He held me tight. "I know. I don't want you to live in fear. I've been thinking about that a lot. I decided that along with the Protection Angels, I'm going to hire human protection. If he sends humans after you, you'll still be protected."

I wanted to argue, but I was out of my league here. I nodded my head. "Until I can protect myself, I'll allow it. I know when I'm in over my head."

He sighed in relief. "Thank you. Thank you for not fighting me on this. As soon as you come into your full powers, I'll get rid of them if that's what you want."

Again, I nodded. I pulled away from him. If I was going to live my life, I had to clear my head and heart. I needed a few minutes to myself. "I'll be ready in a few. I'll meet you downstairs."

He kissed the top of my head. "Don't take too long. You know I can't hold Amy off forever. When that woman has something on her mind, I have a feeling there is no stopping her."

I laughed. "You could say that. She's headstrong and nothing will stop her."

I headed for the closet. Aviel and some of the other angels had gone to our apartment and got the rest of our stuff. He even paid the rent for the rest of our lease. The landlord understood and told Aviel he didn't have to pay, but Aviel insisted.

I grabbed a few things and went back out to the room. Aviel was gone. In a way I wish he would have stayed, but I needed this alone time. Going back into the bathroom, I got myself together. I was ready in less than thirty minutes.

Walking down the stairs, I could hear male voices. I paused just before I reached the bottom.

"What's the plan if he does show up?" one of the male voices said.

"I'll get Violet out. Kemuel, you get Amy to safety. We'll meet back here."

I took the last few steps and walked into the kitchen. "You must be my bodyguards."

All six of them faced me. "It's nice to meet you. I'm Kemuel." He was the one that I heard ask the question a moment ago.

Aviel walked over and took me into his embrace. "This is Gatlin, Tristan, Jodson, Davian, and Zayd." I look at the angels around me and almost want to faint. The male sexiness was almost too much for me to handle.

Gatlin had brown hair with golden strands and baby blue eyes with the same gold throughout. Tristan was like a surfer dude with blonde hair and dark blue eyes that were almost a stormy blue. Jodson's black hair had dark blue streaks. His golden eyes shined bright. Davian's curly brown hair was wild, just like his almost purple eyes. Zayd piercing green eyes felt like they could see right through me. His light brown hair shined, even in the light of the kitchen. Kemuel's dark features made me hesitate to look at him for too long. His bright green eyes and black hair made me want to run and hide for some reason. That was one angel I didn't want to mess with. Ever!

Chapter Twenty-Seven

"Holy shit," Amy said, when she walked into the living room. "Am I in Heaven?"

I shook my head at her, but I saw all the angels give her a smile. Aviel made the introductions and Amy was more than happy to meet them.

"Amy," I said, getting her attention, "they are here to protect us from Lucifer and his followers. They are not here as your playthings."

She stuck her tongue out at me. "You're no fun."

I rolled my eyes at her.

"Are you ladies ready to go?" Aviel asked.

I nodded my head. "Yes."

"Are these hotties coming with us?" Amy said, winking at the group.

"They'll be around," Aviel said. "But you won't see them. If you do, there's a problem and you'll do exactly what Kemuel says."

His tone left no room for argument and Amy was smart enough not to say anything. The angels disappeared and we left the house in Aviel's big SUV.

Amy was talking, but I wasn't really listening. I talked all big in the safety of Aviel's house, but now that we were headed back to town and the fact that Lucifer was really out there and looking for me hit home.

"Are you okay?" Aviel asked.

"Yeah, just wondering if this was the best idea."

"As much as I would like you to, you can't stay in my house forever. You have a job and a life, and I think you need something normal after the last few days."

"I guess. What about the human bodyguards you mentioned?"

"More hot guys?" Amy asked with a grin.

Aviel ignored her. "They're meeting us at the club. I don't want people to realize they are bodyguards, so they'll be dressed for the club and acting like customers."

"Will we know who they are?" I asked.

"Not tonight. I want to see how it goes. The best thing you can do is act normal."

"What about you?"

"I'll be there but you won't see me. I want everything to appear normal. But just remember you'll always be protected tonight."

I nodded and so did Amy. I think the reality was starting to sink in for her too.

When we got to the club Aviel dropped us at the front door. We waved at the bouncer and walked in. It was a little early, so the club wasn't packed yet. As usual, the waitress brought our drinks without being asked.

Even though I couldn't see them, I could feel the Protection Angels in the club. That made me feel a little better.

Several drinks later, I was more relaxed but still a little on edge. Becky and Lana had joined us and they kept trying to get me out onto the dance floor but I wasn't ready to leave the table unattended tonight.

"Go and have fun," Aviel said in my head.

I immediately looked around but didn't see him.

"I'm close Violet, don't worry."

"Can you hear me if I think this?" I said in my head.

"Yes," he said.

"That's both cool and creepy," I thought back to him.

I heard him chuckle in my head and that sent a shiver down my spine.

"Quit doing that."

"You love it."

"Yes, I do but if I can't have you right now then quit making me want you."

"I'll try and accommodate you. But seriously, go have fun. *Everything will be fine. I promise.*"

I decided to take him at his word, and I left the table and found the girls on the dance floor. A few songs later I felt a hand on my back and then a sinister voice in my ear.

"It's time to go, Violet."

The man moved around to the front of me so that it looked like we were dancing. I didn't know who he was, but I had a pretty good idea who he worked for.

"I don't think so," I said, trying to sound confident.

"You'll come with me or your pretty little friends will get hurt."

I automatically looked up to see them suddenly have dance partners.

Getting my head back on straight, I said, "Do you really think we're here alone?"

"Nice try," he said, with a laugh. "You all came in alone and there's been no one at your table. You haven't even been on your phone. There's no one here to protect you. Now, come with me or risk your friend's safety."

I was about to tell him to fuck off when another man was beside me.

"Is this guy bothering you?" he asked.

"Yes. And his buddies are bothering my friends over there." I pointed to my girls.

"Don't worry Miss, we'll take care of them."

At some unseen signal, all four bad guys were suddenly on the ground, hands behind their backs, and were getting zip-tied.

Becky and Lana looked horrified, but I could tell Amy understood what was going on. The bouncers, or my bodyguards since I didn't know exactly who they were, carted off the asshole and his friends. I was sure I'd learn more about them later, but right now I needed a good explanation for what just happened.

I motioned to Becky and Lana to come with me. Amy kind of shooed them and we went to our table.

"What the hell was that all about?" Lana asked.

"Yeah. I was having a good time and they were hot," Becky said.

Hopefully, they would believe the lie I was about to tell. "The bouncer told me it was ordered by Mr. Bishop. They'd been looking for these guys. Something about using the date rape drug on women at different clubs."

Amy nodded. "Yeah, that's right. Dad told me that all clubs were to be on the lookout for them. I guess they picked the wrong club and wrong girls to try it on here."

"Wow," Lana said. "I'm glad we were here then."

"Yep, that's why we only go to this club. My dad will keep us safe."

Another round of drinks came, and I sat back in the booth thinking about what just happened when Aviel interrupted my thoughts.

"I told you I'd keep you safe."

"Those were my human protection, right?"

"Yes. And I see they're as good as I was told they are."

"Thank you."

"Anything for you."

"Any sign of Lucifer or his followers?"

"No, but my angels are on patrol."

"What about Becky and Lana? Someone will know now that they're close to me."

"Don't worry. They'll be protected too."

"Thank you."

"Go back to enjoying your time with your friends. When we find the other eleven there won't be much time for stuff like this."

"Hello? Violet, are you still with us?" Amy asked, getting my attention.

"Uh, yeah, just thinking."

"Here," Amy said, handing me a shot. "To close calls."

We clink our glasses and downed the shot.

"Back to the dance floor," she yelled.

I shook my head but followed her out there. It was only three songs later when I had a bad feeling come over me. *"Aviel? Something's here."*

"Meet me at the back exit and hurry."

Leaving the dance floor, I ran to the back of the club. I knew my friends would be protected and it would be better that I was away from them. Aviel was at the door when I got there.

He took my hand and transported us back to his place.

I sat on the couch and took a deep breath. I still had that bad feeling clinging to me. "What was that?"

"Lucifer."

I was immediately worried. "Amy."

"She's fine. Kemuel got her out as planned."

"Where are they?"

"He would have taken her to another protected place like this. When he's sure it's safe he'll bring her back."

"Oh, good."

"How did you know something wasn't right?" he asked me.

"I could feel it. I had this sudden bad feeling and knew something was there with us. Will I feel that every time he's close?"

"Yes, which is actually a good thing. You'll have some advanced warning to either fight or get out."

Thinking about the way I felt I shuddered. I couldn't even imagine what it would be like if he actually touched me. I'd never known what evil felt like, but I think I just had a taste of it and I didn't like it at all.

Chapter Twenty-Eight

After what seemed like hours, Kemuel, Amy, and another angel teleport in. I was off the couch in less than a heartbeat. "Oh my God! Amy, are you okay?"

She held on to me as tight as I was her. I could feel her shaking. "I'm scared, but I'm okay."

"We felt him trying to follow us or we would have been here sooner," Tristan stated.

Aviel nodded his head. "I figured as much. We'll need to come up with a better way of losing him. He's too determined to get his hands on Violet. We may need to get some Archangel help."

Gatlin flopped down on the couch and laughed. "You really think they're willing to take time away from whatever they're doing to protect a half-breed?"

Anger boiled through me. "This half-breed didn't want to be a part of this bullshit to begin with." I walked out of the room. I couldn't stand being called a half-breed. I didn't even know why. It is what I was, but the way he said it pissed me off.

I slammed the door to our room and went to the bathroom to change. I was tired and all I wanted to do was sleep. Kicking my shoes off, I got undressed. I washed my face and put my PJ's on. When I was done, I heard a knock on the door.

"Who is it?"

The only thing I could hear was a mumble. Since it was a female's voice, I went to open the door.

"Girl, you should have seen what Aviel did to that ol' boy. I didn't think I'd ever see a man as pissed off as Aviel was."

I let her in and closed the door again. I wasn't in the mood to deal with this right now.

"He deserved it. There was no need for him to talk about me like that."

"That's what they all said. Apparently, he speaks before he thinks."

"I don't care what his excuse is. There was no need for it." I walked over to the huge bed, crawled on top of it and sat down with my legs crossed.

Amy did the same thing. "I agree. It was extremely rude. So, tell me what happened at the club that we had to leave that fast. I didn't see anyone near you and then all of a sudden you were running towards the exit. I didn't see him, so what happened? How did you know he was there?"

"Both Aviel and I got this bad feeling and he told me to run. We left before Lucifer could do anything. I'm sure we left before he even got there. I'm just glad you're safe."

"When Kemuel picked me up and rushed me out of there, I thought he'd gone mad. I was so scared. When I started fighting him, he said one word, 'Lucifer.' Then I just froze."

I reached over to her and grabbed her hands. "It's okay to be scared. Hell, I was. Until I'm able to defend myself, I'll continue to be scared out of my mind."

"That's just it. I can't protect myself."

I gave her a sad smile and then I realized something. "Yes, you can. You can take classes; we can take self-defense classes. The angels can't kill humans. Only the humans he sends after us. Why didn't I think of this before? We are all going to learn to defend ourselves." I jumped off the bed and sprinted downstairs. I need to tell Aviel my plan.

Getting to the main floor, I stopped dead in my tracks before I collided with Jodson. He braced me by holding onto my shoulders. "Whoa there, what's wrong?"

I took a step back from him. "Nothing, where's Aviel. I need to talk to him?"

He lowered his arms. "He had to go take a walk. He'll be back. Maybe I can answer your question."

Maybe he could help. After all, they know the art of fighting. They haven't lived this long by running. "Me and the girls want to learn how to defend ourselves against the humans. We don't want to be afraid anymore."

He smiled at me and clapped his hands together. "I thought you'd never ask. We start training tomorrow morning."

Before I could say a thing, he vanished. What the hell just happened?

Strong arms wrapped around me before I could even move. I tilt my head back to see Aviel's alluring eyes. I turned around to face him. "Where did you go?"

He placed a soft kiss on my cheek. "I had to calm down before I destroyed my house. I'm so sorry about earlier. He had no right to say those things."

I placed a hand on his chest. "It's not your apology I want to hear. You did nothing wrong. I would rather just move past it. I want to learn to defend myself from the humans. Jodson said we can start tomorrow morning. I need to get a hold of Becky and Lana."

He took my hand that was on his chest and kissed it. "I think that is a great idea. I should have thought about that."

I looked up at him. "You've been more worried about protecting me than anything else."

"I'm all for making out, but can you not do it in front of me," Amy said, as she walked past us. "Unlike some of us, we don't have a man to kiss up on."

I giggled at her. "No one has stopped you from getting you a man," I yelled after her.

"That may be true, but I haven't found my soulmate like you," she hollered back.

I shook my head at her statement. "Sometimes, I don't understand her."

"I agree with you. She can be a bit of a handful."

"Hey, I heard that. I'm not a handful. I just know what I want." Amy said, as she walked back over to us with her hands on her hips.

"Just because I don't have a man doesn't mean I don't want one. I just haven't found the right guy."

I let go of Aviel to take a step towards her. "Just because you haven't found the right man doesn't mean he isn't out there."

"I know that. I just wish I could find him already. I love my independence, but at the same time I wish I had someone that cared about me as much as I did him."

This time I wrapped her into my arms. It was the same way I felt before Aviel came along. "We will find him, I promise. We just need to stop looking for him at the club. Those guys only have one thing on their mind."

I got a laugh out of her. "Why do you think I go there? If I can't find a man, I at least want to get lucky once in a while." We both laughed while Aviel shook his head at us.

Chapter Twenty-Nine

It had been a stressful night and all I wanted to do was go to bed. Luckily everyone was in agreement with that. I laid in bed and waited for Aviel. He was giving last-minute instructions to the Protection Angels.

When he finally made it to bed, I snuggled up to him. At first, we didn't talk but then my overactive brain had a thought, well a few actually.

"Do angels have to sleep?"

"In Heaven no, but here on Earth, we need some sleep. About an hour a day and we're good to go."

"Is that why sometimes I can't seem to sleep?"

"Probably, you still need some sleep but not as much as a human."

"Why did it seem like having an Archangel help me would be entirely out of the question?"

"Archangels are very different from the rest of us. They only involve themselves in the human world if they are specifically instructed to by God."

"Are they all-powerful or something?"

"They are the most powerful of angels and their main job is protecting Heaven, so they almost never leave."

"So, could you like petition one to help us?"

He chuckled. "It doesn't really work that way. If we get help from an Archangel it's because we really, really need it."

"If they are so powerful, how come it's going to take twelve half-angels to save the world? Surely they'd be a better choice."

"All I can tell you is that's the way it's written."

"That's not cryptic or anything." My next question was both something I really wanted to know, and kind of dreaded at the same time. "How long have you been alive?"

"I truly don't know. But I have existed for hundreds of years or more."

"How do angels come into being?"

Aviel grinned at me. "You are just full of questions tonight."

"I've always been naturally curious. Are you going to tell me?"

"Yes. When an exceptionally pure soul enters Heaven, they have the choice to become an angel."

"Wow. I'm taking it that doesn't happen very often."

"No, it doesn't."

"If that's the case, why is Gatlin such an asshole?"

"He's been an angel a long time and I think sometimes he forgets what it's like to be human."

I let out a big yawn.

Aviel pulled the covers up around us. "I think it's time for you to get some sleep. It seems we've got a big day ahead of training tomorrow. You're going to need your rest."

He kissed my forehead and I closed my eyes. I was asleep in no time.

****

By the time I woke up the next morning, I was feeling a lot better. I think it was the prospect of training. I wanted to learn how to kick some ass if I needed to. Amy and Aviel were in the kitchen when I got there.

"Good morning sleepyhead," Amy said, with a grin.

"Hey."

Aviel came over to me and gave me a quick kiss.

"What are you making?" I asked, noticing the smell in the kitchen.

"Blueberry pancakes and sausage. You guys are going to need to fuel up for the day."

I watched him flip some pancakes. He was beyond sexy standing over the stove.

"What are we going to tell the girls?" I asked.

It was Amy that spoke first. "I think we should tell them I was attacked and Aviel's friends are going to help us learn how to defend ourselves."

"You know they're going to be pissed that we didn't tell them you were attacked."

"I know."

"You get to call them then," I told her.

"Are we doing the training here?" she asked.

Aviel turned to answer her. "Yes. This is the safest place for you."

She got his address and made the calls. The girls were up for learning self-defense, but I could tell by the look on Amy's face that she was getting shit for not telling them sooner.

While she was on the phone, I took the opportunity to stand as close as I could to Aviel and watched him cook breakfast.

"You know, seeing you like this is a real turn on," I whispered to him.

He chuckled. "Don't get me started or Amy will yell at us again for another PDA."

I laughed. "True."

"No smooching," Amy said, as she sat back down at the breakfast bar.

We both laughed, but I took a step away from him anyway. "When are the girls coming?"

"They should be here in a couple of hours."

"How mad were they?" I really wanted to know.

"Pretty mad and wanted to know why I didn't say anything last night. I told them I wasn't ready to talk about it. Just an FYI, they're mad at you too."

"What did I do?"

Amy smirked. "Got yourself a boyfriend and didn't tell them."

"Ooooh, yeah, I guess that kind of slipped my mind with everything going on."

"I told them he was hot, and you wanted to keep him all to yourself."

Aviel let out a laugh at that, but otherwise, said nothing.

"Did you warn them that Aviel's friends are hot but off-limits?"

"Of course."

Aviel set a plate in front of each of us. "Breakfast is served, ladies."

"Thanks," we said in unison.

Amy moaned when she took a bite of the blueberry pancake. "Violet, if you two ever break up, Aviel is mine. I'll have him just for his cooking alone. Wait, never mind, I'll become as big as a house if I ate like this all the time."

I shook my head and dug into my food. It was times like this I was glad for my half-angel DNA. I was sure I could eat a whole stack of them.

By the time the girls got there Jodson and Tristan had also appeared. Aviel had the talk with them about not doing any angel things in front of the girls.

Before we could get started, I was given the third degree by Becky and Lana. I was expecting it so I had my story in place that we met at the club and had an instant connection. They believed me and when they saw him, they both winked at me.

I was sure both of them were drooling when Tristan walked out in a pair of tight yoga pants. I'd never seen a man wear them and I decided that Aviel was going to get a few pairs, because, damn, they looked fine on those angels.

Finally, Jodson joined us and it was time to start the training.

Chapter Thirty

We went to the barn that was at the back of the property. When we walked in I wasn't expecting a full out gym with every machine you could think of and a huge area with mats and mirrors all around it. I stopped in my tracks to take it all in. Aviel came up behind me and wrapped me into his arms with my back to his chest.

"I knew we were going to have to train half-angels. I got prepared as much as I could. This is for all of you. Those mats over there will be where you'll be training for today. I have practice dummies in the back I'll be bringing out later."

"This is amazing. But I have to admit, I don't know what ninety percent of these machines are for."

He chuckled and kissed the top of my head. "We'll all teach you and the girls how to use each of these machines. But for today we are going to work on defense."

The worry hit me full force. "What if I'm not good at this?"

He turned me around and looked me in the eyes. "If you aren't then we'll train harder, but I have a feeling you'll be a natural. Go have fun. I'm going to go to Heaven and see if I can't find another half-angel. I'll be back before you know it."

He leaned down and kissed me. When we were through, the only thing on my mind was, why weren't we in our bedroom? "Hurry back," was all I said, before I pulled away from him to join the ladies. If I remained near him, we wouldn't be staying here. Just saying, that man knows how to turn a woman on.

"I still can't believe you have a man and didn't tell us," Lana said as she stared at Aviel's retreating back.

Becky leaned into me and whispers, "Why are these guys off-limits? Are they gay or something?"

I busted out laughing and shook my head. "Not even close." What excuse can I give her that she will believe? "They don't want relationships right now. They came here for a job and they want to make sure they do it right." It was the closest thing I could think of that came close to the truth.

Her face fell a little. "Oh okay."

I felt really bad for her. I know she'd been wanting to settle down, but that could never happen with an angel. Their home wasn't here and after the war, they'll be called back. That thought made me freeze. What does that mean for me and Aviel? Surely, he wouldn't be able to stay. Would he?

My heart sank down to my feet. *"You will have to leave after the war, won't you?"*

I didn't know if he would be able to hear me while he was in Heaven, but I had to try. When I got no response back, I got my answer.

Jodson clapped his hands. "Alright, ladies, today we're going to learn the basic steps to help defend yourself. Who wants to get this started?"

I watch as Lana, Becky, and Amy raise their hands. I was the only one who didn't want to be here anymore. I needed answers. My heart was breaking just thinking about him having to leave me. Just like my father did with my mother.

I watched as Lana walked to the middle of the mat where Jodson stood. "Okay, I'm going to show you a move that will get you out of any attackers hold." He turned Lana around and held her tight. The fear on her face was clear as she froze in his embrace.

"Lana, you don't need to have fear here, but I'm glad you have it. Let me explain why. Fear will make us do stupid things. Like right now, you're frozen in place because of it. I want to train you to fight around your fears. It's the only way."

He let her go and had her face him once again. "Are you okay?"

She swallowed hard and nodded her head. "I think so."

He smiled at her. "You'll be a pro after we're done. Don't let your fear win. Are you ready?"

She shook her head no, but got in the position anyway. She gave me a weird look then let out a deep breath.

"I want you to stomp my foot, elbow me as hard as you can, and whip your head backward all at the same time."

All of our eyes got big. As I watched Lana, I saw something change in her. Without warning, she did as she was told. I watched in horror as Jodson hit the ground. I rushed over to check on him. "Are you okay?"

His smile was evidence that he wasn't hurt at all. He was playing the part of a human and I was thankful for that. I didn't know if I should tell Lana and Becky or not. I'd have to ask Aviel and the other angels if it would be a good idea. The less they knew about what was really going on, I thought the better off they'd be.

Jodson got up and Tristan took his place. This time it was Becky's turn. I watched both her and Amy take them down. Now it was my turn and my stomach was full of butterflies. The 'what if's' were swimming in my head.

Jodson replaced Tristian as I walked onto the mat.

The ladies encouraged me by saying I had this and it was easier then I thought. I still couldn't shake the feeling I was going to suck at this.

"Don't be nervous. You're letting your fear get the better of you. Take a few deep breaths in," Jodson whispered to me. I nodded at him and turned to face the other direction like my friends had.

I took a deep breath just as Jodson grabbed me. I didn't think, I just did what everyone else did. As soon as my head connected with Jodson, something changed in me. I wanted to fight. I wanted to rip his head off for touching me. I had no idea where the rage was coming from.

I spun around and took a swing, but he grabbed and pulled me to him. "Violet, let it go. If you don't it will overwhelm you."

"I don't give a damn. Get your hands off me before I remove them myself!"

I was pissed and didn't even care why. He let me go and I went after him again. This time I didn't stop. I did everything I could to get a hit on him, but he blocked everything I threw at him. Which only pissed me off even more. That was until Amy got in front of my next move. It was like slow motion as my fist headed straight for her face. I tried everything to stop the momentum to no avail.

Tristian grabbed her and got her out of my path just in time. I ended up hitting him in the side and I heard him grunt. I stood there in shock and panting. No one dared say a word.

I couldn't take it anymore. I whirled around to Jodson. "What the hell just happened to me?"

He walked over to me with his hands in front of him. He was acting like I was going to attack again. At this point, I wasn't sure if I would or not. He leaned in and whispered to me. "Your angel came out to play. You need to learn to let it go when it gets that bad. If not, you'll become dark. Something we're trying to stop."

I stood there not knowing what to do or think. I didn't want to turn dark. "I think we're done for today. Lana, Becky, we will pick this up tomorrow…"

"It will have to wait. I found him," Aviel said, as he walked in. "We need to go now before it's too late."

Lana steps forward with her hands on her hips. "You found who and why do you have to get him?"

Shit! "We've been looking for someone that knew my dad. I wanted to see if he could tell me anything about him."

She gave me an 'I don't believe you look' but didn't say anything else. "Becky, I guess that is our cue to leave. Call me when you're ready to tell us the truth. Bye, Amy."

I watched them leave. I couldn't tell them the truth yet. It was better this way, I hoped. I turned to Aviel. "So, where are we going?"

He brought me into his arms. As soon as I was there I could feel the rage calm. I let out a relieved sigh. "We're going to Germany. Pack a small bag. We have to leave as soon as we can. He's in trouble."

Before I knew it we were standing in the one place I'd always wanted to visit. Germany was more beautiful than I could ever imagine. The old architecture was beyond memorizing. If only we were here to visit, but we weren't. It was time to find the next half-angel. Hopefully, before his troubles found him.

Chapter Thirty-One

LUCA
One Week Ago

I hated my job, but I liked the people, so most days I could handle it. Today was not one of those days. I worked for an American software company in the accounting department. The pay was good, but the bonus was the location. I loved Hamburg, especially the food.

One of my coworkers was waving at me to get my attention. I locked my computer and went over to her.

"What's up, Marnie?"

"My computer is doing that thing again where I can't save anything."

"You know this isn't my job," I reminded her.

"I know," she whined. "but you're right here and you always save me."

I smiled at her because she already knew I would help her. And it was true, if she waited for the IT guy it could be a few hours. It only took me a minute to fix the problem.

"Thank you, Luca, you're the best. Your talents are wasted in accounting."

She said that to me every time I helped her. But she wasn't wrong. I could do so much more than accounting, but even though my father was the CEO of the company I had to start at the bottom. Fresh out of college with a business degree I'd started in the mailroom. That was less than a year ago but sometimes it felt like eons.

By the end of the day, I was so ready to go home. Between dealing with customers that didn't want to pay their bills and finding my work incredibly boring, I was done.

On the train ride home, I let my mind wander to my past. I was born in the US and adopted when I was just a baby. Because of my dad's company we'd lived in England, France, Spain and finally

Germany. We'd moved to Hamburg when I was fourteen. That was eight years ago.

Of all the places we'd lived, I knew Germany the best, after all, my high school and college years had been there. I watched people on their phones and thought that things were the same no matter where you lived.

Erik had Friday afternoons off, so he was home when I got there.

"We're going out," I said, as soon as I walked in the door.

"Rough day?"

"Yeah."

He chuckled. "Guess it doesn't always pay to be the prodigal son."

"Whatever," I said, but smiled. Erik and I met freshman year of college, so he knew all about me starting at the bottom of my dad's software company.

Several hours later, we were at our favorite dance club. I had a pleasant buzz going and we were making the rounds checking out the women. A cute brunette caught my attention, so I asked her to dance. It was hot, sweaty and the music was loud. The rhythmic beat of the music made me feel carefree after the long day.

We danced for a few songs then went our separate ways. When I got back to where Erik was, I was greeted by two beautiful blondes. He handed me a drink and I started talking to the one closest to me. A while later, the women excused themselves. I wasn't sure if they'd be back, but if not, there were a lot of women there to choose from.

I was watching the sea of people move on the dance floor when a strange feeling came over me. It was like someone was watching me, but in a place with this many people, it could be anyone.

Then I saw her. She had hair so blonde it looked white in the dark club. And even from here, I could tell she was stunningly beautiful.

"I'll be back," I yelled to Erik, and headed straight over to the mystery woman.

When I got to where I'd seen her, she was gone. Then I felt a hand on my back and heard a voice in my ear. "Are you looking for me?"

I spun around to see her. She was even more gorgeous up close. "Yeah," I told her.

"Good," she said, and took my hand, leading me to the dance floor.

Not only was she the most beautiful woman I'd ever laid eyes on, but the way she moved when she danced was incredible. I couldn't help but think about what she'd be like in bed. After a few dances, it was clear where this was leading.

"I don't know your name," I said, when we were close.

She smiled in a way that made my whole body take notice. "Evangeline."

"Well, Evangeline, would you like to go to my place?" I said in her ear.

"I'd love to," she said. Even her voice was sexy.

I texted Erik that I was going back to our place and that I wasn't alone. He sent me a thumbs up and Evangeline and I left the club. I started to head to the train when she stopped me.

"My car is over here," she said, and I followed her to a sleek black sports car.

I whistled. "Nice ride."

Smiling, she said, "I know. Get in."

I gave her directions to my place and with the way she drove, we were there in no time. I barely got the apartment door closed before she undid the top of her dress and I watched it fall to the floor. She was completely naked under it. Wearing nothing but her heels, she walked straight into my room. I had a feeling I was in for the ride of my life.

****

When I woke up the next morning, I was alone. I grinned at the ceiling. Evangeline had rocked my world. I got up to use the bathroom and smiled when I saw the mirror. She'd left her number in bright red lipstick.

After I showered, I went to the kitchen and found Erik making coffee.

"Someone got lucky last night," he said.

"Fuck, it was way more than lucky. It was like winning the lottery and finding a buried treasure all rolled into one."

"That good huh?"

"Best I've ever had."

"You going to see her again? I see she left her number." Erik grinned.

"God yes. I think I'm slightly addicted."

He rolled his eyes. "It was just sex, Luca. Even if it was good there's no way it was life-altering."

"You've obviously never had great sex."

Erik chuckled. "You sound like a teenager after having sex with someone more experienced."

I had to laugh at that because he was partially right.

After finishing my second cup of coffee I got ready for the day. I had a bunch of errands to run which I normally hated, but nothing could put me in a bad mood today.

Chapter Thirty-Two

Two hours into my day, and all I could think about was Evangeline. It was like she had a spell on me or something. I still couldn't believe I got lucky with a woman like that. I grabbed my phone and texted her.

Me: I had a great night last night. You want to hang out again sometime?

I put my phone back in my pocket. I really wasn't expecting her to answer me right away. But when my phone beeped, I reached for it.

Evangeline: Last night was amazing, I would love to hang out again. When and where?

I felt like a little boy who got to sit in the front of the dugout of their favorite baseball team. I wanted to fist pump the air, but I didn't.

Me: How about tonight? We can have dinner at Sagners.
Evangeline: Sounds like a plan. I will see you tonight at seven.
Me: See you then.

After getting all my errands done, I headed to get some lunch. If I could even eat, my stomach was filled with knots. What if I screwed this up and she never wanted to see me again? That would fucking suck.

"Luca?"

I turned to see who had called me. A smile graced my face when I saw Carmen standing across the street. I jogged over to her and gave her a hug.

"How have you been? I haven't seen you since college."

She whipped her long brown hair to the side. "I've been good. Got a great job in marketing. How about you? Did your dad give you your dream job?"

I gave her a sarcastic chuckle. "Oh yeah, pops gave me a job alright. I had to start from the bottom and I'm still not where I want to be. Most days I hate my job, others I love it. For now, I'll stick with it. I'm glad you got a great job. I'm actually happy I ran into you. You should hang out with me and Erik sometime."

She giggled. "You two are still hanging out. I thought by now you would be sick of each other. What are you guys doing next weekend?"

I put my hands in my front pocket. "We will be at Club Moondoo. You should come, I know Erik will be happy to see you."

She chuckled. "I'm sure he'll be happy to see me. I broke the man's heart. I doubt he'll be excited."

I leaned into her and whispered, "He hasn't gotten over you. He still thinks if he becomes a better man, you'll come back to him."

She gasped, "Are you serious?"

I nodded my head. "You'll see, that is, if you aren't a chicken shit and actually show up." I gave her a wicked smile.

She puts her hands on her hips. "I ain't no chicken shit you asshole."

I busted out laughing, just as she hit my arm. Once I got my laughter under control I asked, "So, I will see you there then?"

She rolled her eyes. "Fine I'll be there, but if shit hits the fan, it's on you."

"Deal." I gave her a hug before we went our separate ways.

****

I'd changed, I didn't know how many times. I wanted to look good for Evangeline tonight. I was so nervous I couldn't even think straight. I looked at the time and cursed. If I didn't leave now I was going to be late. I grabbed my shoes and put them on. I left just in time to meet the train.

I watched the city fly by as I looked out the window, trying to get my stomach to stop knotting up. I'd never been like this with a woman before. I didn't know what the deal was.

Finally, my stop came up and I got off. Luckily the restaurant was only a block away from the train stop. I looked at my watch and saw I only had ten minutes to spare. I'd never been late in my life and here I was about to be late to my first official date with Evangeline. She had to have a spell on me or something.

"I was wondering if you were going to show up or not."

I turn my head to the side to see Evangeline leaning against the wall of the restaurant.

"Of course, I was just running behind. You ready?" I gave her my arm. She was happily willing to take it.

"I'm glad you asked me out tonight. I wanted to talk to you about last night."

The hostess took us to our table, and I pulled out a chair for her. "What about last night?"

I didn't want to seem eager or even tell her I had the best night of my life.

"I don't normally do that kind of thing. I'm not that kind of woman."

I gave her a smile. "If it makes you feel better, I had an amazing time." I didn't want her to feel guilty about it.

She smiled back at me. "It helps."

The waitress came over and took our orders. We talked while we waited for our food to come. Turned out she was an accountant as well, but unlike me, she loved her job. She just moved here from Spain about a year ago. How I hadn't run into her sooner was beyond me.

She could speak multiple languages and had worked for a lot of major companies. She'd also visited most major cities around the world. I was sitting there wondering how she was interested in a guy like me.

"What are you thinking about?"

I looked up at her. "Nothing really. I'm enjoying your company and getting to know you. I'd like to see you again."

The smile that graced her face was breathtaking. "I would love that."

"Erik and I go to the club every Friday. I was hoping you would join us there."

She looked down at the table. "I was actually hoping to hang out with you sooner than that."

I couldn't help but smile at her. "I think we can arrange that. How about Monday night?"

"I think I can swing that," she said, as she pulled her blonde hair behind her.

The waitress came over to place the bill on the table. "I'm going to leave this here if you need anything else just let me know."

We both said thank you as she walked away. I picked up the bill and placed the money inside and left it as I got up.

"I've had a great time tonight. Do you want to come back to my place?"

I hoped she would say yes. I need her more than I want to admit.

"I had a great night as well. I think I'm going to pass on tonight. I have a lot to do before work on Monday. Especially, if I will be spending the night with you on Monday," she said, as she got up and walked over to me.

I couldn't help but to lean down and capture those lips. If I died right now, I would be a happy man.

Chapter Thirty-Three

I watched as Evangeline walked down the sidewalk. She had a body that went on for days. I had to force myself to turn around and make my way back to the train station.

Erik wasn't home when I got there which meant he probably had a date. I couldn't wait to surprise him with Carmen next week. I should probably warn him, but where was the fun in that?

Feeling a little restless I didn't want to watch TV. Our apartment had a small balcony, so I got a beer and decided to sit out there. We had a good view of the city. I could see both the old and the new mixed together. It was something I loved about Hamburg.

As I took in the busy city, my thoughts went back to Evangeline. She was like the perfect woman. Sexy, smart, and liked to drive fast cars. It was as if she appeared out of nowhere just for me, and I certainly wasn't complaining.

A while later my phone rang. It was my mom.

"Hi mom," I said, when I answered.

"Is everything okay?" she asked.

"Yeah. Why wouldn't it be?"

"I just have this feeling that something was going on with you."

"Everything is fine. In fact, I had a dinner date with a gorgeous woman earlier."

"Where did you meet her?"

"At the club."

"You know you won't meet a nice girl at a place like that Luca."

I rolled my eyes. "She has a good job mom. Some people go there just to dance and blow off steam. Not every woman there is a tart."

She laughed at that. There were a few words mom still used from when we lived in England and I liked to use them whenever I got a chance.

"Very funny son."

"I thought so."

"So, tell me more about this woman you've met."

I told her what I knew about Evangeline and mom actually seemed impressed.

"Well, I hope it works out for you honey."

"Thanks, mom, me, too. And tell dad I'm ready for a promotion."

She laughed. I said that every time I talked to her. I heard a knock on the door.

"Someone's here. I'll talk to you later. Love you."

"Love you, too."

I hung up and went to the door. I was shocked to see Evangeline on the other side.

"Hey," I said with a grin. "Would you like to come in?"

"Actually, I was wondering if you wanted to come somewhere with me."

"Yeah, I'd love to. Let me get my wallet and keys."

I went to my room to get what I needed. I had no idea where she wanted to take me, but I was up for anything with her. A minute later, I was locking the door and we were headed to her car.

Once again, she was driving fast through the sometimes very narrow streets. It actually made me nervous a few times, but I tried not to show it.

"Where are we going?" I finally asked.

"There's a midnight showing of Casablanca. I thought we could go see it."

I was at a loss for words. I loved the old black and white classics, even though no one my age had ever seen them. I used to watch them with mom when I was a kid and still watched them to this day.

"You like old movies?" I asked her.

"Yes. They take you back to a simpler time."

It was official. This woman was made for me. "That's what I think too. Are you even real?"

A beautiful laugh came out of her mouth. "I'm very real, Luca."

She parked and we walked a couple of blocks to an old theater. She already had tickets, so we handed them to the attendant and easily found seats in the almost empty theater. I felt almost giddy when the movie started. I was about to watch one of my favorite movies with a stunningly beautiful woman. Life couldn't get any better than this.

I was wrong about life not getting any better. About halfway through the movie, she reached over and started rubbing the crotch of my jeans. I looked at her, but she appeared to be focused on the movie.

Normally I wasn't an exhibitionist, but it seemed like Evangeline was bringing out parts of me I didn't know existed. As quietly as I could I unzipped the zipper. I was already semi-hard, so it felt good to let my dick escape the confines of my jeans.

As soon as her hand touched me without the pants in the way, I was fully hard. Even though the theater was mostly empty, there were still people here and we had to be careful.

Evangeline grabbed my dick and started stroking it. Sitting still was the hardest thing I'd ever had to do, but I didn't want to give away what was really going on. I knew I wasn't going to last long and before I knew it, I was coming. I practically had to bite my tongue to keep from calling out her name.

When I opened my eyes, I saw that I'd made a mess on her hand and the back of the seat in front of me. Looking over at her she had a very satisfied look on her face. She reached in her purse and pulled out a cloth. After wiping off her hand she cleaned the back of the seat.

I couldn't focus on the movie anymore and when it was over, we went back to her car.

"I get the feeling you've got a little bit of a bad girl streak in you," I said, when I slid into the passenger side.

She laughed. "I've got a lot of bad girl in me. I have to be good at the office, so it has to come out sometime."

"But earlier tonight you said you don't normally do things like go home with a guy you've just met."

"That was true. I'm very picky about who I spend time with, and Luca, I'm really beginning to like spending time with you."

All I could do was smile. I knew it was fast, but I might just be falling for the mysterious Evangeline.

Chapter Thirty-Four

We made it back to her house in the suburbs in record time. I barely made it out of the car before she was on me. I let her lead the way into the house without taking my hands and mouth off of her.

With heavy breaths she asked, "You got a condom?"

I nodded my head and took it out of my back pocket. Picking her up I threw her on the bed while I got undressed. I needed her more than I wanted to admit. My dick was harder than it had ever been. I stalked over to her and ripped her dress off. I looked at her as she laid there, naked for me, with a devilish grin on her face. Putting the condom on I moved so that I was on top of her.

I kissed her neck and rubbed her clit with my dick at the same time. Her moans were making it hard for me to take my time. She grabbed me as she looked at me. "I need you inside me now."

I didn't even hesitate. I thrust inside her with one stroke. Feeling her tighten around me almost undid me. I was in heaven as I fucked her hard. Her moans drove me insane, making me go harder and faster. There was no way I was going to last much longer. I felt her come hard as she screamed my name. I released myself at the same time.

We lay there breathing heavily, staring up at the ceiling. "Wow!"

She turned her body towards me. "Wow is right."

I turned to look at her and took her face in my hands as I kissed her. "What kind of spell do you have over me woman?"

She laughed and slapped my arm playfully. "I was going to ask you the same thing."

"Where have you been all my life?"

She laughed again. "I've been around." She got up and headed to what I was guessing was the bathroom. I laid there thinking how I got so lucky to find her.

"Do you want me to stay the night or do you want me to go home?" I was hoping she said to stay.

She peeked around the corner. "I still have a lot of work to do. I would rather you go home so I can get things done."

My heart sank a little, but I understood. "Yeah, I can see your point." As I stood up it was obvious, I was very ready for her again, but that wasn't happening so I grabbed my clothes and got dressed. Once I was done, I went to the bathroom just as she came out and pulled her to me. I captured her lips with mine. I couldn't help it; I could honestly say I was addicted to her.

When I forced myself to pull away, I rested my forehead on hers. "I'll see you on Monday." I kissed her one more time. I unwillingly let her go and walked out the door.

That night I couldn't sleep. I tossed and turned as my mind wandered. I couldn't get her out of my mind. What the hell was happening to me? I just met the woman. I shouldn't be feeling this strongly towards her yet. Should I?

Finally giving up on sleep, I went to take a shower. I hoped it would help with my restlessness. It was a good thing I didn't work tomorrow. Sundays were when I worked out and relaxed. It was the only day I had that my father didn't have me either working or running errands.

I turned the water on as hot as I could. Getting undressed, I looked into the mirror and noticed I needed to shave. I'd do that after the shower. Jumping in, I let the hot water wash over me. I almost moaned with how good it felt. I didn't realize how stressed out my body was.

Once the water started to turn cold, I got out and wrapped a towel around me. Going to the sink I started to shave my face. When I was done, I finally felt the pull of sleep trying to take me. I was thankful for that because I definitely needed to sleep.

****

Waking up well after I normally did was a shock. It meant I was going to be late starting my workout, and I hated being late for anything. It made my day out of whack.

Throwing the covers off of me, I grabbed my tennis shoes and workout clothes and got dressed. Heading out to the kitchen, I got my shake ready. While it was in the blender, I went to grab my phone from my room. I hated working out without music.

"Starting a little late aren't you," I heard Erik yell.

"You have no idea, man." I walked back into the kitchen and turned off the blender.

"Do I even want to know?"

I laughed at him. "Not really, man. Not really. Want to get lunch later?"

Erik took a seat at the counter. "Sure, where do you want to go?"

"Let's try that new sports bar. I hear the wings are killer."

"Awesome, I'll see you there around one."

I grabbed my shake and headed out. "See you there, bro."

I drank my shake before I even got out the door. I tied my shoes, opened my music app, and clicked on my favorite song, Thunder by Imagine Dragons. It helped to get me in the mood to workout. I jogged to the gym that was over a mile away. I got into my groove and by the time I was done, it was almost time to meet Erik.

I took a quick shower before I headed out. I took the train to the other side of town to the new sports bar. I was kind of excited to eat there. From what I'd heard, it was the new hot spot to hang out, even during the day.

Reaching my stops, I got off, and I slowly jogged over to the bar. Erik was just getting there too.

"Hey man!" I yelled to Erik.

He turned in my direction with a smile on his face. "Man, I just got here and I'm already seeing some fine ass honey's."

I laughed. "What are we waiting for, let's go in and see what the hype is all about."

We walked in to find half-naked woman working. "No wonder this place was highly recommended."

"Dude, I think I just found my favorite place to eat," Erik said.

"I think you're right. Let's get a table and some wings."

Erik nodded and followed me. We grabbed a table just as a hot blonde came up to take our drink order. We told her what we wanted and ordered wings.

"Dude, this place is off the chain. Why haven't we found this place sooner?"

We both laughed until I got the feeling of being watched again. I took a look around. I didn't see anyone even looking this way, but I couldn't shake the feeling.

"Hey, do you have this weird feeling?"

Erik raised his eyebrows. "Like what kind of feeling?"

I tilted my head to the side. "Like we're being watched."

He shook his head. "No, I don't feel or see anyone looking at us or watching us."

I tried to shake the feeling, but it just got worse. When I couldn't take it anymore, I saw there was a guy at the end of the bar that got up and headed our way. I nudged Erik just as the guy stood in front of us.

"We need to talk."

I gave him a funny look. "I think you got the wrong person. Do I even know you?"

He shook his head. "Not yet, but I promise you will want to hear what I have to say."

I debated if I should talk to this man. What if he is Evangeline's husband or something? I never asked her if she was married or had a boyfriend. I guessed I was about to find out.

Chapter Thirty-Five

I looked at Erik. "If I'm not back in ten minutes, call the police."

He gave me a strange look, but nodded. I got up from the table and followed the stranger out of the bar and away from any people.

"You know this is a little creepy right? What do you want?"

"Evangeline isn't who you think she is."

"What are you talking about? Are you her husband or something, because I swear, I didn't know she was married."

"I'm not her husband and she's not married."

"Then what's with the cloak and dagger shit? And who are you?"

"I'm here to warn you. You need to stay away from Evangeline. She's dangerous."

I looked at him like he'd lost his mind. "Sure she likes to drive fast but that doesn't make her dangerous."

The stranger looked like he was getting frustrated. "I can't tell you more, but you need to believe me. She is a very dangerous creature and you need to stay as far away from her as possible. Your life depends on it."

A noise behind me caught my attention. It was just a kid crying, but when I turned back around the stranger was gone. I spun around a few times, but it was like he just disappeared.

Shaking my head, I went back into the sports bar.

"What the hell was that all about?" Erik asked, as I sat next to him.

"I'm not completely sure. He warned me to stay away from Evangeline."

"Who's Evangeline?"

"The woman from the club. We hooked up again last night and I'm seeing her again tomorrow."

"Why would he warn you to stay away from her?"

"No fucking clue. He said she was dangerous, and my life depended on me believing him. Weird right?"

"Extremely. Can't you pick up a woman like a normal guy?"

I snorted and took a drink. Ever since we'd known each other he always said I wasn't a "normal" guy. Sure, I could go on less sleep than him, or eat my way through a buffet and never gain a pound, but that didn't make me different. It was just good genetics, or so I assumed since I didn't know who my birth parents were.

Our wings came and the entire time I was eating I kept thinking about the weirdo with the warning. Maybe he was an ex that wanted her back? But that would mean he would have to be stalking her to know about me. I didn't notice anyone following me last night, but honestly, all I was thinking about was getting her naked again.

By the time we left, Erik had the number of our waitress and I was fully expecting him to have a date with her in the next couple of days. We decided to go to the market to grab some stuff to make dinner. Since I loved to eat, cooking came naturally to me and tonight I was in the mood for butter-poached fish, so I found what I needed, and we went back to our place.

"You know," Erik said, when I put the last of the groceries away. "I think you might want to listen to the strange dude from the bar."

"Huh? Why would I do that?"

"I've dated a lot of people and never once has someone warned me to stay away from them. Maybe she really is bad news."

"The worst thing she's done is drive too fast and give me a hand job in an almost empty movie theater. Yeah, she's really scary."

Erik chuckled. "She really gave you a hand job in a theater?" I nodded. "She's a keeper then. Ignore the mysterious stranger. He was kind of hot though."

I rolled my eyes. Erik really didn't have any sexual boundaries. He'd tried to flirt with me at first until he realized I had no interest in him. "I'm surprised you didn't try and get his number too."

"I might have if he'd come back into the bar."

That made me think about how the guy just seemed to vanish, but that wasn't possible, so I must have just not seen him slip away. "If I see him again, I'll ask him for his number for you."

"Wow, that wasn't sarcastic or anything."

I ignored him and started getting a few things ready for dinner.

Later that night my phone alerted me to a new text. I smiled when I saw who it was.

Evangeline: I'm really looking forward to our date tomorrow
Me: I am too
Evangeline: Where are we going?
Me: It's a surprise
Evangeline: How will I know what to wear?
Me: Something comfortable and shoes you can walk in
Evangeline: Okay? Where are we going?
Me: Meet me at the beer gardens in Altonaer Volkspark
Evangeline: You want me to go to a park?
Me: Yes. I'll see you there at seven.

I wasn't sure if this was the best idea for a second date, but I loved being outside and if she didn't then there was no reason to pursue a relationship. I laughed at myself, who was I kidding, even if she hated it, I still wanted to see her naked as often as I could.

****

Work the next day dragged, and I know it was because I was looking forward to seeing Evangeline. By the time five came I practically ran out of the building. I had a lot to do before our date.

I got to the beer gardens a little bit before seven. I found a table and waited for Evangeline. I loved people watching and this was a great place to do it. A few minutes later, I saw her walking through the crowd of people.

She stood out from everyone around her. It wasn't just her beauty, there was just something about her that made you stand up and take notice. I still couldn't believe she was choosing to spend her valuable time with me. When she saw me, she smiled, and I felt like I'd won the lottery.

"Hey," I said, when she sat down.

"Hey," she said, with that sexy smile.

'Have you been here before?" I asked.

"Can't say that I have. I don't really spend a lot of time outdoors."

"Then you're in for a treat."

"We'll see."

After a quick, but delicious meal I took her to my favorite place in the park. I checked the time; I was right on schedule.

"What are we doing here?" she asked me.

"You'll see. Now close your eyes and don't open them until I say so."

I could tell she wasn't sure what I was up to, but eventually she did as I asked. Setting my bag down I pulled out the two glasses and wine I'd brought with me. I turned Evangeline around to where I wanted her.

"Hold out your hand." She did and I put the glass in it and poured the wine. "Okay, you can open your eyes now."

"Wow."

That was my exact thought every time I came here, and sunset was by far my favorite. "Beautiful isn't it."

"It's certainly something else."

I clinked her glass and we each took a drink of wine.

"Great choice. I love a nice chardonnay." She took another drink and held out her glass for more.

"I was hoping you were a wine lover."

We watched the sun as it sank down until it was almost dark.

"So, how are you liking the outdoors right now?"

"Not too bad. But I think it's the company. Are you ready to get out of here?"

The way she said it made me think really dirty thoughts. I nodded and packed up my bag. I had no idea what she had in mind, but I was really hoping it involved less clothing.

Chapter Thirty-Six

The sun woke me up the next morning. I looked at the clock and realized I wasn't in my bed. A smile graced my face when I turned over until I noticed Evangeline wasn't in the bed. I sat up and looked around the room and saw that the clock said seven-fifteen. "Shit!" I was going to be late for work.

I got up to get dressed. Evangeline was probably already at work. Why didn't she wake me up?

Fuck, my dad is going to be pissed that I'm late. I can hear it now. 'How do you expect me to trust you with the company, when you can't even get here on time?' I really didn't want to deal with that today, especially after last night. It almost made getting yelled at worth it.

Grabbing my shoes, I run out the door and head straight for the train station. One of these days I'll get a car. I just loved riding on the train. I didn't have to worry about traffic, and it gave me time to relax before and after work. It also helped when I'd had way too much to drink. I laughed at myself.

I got to work with one minute to spare. I just hoped my dad didn't see me come in this late. He always says, "If you're not fifteen minutes early, you're late."

Marnie came over to me. "You're pushing it today aren't you? It's a good thing your dad is in meetings this morning."

I let out a relieved sigh. "Yeah, I don't know what got into me this morning. I guess I need the extra sleep."

She giggled. "I get that. I better get back to work."

I nodded at her and got to work myself. I still could believe Evangeline didn't wake me up. What was up with that? The guy's statement came back to me from the sports bar. Maybe she was bad news. I shook my head to get rid of that thought. Maybe she didn't want to wake me up as early as she had to get up.

"Luca! Can I see you in my office?"

Shit! I got up to see what my dad wanted. I sure hoped this wasn't because I was one minute early. I swear, sometimes I couldn't catch a break with him. I walked into his office and stood there until he asked me to take a seat.

"I wanted to talk to you about something."

I nodded in his direction. "Okay. What's up?"

He shook his head. "Sometimes, I don't understand the younger generation. I wanted to talk to you about being a partner in the company."

My heart started to beat against my chest, but I didn't let it show. "You are going to make me partner?"

He nodded. "You've shown me you can handle it. I think it's time you learn the business. I'm not getting any younger."

"Wow, Dad! I would love to."

"Good, now go home and thank your mother. She's the one who pushed this for you. Besides she has been itching to have you over. I'll get all the paperwork drawn up and have it by dinner time. I'll see you at the house tonight."

I stood up and shook his hand. "Thank you, Dad, I won't let you down."

He looked up at me. "You better not."

I left his office in a daze. I never thought this day would come. At least, not while I was so young.

****

Just as I got to my parent's house my phone chimes with a text.

Evangeline: I'm sorry I didn't wake you up. I had an emergency at work at three o'clock this morning. I hope you can forgive me.

Me: It's fine. I'll have to learn to set my own alarm. I have good news. I got partner in my father's company.

Evangeline: That's awesome. We should celebrate tonight.

Me: I can't tonight. I'm having dinner with my parents. How about tomorrow?

Evangeline: Yeah, sure. Text me later.

Is there something wrong, I asked myself.

Me: Ok, sure. Is everything ok?

She didn't answer me back. That was weird. I put my phone back in my pocket and headed inside. "Mom! Where are you?"

"There's my baby. How have you been? I haven't seen you in ages it seems."

I smiled at her. "It's only been a week in a half since I saw you."

She slapped my arm. "That has been the longest week in a half. I take it your father told you the good news."

I give her a tight hug. "Yeah, thanks to you. So, thank you for that. I thought I was going to be fifty before he made me partner."

She kissed my cheek. "You're welcome. You deserve it. You've done everything he's asked you to do. He was just being a stubborn mule."

I laughed and kissed the top of her head. "I'm starving, what do you have to eat?"

She laughed as she said, "You know where the kitchen is. You're a better cook than I am. I could use some breakfast."

We went into the kitchen and she watched me cook for the both of us. I was in the mood for blueberry pancakes with ice cream. When I was done making them, we headed out to the patio and we caught up. I even told her about Evangeline.

"I want to meet this woman. I want to make sure she is good for you."

"Mom, we aren't there yet. I've only seen her three times. Let me see where this is going to go before I commit to her. Please."

She gave me a small smile. "Fine, but you better be treating her like a lady. I don't want to hear you are just using her for sex. I raised you better than that."

"Mom! I am not talking about my sex life with you. Please just stop. We can talk about anything you want but that."

I watched as her serious look turned into a mischievous grin. "I love watching you blush, and I've still got the touch," she said, as she laughed.

I just shook my head at her and ate my food. The only thing ruining this moment was that I couldn't get rid of the nagging feeling about Evangeline. Her last text was worrying me, and I didn't know why.

Chapter Thirty-Seven

I spent the day with mom. We went to the market and got all the ingredients for dinner. Whenever I visited my parents, I always ended up cooking, but I didn't mind.

Mom was on the phone and I was chopping vegetables. Since I'd done this hundreds of times my thoughts went to Evangeline. I hadn't heard from her since the text this morning. I wasn't an expert on women by any means, but it seemed like she was mad that I couldn't meet her tonight. I didn't understand that. It's not like we'd been dating for months or even that we were exclusive, so it didn't make any sense to me.

Mom ended her call and sat down at the raised kitchen counter, smiling at me. "You look like you're thinking really hard son."

"You know me, a million thoughts going on at once."

She looked like she didn't believe me, and she'd be right. Mom was always good at telling when I was lying, but luckily, she didn't call me on it this time.

As I was cooking mom started telling me about what my cousins were up to. It had been a long time since I'd seen them, and it was hard for me to believe they were already in high school.

"You should go visit them sometime," mom said.

"That would be great. It's been a few years since we went back to the US. And now that dad has finally come to his senses and promoted me, I doubt I can get back there anytime soon."

"Well, since you haven't actually taken over anything, I bet I could use my powers of persuasion to convince him to give you time off to see them."

I laughed. "If anyone could do it, it would be you."

Dad got home just as I was putting the finishing touches on dinner.

"It smells great in here," he said, as he walked into the kitchen. "Luca must be cooking." Dad winked at me. He was always teasing mom about me being a better cook than she was.

"I'm going to change and be right back. I'm starving." He gave mom a kiss as he walked by her.

My dad was like dealing with two different people. At home, he was fun and loving, but at the office it was like working for a dictator. I still had trouble adjusting to work dad sometimes.

We sat down for dinner and I mostly listened as mom told us how her mother was doing. For a seventy-something-year-old lady, she sure seemed to keep busy, but maybe that was her secret. As I listened, my thoughts turned to my mom and dad. I had to admit I was very lucky that they were the ones to adopt me, but that got me thinking about my birth parents.

When there was a lull in the conversation, I decided to ask them about it. "This is totally out of the blue, and I don't know why I haven't asked before, but what do you know about my birth parents?"

They both looked at me like they didn't know what to say.

It was dad who spoke first. "Well son, all we were told was that your mother came into the hospital alone. They asked her about the father and all she said was that he was gone. Then unfortunately she died while giving birth to you."

"Why are you asking?" Mom wanted to know.

"No real reason. Just hearing about grandma made me realize I didn't know anything about my birth parents. No big deal, mom. I know I have the best parents in the world, and I wouldn't change a thing."

Mom smiled and I could tell by her smile what was going to come out of her mouth next.

She looked at dad. "Speaking of being the best parents in the world, I think our son could use a little time off before he gets into the corporate world. His cousins miss him, and I think it would do my mom good if she could see Luca."

I could tell dad was fighting a smile. He was trying to be the hard-nosed CEO as well as dad. It was a losing battle and he knew it.

"Fine. Finish the rest of the week and you can go see your cousins in Florida."

"Thank you, honey," mom said, and leaned over to give him a kiss on the cheek.

"Thanks dad. I promise not to screw this up."

"You'd better not." He sounded stern, but had a smile on his face.

After dinner, I checked my phone, hoping for a text from Evangeline, but the only message I had was from Erik telling me he was going out. I figured he had a date with that waitress from the bar the other day.

I said goodbye to mom and dad and made my way home. I was about to open the apartment door when I saw a piece of paper sticking out from under the door. I unlocked the door, picked it up and went in. I opened it and was shocked by what it said.

You need to stay away from Evangeline. She is very dangerous to you. Your life depends on it.

What the fuck? Not only was the note freaking me out, but someone knew where I lived.

The knock on the door scared the shit out of me. I looked through the peephole and saw Evangeline. Talk about weird timing. I shoved the note into my pocket and opened the door.

"Hey," she said, with that sexy smile of hers.

"Uh, hey. What are you doing here? Not that I don't want you here, I'm just surprised. I didn't hear from you all day."

She just laughed at me and walked inside. "I'm here to celebrate your good news." Then she undid her long coat and let it fall to the floor. She was standing there in nothing but her heels.

"Fuck," I whispered to myself. She was like the perfect woman and I still couldn't believe I was so lucky. I followed her to the bedroom, a very happy man.

Chapter Thirty-Eight

The next morning, my alarm woke me up at five-thirty. I rolled over to shut it off. Last night there was something different about Evangeline, either that or the warnings were getting to me. I needed more information about her.

I got up and got dressed in my workout clothes. Since I didn't have to be at the office until eight, I ran most mornings. Putting on my running shoes and I headed out the door. I let the pounding of my feet carry me away.

I couldn't stop thinking about how the person who left me the note knew where I lived. It was kind of creeping me out. If I would have come home five minutes later, would Evangeline have found the note? How did she even know I was home? Was she stalking me? I had more questions than answers.

Getting back to the apartment, I hopped into the shower and got ready for my day. I still wish I knew who left me that note. Once I was done with the shower, I grabbed something small to eat and headed to the train station.

Sitting in the back, I took out my phone and texted my cousin Damon.

> *Me: Hey bro, guess what?*
> *Damon: You're not an asshole anymore?*
> *Me: Ha-ha, I'm still an asshole. I'll be coming to Florida soon.*
> *Damon: Awesome. I can't wait until you get here. I have so many things to show you.*
> *Me: Sounds great. Don't tell Sam I'm coming. I want to surprise her.*
> *Damon: My lips are sealed. She is going to be excited when she sees you.*
> *Me: That's the plan man, that's the plan. I'll give you more info when I can. See you soon.*
> *Damon: Sounds good. Bye, cos.*

Me: Bye homie.

Man, I couldn't wait to see them. It had been way too long. It was hard to believe they were in high school already. Time flew way too fast.

I looked up from my phone and spotted the guy from the sports bar. I'd had enough of this crap. I needed to know what the hell the deal was with him and Evangeline. I got up and walked over to him.

"What the hell, you stalking me now?"

The dude smirked at me. "No, but since you're here, I wanted to warn you again about Evangeline. I know you want answers. Meet me tonight at the park across from your apartment at eight. I will give you all the answers I can."

I was about to say something, when the train stopped, and he was gone. I got off the train since it was my stop anyway. I looked around for him, but again it was like he disappeared into thin air. I know that couldn't be possible.

Shaking my head at myself, I walked the rest of the way to work. Could that guy really give me answers and proof? After last night, I was starting to think about things differently. Like she had two different lives or something. Maybe I was just making excuses about what was really going on because I didn't want to lose her. Not that we're together, but she's been the best woman I'd been with and that was saying something. I really wanted this to work, but if she was lying to me about who she was , that was a deal-breaker. I couldn't stand liars, or cheaters for that matter.

Once I got inside, I headed to my dad's office. "Hey dad, I was wondering if you wanted to have lunch today."

He looked up from his computer with a smile. "Sounds good. Where do you want to go?"

I shrugged my shoulders. "Surprise me. I'm down for anything."

He shook his head. "I'll see you at one o'clock."

I nodded and went to my desk. Once I logged on, an email came through from Evangeline.

Hey, you, I'm wondering if you want to hang out tonight. I miss you.

I sat there and read it twice. I really need answers and the only way to do that is to show up to meet that guy. So, I wrote her back.

I would love to, but I have plans already. We can hang out tomorrow if that is ok.

I hit send and got to work. An hour later I got another email from Evangeline.

Why do I have a feeling you don't want to be with me anymore? Yesterday you spent time with your parents and now you have plans tonight. You know what, don't worry about it. Have a nice life.

What the fuck was up with that shit? I didn't answer her right away. I was pissed she thought all my time needed to be spent with her. And for her to get upset at me for spending time with my parents was fucking ridiculous.

I looked up at the clock and saw it was five minutes to one. I logged off my computer and walked to my dad's office. I knocked on the door and waited for him to invite me in.

"Come in."

I opened the door and peeked in. "Are you almost ready for lunch?"

He nodded. "Give me a few minutes. I need to finish this email."

"I'll meet you at the elevators."

He waved me off. I shut the door and went over to Marnie to tell her that I'd gotten the Jacobs' files ready for her.

"Hey Marnie, I finished those files for you. When I get back from lunch, I'll send them to you."

She turned in her chair and smiled at me. "Sounds good. Have a great lunch with your dad."

"I plan on it."

I went back to waiting by the elevators and as soon as they opened up, there was a pissed off Evangeline. What the fuck is she doing here? She stalked over to me and slapped me across the face.

"How dare you ignore me? How dare you play games with me?"

I held my cheek in shock. Who the fuck is this woman. "First off, I'm not ignoring you. Second off, don't come here starting shit in my workplace."

"Don't you dare raise your voice to me? Do you even know who I am?"

Apparently, I didn't. "I know you're making a fool of yourself right now. You need to leave before I get you escorted out."

"This isn't over. I will see you tonight." She turned around and left. Again, what the fuck is up with this chick? I won't be seeing her tonight or ever after this stunt.

My dad came out of his office with a disappointed look. "Dad, I'm sorry. I didn't know she even knew where I worked. I can explain over lunch. I swear this is never going to happen again."

He shook his head. "It better not. I don't want your, or anyone else's drama, here at work. Keep that shit outside these doors when you come to work."

I nodded at him and gestured we leave before things got worse. I just hope this didn't ruin lunch.

Chapter Thirty-Nine

I tried to put the incident with Evangeline out of my mind during lunch. A work lunch with dad was just like a meeting, so if I wasn't paying attention he'd know. We talked about what my new role would be. I had to admit, I was excited to finally learn how the business really worked.

Luckily, the rest of the day at the office was uneventful. I still couldn't believe that Evangeline had acted like that. I mean, who did she think she was? She acted like a jealous wife rather than someone I'd had sex with a few times. I was definitely starting to think there was something off about her.

Instead of going home, I went to the outdoor market. If I was going to visit my family in Florida, I better get some cool things to take to them. As I was shopping, I stopped at a few food vendors and considered that dinner.

I made it back to my apartment with enough time to drop off my bags and head over to the park. I hoped I wasn't making a huge mistake by agreeing to listen to what the stranger had to say.

At exactly eight, I entered the park and looked for the guy I was supposed to meet. It wasn't a big park, but I didn't see him. I waited a few minutes and decided this was obviously a waste of time.

"Fuck," I said, when I turned to leave. He was suddenly standing right in front of me.

"We need to have this conversation somewhere else. It's no longer safe here." Then he started walking away.

I debated following him. Then I thought about what happened at work and I wanted answers, even if they were from a disappearing mystery guy. I was a few steps behind him as he turned the corner and went into a small pub. Taking a seat at a booth in the back, he motioned for me to join him.

"You know this is seriously weird," I said.

He didn't say anything because the waitress came over to the table and asked what we wanted. I figured I was going to need a drink for this conversation, so I ordered a beer. My mysterious friend didn't want anything.

Not wanting to be interrupted we didn't say anything until after she brought my beer. I took a big drink and waited to hear what he had to say. Finally, he spoke.

"Do you agree that there is good and bad in this world?"

Weird question, but I answered. "Yeah, of course there is."

"Do you believe there are things in this world that can't be explained?"

"Sure, I guess." I was already starting to get frustrated, so I took another long drink. "Can you get to the point already?"

He sighed like he was frustrated with the conversation, too. "You have to understand that there are things I want to tell you, but I'm bound by a higher power and I can't. Trust me, this would be so much easier if I could."

"You know that doesn't make any sense, right?"

"I'm doing my best to explain this to you, but I have limitations that prevent me from saying certain things. So, on that note, do you believe in Heaven and Hell?"

"I don't know. I guess I never really thought about it."

"Okay, fair enough. Let's try this one. Do you think you are different from everyone else?"

I started to say no but something stopped me. I took a minute to really think about it. "Yeah, sometimes I feel like there's something different about me, but that's the same for everyone, right?"

"Not necessarily. You're different."

"Okay, why?"

"I can't tell you, but I have a feeling that you'll find out soon enough."

"That's not cryptic or anything. So, what does all this have to do with Evangeline?"

"Everything. She's not what you think she is?"

I was about to argue when I realized that he said what, not who. "Wait a minute, what do you mean, what is she?"

"I can't say more on that but just know that she's not from anywhere close to here."

"You mean, Germany?"

"Farther than that."

"Europe?"

"Farther."

"Asia? North America? South America? Antarctica?"

"Farther."

"There's nothing farther away from here than Antarctica."

"You're thinking too earthly. And that's all I can say about that. I have to go but remember, Evangeline is extremely dangerous to you. Stay away if you can."

Then, right before my eyes, he vanished. I blinked a few times, but he was still gone. I looked at my beer and pushed it away from me. I left money on the table and went home.

Thankfully Erik was there when I walked in. "Erik, I think I'm going crazy."

"What are you talking about?"

I told him everything. About the note, Evangeline's behavior and then finally the conversation I'd just had at the pub. "Then he freaking disappeared. I mean like poof, just gone. I had to have been seeing things, right?"

"I really don't know what to tell you man, but I don't think you're going crazy. I can't explain the whole vanishing act, but something is telling me not to dismiss this guy. Especially, after the whole Evangeline slapping you thing today."

"I'm worried what she might do if she comes over here tonight."

"Can't blame you for that. But I'm not going anywhere tonight, so I'll be here if you need me. Why don't you change and join me. We'll watch some TV and chill out for a bit."

"Yeah, that sounds good."

A couple of hours later, I decided to go to bed. I made sure the front door was locked as well as all the windows and the glass balcony door. We were a few floors up, but between her behavior today and the warning I got; I wouldn't put anything past Evangeline. I wasn't sure if I was going to be able to sleep or not. I just hoped she didn't give me a reason not to.

Chapter Forty

It was Friday and I couldn't be happier. I hadn't heard from Evangeline or the creepy mystery man and I finally got to go see my cousins. My flight left at five am tomorrow morning. Tonight, I'll celebrate with Erik and Carmen, even though he didn't know she'd be there. I couldn't wait to see his face.

"Luca, you got a minute?"

I turned to my father's voice. "Yeah, I'll be there in a moment."

I logged off my computer and headed into his office. "What's up pops?"

He didn't look at me when he said, "Take a seat."

Sitting down, I waited for him to talk.

"I know you're leaving tomorrow morning, but I wanted to talk to you about this new client I hope to get. She is in need of a business consultant and she only wants to work with you."

I knew it was too good to be true to get out of here for a while. "Can it wait until I get back from Florida?"

He shook his head. "She wants to meet with you today. She said she'll deal with you and you only. We need to get her as a client. This will make a name for you."

I put my head in my hands and placed my elbows on my legs. How does this woman even know about me? "Fine, but I can still go to Florida tomorrow right?"

"About that, it's my understanding that she needs this ASAP. I know you were looking forward to seeing your cousins. Maybe I can arrange for them to come here instead. I'm sure your grandmother would love to visit."

I stood to leave, but my father wouldn't let me. "Dad, that isn't the point. I needed a break from here before I committed my life to this place. Don't get me wrong, I am excited to become a partner. I was just hoping to have one week to relax and enjoy my family."

"I understand and I promise I will find a way to make this up to you."

"Fantastic, I'll cancel all my plans," I said sarcastically. "She better be paying top dollar."

I didn't turn around, I just walked out. There was nothing he could do to make this up, but that was my life now. I'd still like to know who this woman was. It hasn't even been announced that I was a partner yet.

I went to my desk and cancelled my flight, then I went over to Marnie. "You got the file on this new client I'm supposed to meet with?"

She handed me a file without turning my way. "Here you go."

I pulled it out of her hand and walked back to my desk. Opening the file, I read the name.

Violet Lathan
Age: 22
Sex: Female
Occupation: Marketing

That was all the file said about her. Which was odd considering we gave them a questionnaire to fill out before we ever met with them. We never took a client without it being filled completely out. What made her so special? Apparently, I would find out this afternoon.

Instead of dealing with that right now, I decided to go get an early lunch. I texted Carmen to make sure she was still meeting us tonight.

Me: Hey Carmen. Are you still coming tonight?

It took her a few minutes to answer me back.

Carmen: If you're sure this is a good idea, I'll be there.
Me: I'm positive. We'll see you at eight tonight.
Carmen: I'll see you there.

I smiled at my phone. This was going to be epic. I knew he still loved her. I just hoped this went as planned. I took the elevator down to the ground floor and headed out to my favorite spot to eat. That was, until I spotted Evangeline standing just outside the door looking regal as hell.

I debated if I really wanted to deal with her or not. Making up my mind, I decided to get this over with. I walked out the door and stood there waiting for her to notice me. It didn't take long. When she spotted me, she smiled like it was just a normal day.

"Luca, I'm glad I got to see you today."

What the actual fuck was wrong with this chick? "Yeah, I'm sure. Are you here to smack me again?"

She pouted as she walked over to me. "I wanted to tell you how sorry I am about that. I don't know what got into me. I promise it won't happen again," she said, as she played with my shirt.

I pushed her hands away from me. "Look, I don't know what game you're playing, but I'm not playing it. I don't want to deal with this drama. So, you go do you and I'll go do me."

There was no way I was going to be that guy that would cave for a woman like this.

She pouted even more. "But I said I was sorry and it wouldn't happen again. Can we just start over?"

I shook my head. "I'm sorry but no. Now, if you'll excuse me, I need to get something to eat before this meeting this afternoon with Miss Lathan."

I walked away from her as her jaw dropped. If I was younger, I would have fallen for the pouty lip. But now, I had too much riding on my life to have drama stir up trouble and ruin everything.

Chapter Forty-One

By the time I got my food and walked out of the bistro, Evangeline was gone. I hoped that was the last I'd see of her, but somehow, I doubted it. She didn't seem like the kind of woman that took no for an answer.

I headed back to the office to eat my lunch in my brand new office. Despite having to cancel my vacation I still smiled as I looked around. Right now, the walls were bare, but I'd get to decorate it any way I wanted.

After I finished eating, I looked at the file for Violet Lathan again. She was only twenty-two. That seems kind of young to be paying the kind of money I knew we'd be asking. Then I thought about it, I was the same age and I had my own office and stood to take over my father's business, so I guessed age really has nothing to do with it.

I still didn't understand why the whole questionnaire wasn't in the file. How was I supposed to know how to help her if there was nothing to go on? Just when I decided to Google her my phone rang. It was dad's assistant letting me know that Miss Lathan was here to see me. I made sure my tie was straight and walked down the hall to greet her.

I saw two people standing at the reception desk. They were not what I was expecting at all. The woman was tall and beautiful, but she was wearing jeans, a sweater, and sneakers. The man was also tall and handsome, but there was something different about him that I couldn't put my finger on. I realized I was staring at them. I snapped out of it and walked over to greet them.

"Miss Lathan, I'm Luca Maier. Please come with me."

They followed me to my office and sat in the chairs I offered them.

"Can I get either of you something to drink?" I asked.

"No, we're fine, thank you," the woman I assumed to be Violet said.

The man she was with got up, closed the door and shut the blinds. I thought that was a little strange, but maybe they were the type that liked privacy.

"So, I understand you requested me personally, what can I do for you?"

They looked at each other and the man nodded. Violet began to speak.

"This is probably going to sound crazy to you, but you're in very grave danger."

I looked at her like she was nuts.

"Before you throw us out of here, has anything strange happened to you recently? Met anyone that seemed a little different or had an experience that didn't make a whole lot of sense?"

I was about to say no, but then I thought about the mysterious stranger disappearing in the pub the other night.

"I don't see what you're getting at," I said to her.

"Show him the picture Aviel."

Aviel, who I now assumed was the guy, took a picture out of his jacket and handed it to me. It was the man who'd been warning me about Evangeline.

"Who is this guy?" I asked.

"Have you seen him?" she asked in return.

"Yes. Now, who is he?"

Aviel leaned forward and said in a low voice, "He was sent here with a message for you. Did you get it?"

"Maybe, what was the message?"

"That is only for you to know. But it's important for you to tell us what he said to you."

"Why should I tell you two anything? I know nothing about you. I was told an important client needed to meet with me, but it's clear you aren't clients."

Violet looked me directly in the eye. "We're here to save your life. Trust me, I know how crazy this sounds. Just a week ago, I was living my life without a care in the world. But then I saw and learned things that at first, I couldn't believe."

"You realize that makes no sense at all, right."

"If we show you something, can you promise not to freak out?"

"What kind of question is that? How can I promise something like that when I don't have a clue what you're talking about?"

Violet stood up and started pacing. "Okay fair enough," she said. "Aviel is going to move from one side of this office to the other, but it won't be in a manner that you've ever seen before." Then she nodded at Aviel.

I was looking right at him when he just disappeared and was suddenly behind me.

"What the fuck," I practically yelled. Then, poof, he was back where he started. I sat down because I was sure I was seeing things.

Both of them sat down as well and Violet started talking. "I know you think you might be crazy, but there are things around us that most people have no knowledge about."

"What are you?" I finally asked, directing my question at Aviel.

"I'm an angel," he said like this was an everyday occurrence.

"And you?" I asked Violet.

"I'm half-human and half-angel, and so are you."

I decided I was done with these two and I wasn't going to listen to anything else they had to say. "I'd like you to leave. I don't know what's going on here, but I don't appreciate you wasting my time and ruining my vacation."

A look passed between them, but they both stood and walked out of my office. I was so pissed off that I shut down my computer and stormed out of the office. My phone was ringing, but I ignored it. It was probably my father but what was I going to tell him? An angel came in pretending to be a client. I didn't think so.

I wandered around for a while before I finally made my way home.

Erik was in the living room when I walked in. "You're home early. Packing for your vacation?"

"Nope," I said, with a hint of anger. "My vacation was canceled for a very important new client I had to meet this afternoon. Turned out it was a couple of crazy people pretending to be angels."

"Um … what?"

I filled him in on the whole "meeting".

"So, he just like transported across your office?"

"I think it was some kind of illusion. I don't know what the point of it was, but I'm still pissed. Oh, I almost forgot, I went to my favorite bistro to get lunch and Evangeline was waiting for me and acted like nothing had happened. What a fucking crazy day."

"Good thing we're going out. I think you need to blow off some steam."

That made me think about Carmen being there tonight. After what happened today, I don't think I could handle it if anything else went wrong so I decided to tell him.

"Uh, Erik, about tonight, Carmen is going to be there."

"What? Carmen from college?"

"Yeah, I ran into her earlier this week and invited her out tonight. I was going to have it be a surprise but after the day I just had I can't handle any more drama."

He didn't say anything for a minute.

"Are you okay?"

"I think so. I'm just surprised, I guess. I've never forgotten about her."

"I know, that's why I invited her to the club tonight. Are you okay with this?"

"Yeah, sure, it'll be nice to see her. I'd better get ready."

I laughed to myself. It was only three, five hours until I said we'd meet her. I took off my suit jacket, undid my tie, and grabbed a beer. The balcony seemed like a good place to decompress after the frustrating day.

Chapter Forty-Two

I couldn't believe the day I'd had. Now that I had time to really think about the whole ordeal, I had to say that was some kind of trick that guy did. What was up with them thinking they were angels and then expect me to think I was a half-angel?

They must have thought it was funny to play a trick on me like that. And to miss out on seeing my family because of it wasn't sitting well with me. I couldn't believe those people would even play a prank like that. I shook my head at my own self for dwelling on it. What's done is done. I really needed to call my dad back. He had been calling me non-stop. I grabbed my phone and dialed his number. He answered on the first ring.

"What the hell happened?"

I sighed and told him everything that happened. There was a pause on his end.

"So, all of this was a joke? A sick joke to top it off. Son, I'm sorry for making you miss your trip for this. If I'd have known, I would have handled it myself."

"Dad, there's no way you could have known. Except, she never filled out the questionnaire. How did she even get past that?"

"What do you mean, she didn't fill it out? If that is the case, she should never have been seen."

"Someone needs to answer for that."

"I agree. Let me look into that and I'll get back to you."

"Sure dad, I'll talk to you later."

I hung up the phone and went back inside. Since there were still a few hours before we left for the club, I decided to go for a run. I needed to let some of this stress out before tonight, or I wouldn't even want to be around myself, never mind anyone else.

Changing my clothes, I grabbed my shoes and put them on.

"I'm going to go for a run. If you need me, call me," I yelled to Erik.

Hitting the pavement, I put in my earbuds and turned the volume up. I let the pavement take me away and clear my mind to the point I wasn't even thinking anymore, I was just running.

I looked at my watch and saw I only had forty minutes to get back to the apartment and clean up. I turned around and saw Violet and Aviel standing there talking. Damn it, I didn't have time for that shit. I took off running as fast as I could back. There was no way they were going to ruin my night like they did my trip.

I got back to the apartment in record time. I hopped into the shower and was ready in twenty minutes. I headed out to the living room.

"About time you get your ass out here. I was about to leave you here."

I laughed at Erik. "You know I wouldn't miss club night. Besides, I certainly wouldn't miss this reunion with Carmen. It's been a long time coming."

He slapped my shoulder. "If this goes south, I'm blaming you, my friend."

I chuckled this time. "I assure you, this will probably go south."

This time he punched my arm. "I'm not that bad of a person, man."

I laughed hard this time. "You are a player, player. It will go south."

He stared at me before he said, "Fuck you man. It's not my fault the ladies love me."

I laughed as I smacked him on the shoulder. "True. Let's go, I'm ready to get my drink on and forget all about today."

Hopefully, Violet and Aviel didn't ruin my night by showing up. I didn't need any more drama or stress.

We got to the club just in time to meet up with Carmen.

"Hey guys!" she yells across the street from us.

I gave her a smile. "I'm so glad you made it," I said, as she approached us. I gave her a bear hug. Her laughter was like music to my ears.

"Put me down you baboon," she said while smiling. I missed her more than I realized.

I looked over at Erik and he was standing there with his hands in his pockets looking at the ground.

"Erik, look who it is." Trying to get him to at least acknowledge her.

He looked up and gave her a pitiful smile. "It's great seeing you. How have you been?"

She tossed her hair behind her shoulder and smiled at him. "Life has been good. How about you?"

He shuffled his feet. "You know. Can't complain, I guess. At least, I get to live with my best friend, so that's a plus."

She looked between the both of us. "Are you ready to go inside?"

I held my arm out to her. "I'm ready when you are, beautiful."

That smile I remembered so much appeared on her face as she took my arm. Please let tonight go smoothly so we can all have a great time.

Chapter Forty-Three

I watched as Erik and Carmen got reacquainted. I could see the spark was still there, but I knew both of them were trying to act casual. It wouldn't surprise me if they ended up sleeping together tonight.

Taking a drink of my beer I looked around the club. This was supposed to be a night to relax but I was on edge. I was waiting for something to happen. Whether it was Evangeline showing up or the crazy pair of Violet and Aviel, I didn't know, but I had a feeling it was going to be something.

Erik and Carmen went to the dance floor while I sat back and looked around the club. It was dark, but I was able to see everything clearly. I wanted to get falling-down drunk, but I knew I needed to keep my head on straight tonight. A flash of blonde caught my attention and my first thought was Evangeline, but it turned out to be no one.

"You look tense, want to dance?" a female voice said in my ear.

My head snapped around. Something about her looked familiar, but I didn't know who she was. "I'm fine," I said. I really didn't need to get involved with another woman, even if it was just a dance.

"Your loss," she said, and walked away.

I watched her and she found another dance partner, but she kept her eyes on me. Yeah, I found that strange, so I tried to keep my eye on her, but she was soon swallowed up by the crowd.

"Hey man," Erik said, as he handed me another beer. "You okay?"

"Yeah, just a little on edge."

"I totally get that. Any sign of the crazy bitch?"

"No, but I have a feeling she's going to show up."

"Just keep your eyes open. I'll help in any way I can."

"Thanks, man."

I knew Carmen was wondering what we were talking about, but I really didn't feel like going into it, especially in a loud club. Thankfully,

Erik took her back to the dance floor. My eyes were continually scanning the club for anything out of the ordinary. So far over the last hour, everything seemed to be normal. Maybe I was overreacting and just needed to relax.

Two more drinks later, and I was feeling a little bit less tense. Someone sat beside me. I thought it was Carmen until I saw it was the girl from earlier.

"You look a little bit more relaxed."

"Maybe." I didn't owe her any explanation, so I wasn't going to give one.

"Dance?"

"No, not really in the mood."

"Bad breakup?"

"No." I hoped she would get the hint and go away. I didn't want to be mean but with the mood, I was in she wasn't making it easy.

"I was hoping to do this the easy way, but it looks like that's not going to happen."

"What are you talking about?" I was really confused. Then I felt something poke into my side. I looked down and she had a gun on me. "What the fuck?"

She shoved the gun further into my ribs. "You are going to come with me, nice and easy. If you put up a fight or make a scene your friends are going to get hurt."

Immediately I looked to where I'd last seen Erik and Carmen. There were two very large men hovering around them. "Fine, I'll go with you, just let me text him that I'm going home, otherwise he'll know something is going on."

"Show me your phone."

I put it on the table and texted Erik that I was leaving. When the woman with the gun was satisfied, she motioned for me to leave. I headed for the front door, but she pushed me towards the back of the club.

It took a few minutes to get through the crowd, but we managed to do it without incident. Every time someone bumped me, I thought I was going to get shot. I'd never been so nervous or scared in my life.

When I saw the exit, I was sure this was the end of my life. A man dressed all in black opened the door and shoved me out. I was both surprised and not surprised at who was standing there waiting for me.

Evangeline was dressed like she was going to a fancy dinner, but I didn't let that fool me. The mystery man's warning came roaring through my head. "Luca, you've been ignoring me."

"I have that tendency when someone acts like a crazy bitch."

"Tsk, tsk, it's not nice to call people names. Didn't your mother teach you that."

"What the fuck do you want?"

"I want you. Well actually, he wants you. See, you're special and you don't even know it. We can't let you live, or you'll ruin all of his hard work."

Now I knew she was officially crazy.

"I can tell you don't believe me, but you will. He'll be here shortly."

"Who will be here?" I figured if I kept her talking, I could figure a way out of this.

"Lucifer of course."

"You mean the guy from the TV show?"

"Humans are so stupid. Lucifer, the fallen angel who is set to take over Heaven."

Despite the situation, I had to laugh. "You've lost your mind," I said, but then I felt it. Something was coming and it wasn't good. My whole body shuttered with the feeling.

Evangeline smiled. "He's close. I can tell you feel it."

The next thing I knew there was a flash of light and Evangeline was thrown halfway down the alley. The woman with the gun was knocked unconscious or something because she just collapsed where she stood. That left the big guy who'd opened the door. Someone swung a bat and he went down too.

"We need to get out of here right now," the voice with the bat said.

I looked to my right and saw it was Violet.

"Take him first," she said to Aviel.

"What the fuck is going on?" I wanted to know.

"No time," she said. "Now Aviel."

He touched my arm and I was suddenly in my apartment. "I'll be right back," he said, and disappeared. A second later he was back with Violet.

She turned to look at me. "Luca, you need to pack a bag as fast as you can. It won't take them long to figure out where we took you."

"I demand to know what the fuck is happening," I yelled.

She got right in my face. "If you stay here you will die. Lucifer wants you dead and unless you come with us, he'll get what he wants. Now, go pack a bag. You have two minutes."

Violet pushed me in the direction of my room. I didn't know what to do, but I did just see Evangeline taken out with a ball of light and I was instantly transported to my apartment. I was slowly understanding that there were things in this world I knew nothing about.

Since I wanted to live and they hadn't tried to hurt me, I grabbed a few things and shoved them in a bag. I walked out to the living room. "Okay, I'm ready." I had no idea what was happening, but when Violet reached out to touch me, I suddenly felt like everything was going to be alright.

Chapter Forty-Four

I was about to ask where we were going, but Aviel did his blinky thing again. We were standing in a living room of a house I had never been to before.

"You're safe here. We'll answer all your questions if you're ready to listen," Aviel said.

I didn't have a choice. I needed to know what the hell was going on, then I needed to know what they knew. I took a seat and put my arms on the back of it. "I'm listening."

Violet sat in the chair in front of me while Aviel stood behind her. "First, I want to ask a few questions. Have you ever wondered why you don't gain weight or are faster than others?" Violet asked.

I was about to say we were back to this again, but I knew she was right, so I just nodded.

"I know you don't want to believe us, but I hope you will at least try to listen."

"I said I would." That came out a little more assholely than I wanted. "Sorry, I just want to know what the hell is going on."

She nodded her head in understanding. "I was just like you a couple of weeks ago. Working, living life to the fullest." She looked over her shoulder at Aviel and smiled then brought her attention back my way. "I'll get right to the point. I'm a half-angel and Evangeline is a Dark Angel, one of Lucifer's followers…"

I interrupted her because I needed to know who this man was. "Who is this Lucifer and why did I feel like fleeing as soon as he got close?"

They looked between each other before Aviel answered me. "He is the devil himself. Evangeline wasn't lying to you about that." He raised his hands before I could say a thing. "I know you're having a hard time believing us. But how can you not see there are things out there even you can't deny anymore? Like me. I'm a full-blooded angel that can teleport."

I opened my mouth to say something but closed it again. He was right, I couldn't deny things anymore. "As much as I want to deny this, I just can't. I'm still trying to wrap my head around being a half-angel. How can you tell that I'm half anything?"

Aviel sat on the arm of the chair. "Your soul is brighter than a human, but not as bright as a full angel."

"Why is Lucifer after me?"

"He is after all half-angels," Violet said. "We are the only thing that can stop him. There are ten others we have to find before he takes over Heaven, and then Earth after that."

"Say what? You expect me to believe I'm going to fight him and survive?" I was freaking the fuck out. I felt how powerful that bastard was.

Violet came over and sat next to me and held out her hand. "Let me see your hand."

I hesitated for a split second before I gave her my hand. That was when I felt the hum of something just underneath my skin. It felt like power. "What is that?" I asked in amazement.

"That's the power I've been working on. We can teach you too. But you have to be willing. If you leave, the world as we know it will end because he will kill you."

That was kind of blunt. If I stay, I live but will have to save the world. If I leave, I die. "I guess I don't have much of a choice, do I?"

Aviel came over and took Violet into his arms. "You have free will. We can't make you stay, but we hope you will and learn how to gain your powers to help save the world."

Horror struck me. "You need to get Erik and Carmen somewhere safe. They will kill them." My panic was almost overriding all of my senses.

Aviel placed a hand on me and everything went calm. "We already have them somewhere safe. We'll bring them to you when you're ready. But they can't know about this until we know they won't say anything to anyone."

I let his words wash over me. "Thank you. I would like to see them. I have a lot to explain to them. I promise they won't say a word. They may freak out or call us liars at first. Well, Carmen anyway. Erik takes things differently.

Aviel nodded his head and reached for me. "I'll be back my love." He kissed her, and before I knew it we were in a different place again.

"Luca! Thank the gods you are okay." I turned to see Carmen coming at me. I opened my arms to give her a hug.

"I'm just glad you guys are okay."

Erik slapped me on the back. "What is going on, Luca?"

"It's a long story. The short version is we need to keep hiding for a little while longer. Once I figure everything out, I'll fill you in. For now, I need both of you to stay here and stay safe."

Carmen stepped out of my embrace. "I have to go to work. I can't miss it or I'll be fired. I can't lose this job." I could tell she was starting to have an anxiety attack.

I placed my hands on her shoulders. "Breathe Carmen. You won't get fired. We'll figure out a way for you to keep your job, but right now, I need you to calm down before you pass out."

She took a few slow breaths. When she was done, she nodded her head at me. "Thank you. What do you have in mind about keeping our jobs?"

I turned to Aviel for answers because I didn't have a clue. He bowed his head at me and took the floor.

"I can come up with something, but Luca is right. All of your lives are in danger." He looked me in the eyes. "Your parents are at a different safe house. If you'd like to be with them, I'll take you over there or you can stay here."

I shook my head. "I can't face them right now. I need more answers before I see my father. He isn't the most levelheaded man when he is pissed."

I turned back to my friends. "If you guys want to go there you're more than welcome. I'll be back soon with more answers. You guys stay safe. I love you both."

I walked over to Aviel so we could leave. I was ready to sit down and listen to everything. I just needed to know how much I could trust them. Hopefully, what they tell me won't freak me out any more than it already had.

Chapter Forty-Five

It was hard leaving Erik and Carmen behind, but I needed to. There was no way I could explain what was going on until I understood it myself. Aviel transported us back to the same living room we'd just come from.

"I'll be right there," Violet said, from another room.

I didn't feel like sitting so I started pacing. But that was driving me crazy, so I looked around the room. It was like any other living room I'd ever been in. A couch, a couple of chairs, and a TV. There were even pictures on the walls.

"Where are we?" I asked Aviel.

"This is a safe house we use from time to time."

"I mean, where are we in the world?"

"Oh, sorry. This house is located in London."

"So, can you transport anywhere in the blink of an eye?"

"Yes."

"That must come in handy."

He smiled. "It does."

Violet walked in with a couple of plates in her hands. "I made a snack."

I looked at what she had and despite the situation, I let out a small laugh.

"What's so funny?" she asked.

"That's something I used to eat after school when I was seven."

"What's wrong with it?"

"It's processed cheese cut into squares and crackers. That's not a snack."

"I don't cook so this is the best you're going to get. Unless you think you can do better?"

I think I pissed her off, which I totally didn't mean to do. "I'm sorry. I'm scared and nervous and I was taking it out on you."

"Apology accepted. Trust me, Luca, I know exactly what you're going through. I was leading a nice normal life and poof; I'm a half-angel and the devil wants to kill me."

"I think it's time I started asking the questions I need answers to."

Violet put the plates on the coffee table, and we all sat down. "What do you want to know?" she asked.

"Tell me more about this whole saving the world thing."

"It started over a hundred years ago," Aviel said. "Lucifer was gaining followers, both on Earth and in Heaven. We worked hard to find and eliminate them all, and thought we were winning, but they'd just gotten better at hiding. We recently learned that he had many more on his side than we'd originally thought. Now we're trying to stop him for good."

"What does he want?"

"To take over Heaven and Earth."

"So, Heaven is like a real place?"

"Yes, and when you're ready we'll take you there."

"Like permanently?"

"To visit," Violet said. "We can only be there for short amounts of time. The human part of us seems to know we really shouldn't be there yet."

"How am I half-angel? That really doesn't seem possible."

"It's not supposed to be," Aviel said. "Technically, angels aren't supposed to interact with humans unless it's to protect them or ferry their soul to Heaven. But on very rare occasions an angel falls in love with a human. That's what happened to your parents, same with Violet."

Violet looked at me. "I didn't know my parents either," she said. "My mother died giving birth to me. I was raised by my aunt."

"Do you know who my birth parents are?" I asked Aviel.

"Yes. Your mother was human, and your father is a Protection Angel. You'll get to meet them when you're ready. They are both in Heaven."

I took that in and let it roll around my head. That was already a lot of information and I'd only asked a few questions. Then I thought of something that I really wanted to know. "You said something about half-angels saving the world, what were you talking about?"

"There are presently twelve half-angels on Earth. Those twelve are going to be the ones that will defeat Lucifer and stop him from taking over."

"How is that possible?"

"Of course, we don't know the outcome, but I think the key is going to be the human part of you. It's physically impossible for an angel to kill a human or even a half-human. You will learn to develop your angel side, but your human side is important too."

"So, basically you have no idea what's going to happen or how we're going to do this."

Violet grinned. "Yep, that's the gist of it."

I shook my head. "Where are the other half-angels?"

"We don't know," he said. "You aren't exactly the easiest to find."

"I thought you said that our souls shine brighter, or some shit like that."

Violet laughed. "I like you. That part is true, but unlike a human soul that shines all the time, ours only shine when we access the angel part of us. That's why we're hard to find."

"So how many halfies have you found?" I asked Aviel.

"Just you two. It's our job to find the other ten, then train you for the upcoming war."

"That doesn't sound like a big task or anything."

"It's either that or let Lucifer win, and that's not an option. You felt him tonight for just a brief second. Now imagine that feeling times a hundred."

I shuddered. I could go the rest of my life and never need to feel that again. It had been a cold and dreadful feeling. "Point taken. What do we do now?"

"You need to rest. Your friends and family are in a safe place. They are surrounded by Protection Angels and humans that were former military. There's no way Lucifer or his followers, human or angels, will be getting to them."

"I guess I'll have to take your word for it, but if anything happens to them it's on you." I was suddenly really tired.

Violet stood up. "Let me show you to your room." I followed her to a large bedroom. "We'll be here with you the whole night. There are also angels patrolling the property. We'll be safe."

"Can I use my phone?" I asked, then felt in my pocket and realized it wasn't there. "I can't find my phone."

"Your phone isn't here. Aviel made sure it was left at your apartment. We didn't want to take any chances. Technology can be just as dangerous as a bad angel. We'll get you a new one tomorrow. You should be able to find everything you need in here. See you in the morning."

She left the room and closed the door. I rummaged through the drawers, found a pair of pajama pants, and went into the attached bathroom. After a quick shower, I crawled into the bed and went over everything that had happened in the last couple of hours. Life, as I knew, had just changed drastically and I knew there was no going back.

Chapter Forty-Six

The next morning, I woke up with knots in my stomach. Was this all a nightmare? When I opened my eyes and saw I was in the bedroom from last night, I knew it wasn't. What the fuck did I get myself into? How the hell are twelve half-angels going to take down the devil himself?

The smell of food caught my attention and my stomach growled. I threw the covers back and hopped out of bed. Placing my hand on the doorknob, I hesitated. Did I really want to face this right now? Shaking my head at myself, I opened the door and walked to the kitchen where I heard Violet and Aviel speaking.

"I feel sorry for Luca, I know what it's like to have your life turned upside down. I'm also proud of him for taking it all in. What if the others are going to be harder to convince? We don't have much time to get all of them and train them before Lucifer tries to kill us all."

There was a brief pause before Aviel answered her. "I have a feeling Luca and you are the key to getting the others on board. Will they deny things at first? Of course. Who wouldn't if they don't believe angels are real."

"You're right, babe. Maybe I'm just overreacting again..."

I took that time to make myself known. "It smells good in here. What's for breakfast?" I didn't want her to get worked up over things. It would do none of us any good.

She and Aviel looked my way. "Beignets. Hope you like them. I figured we would eat something small for breakfast and get to training. The faster you learn the better," Aviel said.

"Alright, I get that. But I still have a few more questions from last night. If that's okay?"

Violet jumped down the barstool and came over to me. Without warning, she was hugging me. "You can ask all the questions you want. If we don't have the answer, we'll figure out a way to find it."

I hugged her back because let's face it, she was the sweetest thing I'd ever met, and her energy was addicting. "Thank you." I let her go and went straight to the food and piled my plate up. I sat down across the island from them so I could see them better when I asked my questions.

I took a bite of the beignet and it melted into my mouth. I swear I think I groaned, but I didn't care, it was that good. It kind of made the situation a little bit more bearable.

We ate in silence for a few more minutes before I got the nerve to ask the one question that had been on my mind. I swallowed the bite I just took and asked the hardest thing I've ever asked before. "Did my parents even love me?"

Violet was the one to answer me. "The only way you will ever know is to ask them yourself. But we would never make you meet them if you didn't want to. I've been up to heaven and I haven't seen my parents yet. But I know they love me. I'm just being a chicken shit to see mine."

I laughed at her. "I guess we're in the same boat. I don't know if I'm ready to meet my real parents yet. The people who raised me will always be my parents. They loved me from the start even, when they didn't have to."

I could see a tear in her eye before she spoke again. "I feel the same with my aunt. She is my world. I don't want to deceive her like that…"

"Violet, you could never deceive me. If you can get a chance at meeting them you need to. I promise your mother wants to meet you, but she would never make you feel bad in any way. Take the chance to get to know your parents," a woman that kind of looks like Violet walked in with a man I was assuming was another angel.

Violet jumped down and ran to her arms and held her. Violet looked up to her and asked, "Are you sure? You've been my mom and aunt my whole life."

Her aunt took Violet's face into her hands. "You listen to me. Your mom is an amazing woman. I want you to get to know her, your dad too. I'll not be hurt one bit."

Violet nodded at her as she wiped the tears off her face. "Thank you. I'm so glad you're here. You want a beignet?"

She smiled at her niece and nodded. When she turned in my direction, she gave me an encouraging smile. "I think you should get to know your parents as well. You never know, you might get the answers that have been swirling around in your head."

I stared at her. How did she know I had questions?

"I can tell you have questions. Every child that has lost their parents or their parents gave their babies up for adoption, have questions."

"Who are you? I know you are her aunt but are you an angel too?"

This got a laugh out of both Violet and the new lady. "Oh, child I am not an angel. I'm a regular human. My name is Milana. You must be Luca?"

I nodded at her. "If you're not an angel, how do you know what someone is feeling inside?"

This time Violet laughed and answered me. "She is in tune with people's feelings. You can say she's an empath."

I didn't know what else to say so I just sat there eating my last beignet. I thought about everything. Did I really want to meet my real parents? It wasn't like they could have raised me when my mother died giving birth to me. This brought up another set of questions.

"Were all the human's women and the maled angels?"

"Yes," Aviel siad.

"Did all the mothers die giving birth?"

Aviel looked like he didn't want to answer, but he did. "Yes, that was the punishment. Even though it backfired. Once the women went to heaven, they found their lovers and refused to leave their sides."

I could see the women putting up a fight to get what they want and that put a smile on my face. "Maybe one day I'll meet them, but for now I want to get started with training."

In my heart, I knew I wanted to meet my parents and ask them every question I had. I would like to have a connection with them and that was why I hesitated. What if they didn't want the same thing? I didn't think I could handle that.

Chapter Forty-Seven

I was the last one finished eating. The truth was, I think I was stalling. Violet's aunt volunteered to clean the kitchen so we could start training. I had no idea what that involved, but I was about to find out.

We left the house and walked around to the back. There was another building that was almost as big as the house itself. Inside it looked like a high-end gym. There were all sorts of workout machines on one side, but more than half of the room was an empty space.

The man who'd been with Violet's aunt had come with us to the training room. He walked ahead of us and stopped. He turned to face me.

"Luca, my name is Jodson. I'm a Protection Angel but I'll also be the one doing the majority of your training."

"Hey." I really didn't know what to say in this situation.

"Have you had any self-defense or military training?" he asked me.

"No."

"Okay. Violet, do you want to show him what we've been working on?"

"Uh, okay," she said, looking a little unsure of herself.

"Just remember to stop when you feel the rage," Jodson told her.

I thought that was a strange thing to say, but then she stepped up to him and all I could do was watch. Jodson lunged at her and faster than I could see she was on him. It was a blur of motion. I wasn't even sure who was winning or if it was even a contest. Finally, he yelled stop and was instantly on the other side of the room. Violet turned around and looked pissed off at the world.

"What the hell was that?" I wanted to know. Violet seemed like an exceedingly kind person but right now she looked like she wanted to kill something.

Aviel slowly walked over to her and started whispering in her ear. Eventually, I saw her relax and she looked like the woman I ate breakfast with. She walked over to me.

"That is what can happen if you don't listen to your human side. For some reason, I have trouble controlling it."

"I don't understand."

"The first time I did this I lost control and wanted to rip Jodson's head off. My best friend stepped in the way and I didn't stop. I could have killed her if he hadn't acted fast and got her out of the way. I don't know how it'll be for you but when I start to fight it's like something takes over and I'm not myself. That's what I have to learn more than anything. The fighting came naturally, but I have no idea why the rage comes out. If I don't learn to control it I could become dark."

"Dark like Evangeline?"

"Yes. And I really don't want that to happen. Now, it's your turn."

"What do I do?"

Jodson stepped forward. "Just try and attack me. We need to see how you'll react."

That sounded ominous, but I guessed it was time to learn what I was made of. I ran at him. The next thing I knew I was on the ground with him on top of me.

"That was a good start," he said, helping me up. "What were you thinking about?"

"Stopping you from getting to my mom."

"Did you feel any anger?"

"No."

"Good. Keep those same thoughts and come at me again."

I lasted a bit longer the next time, but not much. We went at this until I was exhausted.

"That's enough for now," Jodson said. "Let's go back into the house and feed you."

I was about to argue when I realized I was starving. It took all my remaining energy to walk back to the house, but I suddenly felt a little better when I smelled something amazing coming from the kitchen. I guessed Violet's aunt had been busy.

She pulled a big pan of lasagna out of the oven just as we walked in. "You're right on time," she said. "Sit at the table. The salad and bread are already there."

Violet looked as eager as I felt. "My aunt makes the best lasagna ever," she said, taking a seat.

I helped myself to salad and bread. Just when I was finishing that, a big plate of lasagna was placed in front of me. I was so hungry that I didn't even wait for anyone else, I just dug in. When I heard Violet laugh, I looked up from my plate.

"Told you it was good," she said.

I had to laugh at myself because I'd already eaten half of it and everyone else had just barely started. "Sorry," I said, to no one in particular.

"No worries," she said. "Using your angel side will use your energy way faster than anything you can do as a human."

"Will that get better?" I asked Aviel.

"I think so," he said. "This is new to all of us. Half-angels aren't supposed to exist so we're all on a learning curve."

"You did really well today Luca," Jodson told me. "At any point did you feel anger, hatred, or rage?"

"No. Was I supposed to?"

"No. It's just that this went so differently from Violet's first training session. But I think I know what the difference was. Did you think about protection the whole time you were fighting me?"

"Yes. I wasn't going to let anything get to someone I cared about."

He turned to look at Violet. "Do you remember what you were thinking about when we first did this?"

"Yeah," she said. "I was scared."

"And what do you normally do when you're scared?" he asked her.

"I get mad."

It was Aviel that spoke next. "I think I see where you're going with this. It seems that your state of mind is important to how your training will go. This is good to know. We can use this when we find the other half-angels."

Violet put her fork down. "So how does this help me? I don't want to turn dark but as soon as I start fighting, I get mad."

"We'll have to find a way to change your mindset," Jodson told her.

I had an idea. "Maybe think about protecting your aunt. Protection can be a powerful feeling, but it's a good one."

"That might work," Aviel said. "We'll try that later this afternoon."

"So, what's next?" I asked them.

Aviel looked at me. "After you've gotten your energy back, we're going to start tapping into the angel side of you," he said.

Violet smiled. "This is where it gets fun."

She looked like a kid in a candy store. I had to admit I was excited to see what the angel side of me could do.

Chapter Forty-Eight

Aviel and Violet were sitting across from me. When they said this was going to be fun, I didn't expect to feel power coursing through me. At first, it scared the shit out of me. Especially when Aviel did his power vibe in my arm. I'm not the type of man to scream like a bitch, but I almost did.

"Now that you have access to your powers, with more practice you'll be able to run faster, jump higher, and fight with more speed," Aviel said.

Violet hadn't stopped smiling since we started. She even showed me a few tricks with making a ball of energy in my hands. It was small, but I got it. Now that I knew the energy was around me, my body was filled with it. Like it was like having a heating blanket wrapped around me.

"Are you ready to see what you've got now that you can access your powers?" Jodson asked.

It was my turn to smile. "Hell yes, let's do this." I jumped up and headed for the back building. I couldn't help the excitement that went through me. I wanted to see if I had what it took to take down a real angel.

What I wasn't expecting was to get my ass handed to me the first go around. I think I went down faster than the first time.

Jodson stood above me and looked down at me. "What was that? You were doing so much better in the beginning."

I sat up. "I don't know. I think my attention was on trying to find the energy in here."

Jodson nodded at me. "That's what I thought. It will come to you when you need it the most. The more you practice, you won't even have to think about it for it to come to you."

I stood up and faced Violet. "Hey, I have an idea. Why don't you spar with me? Maybe you need someone different." The horror that crossed her face, made me rethink my words. "It's okay if you don't want to."

Jodson and Aviel both agreed with me. "I think it is worth a shot," Aviel said.

"What if I hurt him or my rage comes out. He can't get away from me fast enough."

Aviel pulled her into his arms. "This is your chance to change your mindset, love."

I could see she was thinking about it. "Okay, I'll try. Jodson if my rage hits I need you to get him away from me."

"I promise I will."

She stepped up to me and I said to her, "Just think about protecting your aunt. Don't be scared of me. We are just two people having fun."

"Okay, I'll try. Thank you for trying to help me."

I surprised her by giving her a hug. It took her a few seconds to hug me back.

I got into my fighting stance. I let her come after me. She took me by surprise with how fast she was. I almost didn't get my guard up in time. I pushed her back and she came at me again. I didn't see the rage in her eyes, I saw determination. We did this for almost twenty minutes until Jodson stopped us.

"Violet, I'm so proud of you. I'm glad this worked," Aviel said, as he kissed the top of her head.

She smiled up at him, out of breath. "Me, too. I did what he said to do, and I did it."

I walked over to them and gave her another hug. "See, you just needed a fresh face."

She laughed and smacked my arm and I joined her laughter. I wish I would have trusted them sooner.

"What's next? How do we find the next halfie?"

Aviel turned Violet in his arms to where she was facing me. "I go up to Heaven and look for the next one. I would take you, but I never know how long I'll be there. Like Violet has said, your human body doesn't let you stay up there long."

"Oh. What do we do while you're gone? Can we ever leave?"

"It's not safe to leave, but you can go to any of the safe houses if you want to."

I let out a sigh, no more clubbing or anything else fun. "That sucks, but get it, I really do."

Thanks, Lucifer for fucking up my life. I couldn't wait to kick his ass.

"All we ever do is fight and practice gaining our powers, oh and the food is always amazing." Violet said.

"Sounds like we're in a high-end prison. I would like to see Erik and Carmen. I promised them answers."

"I'll take you over there. I'm sure they're worried about you," Jodson said

He put his hand on my shoulder, and we were standing in the backyard of a country looking house. "Where are we in the world today?"

"We are in a small town in England."

The back door opened and out came Carmen. "It's about time you came back. I was getting worried about you." She gave me a hug.

"Dude, I thought I wasn't going to see you again. What the hell is going on?"

"Let's go inside and I will explain everything."

I followed them inside and took a seat across from them. I told them everything I knew, and I even showed them what I could do. When I was done Erik had a huge smile on his face.

"I knew you were different. This explains a lot, man. It must be nice to never gain weight."

I laughed at him. "Out of all of that, you are worried about me not gaining weight. Dude, your priorities are messed up."

"So, you're a half-angel?" Carmen asked

"From what I understand."

I could see the wheels turning in her head. "You and eleven other half-angels have to take on Lucifer?"

I sighed because I knew where this was leading. "You guys are not helping. You'd get killed and I couldn't live with myself if something happened to you."

They looked at each other before they looked back at me. "If there is anything we can do. You know we'll be there."

"There is one thing you can do; I need you to look after my parent's and make sure my father behaves himself. I don't need him to be a loose cannon."

They both nodded at me. "We'll try our hardest, but you know your father."

I shook my head because I know how true that was. Now, I just had to go see my parents and tell them what was going on. I hoped it wouldn't freak them out.

Chapter Forty-Nine

I stayed with Erik and Carmen for a while, before I worked up the nerve to go see my parents. Before I got Jodson to take me to them, I asked him a question.

"What did you tell my parents about why they were being put in a safe house?"

"That there was a threat to their lives, and they needed to stay there until it was safe."

"And were they transported by an angel or vehicle?"

"From what I understand they were taken in a car to a safe house about two hours away from Hamburg."

"So, they have no idea what's really going on?"

"Not as far as I know."

"I have a feeling this conversation isn't going to go well. You might as well take me there. It'll just get worse the longer I put it off."

Jodson laughed and touched my arm. We were now standing outside of a small house in the country. I knocked on the door. Someone that I was assuming was another angel opened it. We walked in and the two angels were suddenly gone. Great, I wasn't even going to have any backup.

"Mom? Dad? Are you here?" I called out.

"Luca! is that you?" mom said.

"Yeah, I'm here."

Mom came around the corner and hugged me like her life depended on it. "I've been so worried about you. No one would tell us anything. We didn't know where you were or if you were okay."

"I'm fine mom, as you can see. Where's dad? I need to talk to you two."

"Probably outside looking for a way to escape. Your father's not exactly the type of man that takes orders very well."

I had to chuckle at that. Dad was the one to give orders, not take them. I found the back door and yelled for him. After the third time, I saw him come running across the backyard.

My dad wasn't one for hugging people, but when he got to me, he hugged me just like mom did.

"We were worried about you son. What's going on?"

"I have all the answers you need. Let's go into the house and I'll tell you everything."

We went into the house and to the living room. I took a minute to collect my thoughts, then started talking.

"First of all, I want you to listen to everything I have to say before you start asking questions. And believe me, you'll have questions. Also, everything I'm about to say is one hundred percent true. It's going to sound crazy, but I'll be able to prove it to you.

"They were right in telling you your lives are in danger, but it has nothing to do with the company. It's because of me, or actually, because of who my birth parents were. Here's the part that's going to sound unbelievable. My birth father was an angel, like he lives in Heaven angel. And because of that, I'm half-angel. Lucifer, as in the devil himself, has started a war in Heaven that will spill down to Earth. Only me and eleven other half-angels can stop him and save the world." I took in another deep breath before I continued.

"Violet and Aviel were really telling the truth the other day in my office. Friday night I was taken at gunpoint at the club. Evangeline, the woman I'd been sleeping with, turned out to be a Dark Angel and they were waiting on Lucifer to come kill me. Violet and Aviel saved my life. That's why you guys are here."

I waited for them to say something. What I didn't expect was that they would start laughing.

"That's quite a story son," dad said. "If you wanted to get back at me for making you cancel your vacation you could have gone to a little less trouble."

Great, they thought it was a joke. I was in touch with enough of my angel side that I hoped I could prove to them that I was telling the truth.

"Mom, Dad, this isn't a prank to get back at you. Watch this," I said, and tapped into the part of me that allowed me to create energy out of the air. A small white glowing ball appeared in my hand.

My parents looked at me, but I could tell they weren't convinced.

"Nice trick," dad said. "Can you teach me?"

Where was a damn angel when you needed one? Then I had an idea. I took out the phone that Aviel had given me this morning and called Violet.

"Hey," she said, "how's it going?"

"Not good. My parents think this is all some joke and I don't know how to convince them."

"Where's Jodson?"

"I don't know. He disappeared when we got here."

"Why don't you call him?"

"I don't have his number."

Violet started laughing. "I mean just call his name. He'll come to you."

"That might have been helpful information an hour ago."

"Sorry. But call him, he'll be able to help."

"Okay. Thanks, Violet."

I hung up. "Jodson," I called out to the room.

"Yes," he suddenly said from behind me.

Mom screamed and dad reached for something to use as a weapon.

"Stop," I yelled. "This is Jodson, he's one of the good guys. He's here to prove that I'm telling the truth."

"Sorry if I scared you, Mrs. Maier," he said. "That wasn't my intention. Mr. Maier, my apologies."

Jodson didn't move and mom and dad seemed to calm down a little.

"Who are you?" dad finally asked Jodson.

"I'm a Protection Angel. My duty is to protect humans in need and right now I'm here for your son. The one that brought you here is a Warrior Angel. There are also several Protection Angels here to keep you safe."

"How can I be sure you're telling us the truth?" dad asked.

The next thing I knew Jodson was standing there with his wings out. I think mom made a yelping sound, but I was too mesmerized at the sight in front of me. I'd never seen anything like it before. His wings were white with blue tips and stretched at least four feet out on either side of him. It was absolutely amazing.

Mom got off the couch and walked over to him. "May I touch them?" Jodson nodded. Mom ran her hand over the edge of one of his wings. "They're real," she whispered. "Come see." She motioned dad over to her.

He slowly made his way over to them. He reached out and did the same thing mom did, then he turned to me. "I'm sorry we didn't believe you, son."

"It's okay, Dad. Hell, I didn't believe it and it was happening to me. Thank you Jodson."

"You're welcome," he said and disappeared.

Mom and dad both looked around the room.

"He's gone," I told them. "It's just a thing they do. Now, I'm sure you have a lot of questions. I'll do my best to answer them."

We all sat down and spent the next few hours talking. I was really glad they believed me and understood what the situation was.

I called Jodson to take me back to Violet. Now that I knew my family and friends were safe, I was ready to put everything I had into becoming the best half-angel I could be.

Chapter Fifty

A week had gone by. I moved Erik and Carmen with my parent's. It was just easier for me when they were in the same place. Teleporting took a toll on me when I got tossed around too much. I refused to say anything to anyone though.

The training got more intense and the result was my body had never been more toned and in tune with my angel side. I was faster and stronger than ever before. "Damn, boy. You're getting good. We might need to bring in some more Warrior Angels," Jodson said.

I took the towel he offered and wiped my face off. "Thanks, if there is one thing about me, it's I have a competitive side." I turned to watch Violet's fight. She had come a long way since our first sparring match. She didn't let her rage control her anymore. "Nice form, Violet."

I caught a slight smile on her face before she called it quits. We had been at it for hours. I looked up at the clock and saw it was almost six pm. I promised my parents I would have dinner with them, Erik and Carmen. It had been a few days since I went to see them. I wanted to train as much as I could.

Violet walked over to me wiping her face off. "You better get showered. You don't want to be late for dinner. I've met your father and I get the feeling he doesn't like anyone to be late."

I laughed and nodded my head. "How right you are. Jodson you don't mind taking me over there, would you?"

"Actually, I have dinner plans myself, but Tristan said he'd be available to take you."

Violet got a smile on her face. "You have a date with Cassandra Daye?"

I watched as he blushed. "As a matter of fact, I do, since you want to be all up in my business."

We both laughed at him. "Alright, both of you go shower. You both stink." Then he was gone. I looked over at Violet and laughed.

Violet tilted her head. "You better get going. I'll see you later."

I gave her a hug and took off to my room to shower and change. I may have only known these guys for a short time, but they had become family.

I got a text from Carmen just as I was getting out the shower.

Carmen: You have two mins to get here.

Me: Don't remind me. I'm hurrying. I will be there.

I got dressed and called out for Tristan. He popped up before I even finished his name and he grabbed a hold of me, and we were at my parent's safe house right on time.

"I'm here."

I followed the smell of the food. Just smelling it made my stomach growl.

I heard my father's voice before I even got a chance to get into the dining room.

"You're late!"

I shook my head. Here we go. I'll have to listen to this for the next twenty minutes.

"I'm right on time," I said, as I walked into the dining room.

"Being on time means you are fifteen minutes early, not when we should have been eating already."

"Dad, can we not argue about this. I just got done training and I'm starving."

He stared at me as I took a seat at the table. "You're right, I'd rather not argue tonight."

"Thank you. Hey mom, Erik, Carmen. How was your day?"

Mom was the one who smiled before she answered. "Same old, same old. I know if I don't get out of this house soon, I'm going to go crazy."

"I second that," both Erik and Carmen said.

I felt the tug of guilt wash over me. "I'm sorry. If it wasn't for me, you wouldn't be here."

Erik slapped me on my shoulder. "Hey man, this isn't your fault. It's Lucifer's fault. If he wasn't hell-bent on killing you, we wouldn't be here."

I shook my head. "We can go over the if's all day long. We're never going to agree whose fault this is. Mom, this looks amazing."

"Thank you, son. Let's dig in."

We ate in silence for a bit , before Erik asked me. "You want to watch Game of Thrones when we get done? I heard the fourth season is better than the other three."

I smiled at this. "You know I'm in for that."

Carmen laughed at us. "Boys and their shows. How can you even handle all the guts and gore?"

We looked at each other before turning our attention back to Carmen. "That's the best part," we said at the same time and laughed.

"Alright you two, let's not talk about that kind of stuff over dinner," mom chastised us.

Erik and I laughed and stuffed our faces so we could go watch the show. I hadn't hung out with Erik like this in what felt like months. I missed it a lot.

When we were done, we raced each other to his room to watch it. When I got there way before him, I laughed.

When he finally got there he was panting. "Dude, you got faster."

I plopped down on the chair and laughed. "This is what training has done."

He looked to be thinking. "Is there any way I could train too. Just to get out of here for a while."

"I can ask. I don't see why not."

He rubbed his hands together as he smiled. "Awesome. I can't wait. Let's get our game on."

He turned the TV on, we watched Game of Thrones for a few hours and I was content for the time being.

Chapter Fifty-One

The next day, Aviel joined us for breakfast. We'd hardly seen him in the last week. He'd been in Heaven trying to find any sign of the other ten half-angels.

"Hey Aviel, how's it going up there?" I asked.

"Slow. I was sure I'd have found at least one of them by now. You know, you haven't been up there yet. Are you ready to see what it's like?"

I'd been so busy training I hadn't given it much thought. Did I want to go? Yeah, I thought it was time I did.

"Yes, I'm ready."

"We can only spend about an hour up there before your body will tell you it's time to leave. As soon as you're ready we can go."

I decided if I was going to do this, I'd better do it on a full stomach. Aunt Milana, she insisted we all call her that, was a great cook and this morning she'd made bacon, cheese, and mushroom omelettes. After I finished my second one, I was ready.

"Okay, Aviel, let's do this."

"Good luck," Violet said, and hugged me.

Aviel held out his hand and I took it. I blinked and I instantly knew we'd left Earth. Looking around I could just feel that this was Heaven. I felt a sense of peace and comfort like I'd never felt before.

We started walking around. I hadn't asked anyone what it would be like so seeing "people" doing normal things like walking a dog or eating a sandwich surprised me. But one thing I could tell was that everyone was happy, no matter what they were doing. We walked around for a little while longer. I saw people laughing and dancing with each other.

All too soon I wasn't feeling great. Aviel noticed and took me back to the safe house.

Violet was waiting for me with a plate of brownies. I ate a few and started feeling better. Then I ate a couple more just because they were delicious.

"So, what did you think?" she asked.

"It was so ordinary, but at the same time amazing."

"I know right. It's hard to put into words."

"So, what's the plan for the rest of the day?" I asked.

"The day is pretty much over," Violet said. "Look outside."

When I did, I noticed it was getting dark. I didn't understand what was going on. It had been morning when we left to go to Heaven. "What the hell? What time is it?"

"After seven," she said. "Time works differently up there. Aunt Milana left your dinner in the microwave when you're ready to eat it. I'm going to go read for a while. Come find me if you have any questions."

Aviel hadn't stayed when he dropped me off. I guess he knew Violet would be able to tell me what I needed to know. I heated my dinner and I got out my phone and started looking up half-angels. I don't know why, but suddenly, being called a half-angel was bothering me. If we were going to save the world, we needed a cool name like the Avengers or something.

Everything I found kept bringing me back to the word Nephilim. I guess technically that's what we were, but that really just didn't feel right for this situation. I wanted something different and unique. I'd keep thinking about it and maybe it would come to me.

After cleaning my plate, I went to the living room and eventually found something to watch. I must have fallen asleep because the next thing I knew, I was suddenly sitting up straight on the couch. The edge of a dream was sitting there, and I had a strong feeling I was supposed to remember something about it.

I closed my eyes and tried to recall it, but it was slipping away. Then one word simply stood out like a flash of lighting, Quira. That was the word I'd been searching for all night. It was what I was going to call us. I just hoped everyone else was on board with it.

****

Violet and I were in the back building training, again. We'd been at it for what seemed like forever some days. We were in the middle of sparing when I just stopped. She ended up kicking me with a roundhouse that sent me flying halfway across the room.

She came running over to me. "Luca, are you okay? I didn't mean to get you like that."

It took a minute but when I did a survey of my body, I realized I was fine. "Yeah, I'm okay," I said sitting up.

"Why did you just stop like that?"

"I'm tired of just training. We can train every day for the rest of our lives but unless we get some real-world experience, we aren't going to really know how to fight them."

"What are you suggesting?"

Lowering my voice, I said, "I think we should sneak out and see if we can find a Dark Angel to fight."

"That sounds crazy Luca. We could get hurt, or worse, killed. Then what happens to saving the world?"

"We're eventually going to have to face a Dark Angel or one of their human followers. Why not do it before we find the other Quira."

"What's a Quira?"

"Us, half-angels. I decided last night that we needed a name since I was tired of hearing half-angels all the time and Quira came to me in a dream. What do you think?"

"I don't really know. I guess I'll give it some time. Anyway, back to your crazy idea. I know we're going to have to face them, but don't you think we should run this by one of the Protection Angels? I mean, how are we even going to know how to find a Dark Angel?"

"I hadn't thought about that," I admitted.

"It's not like we can wander around asking people if they're one of Lucifer's followers. And, we don't want to attract attention to this place either."

"You're right, again," I told her.

She smirked. "Why don't we do this, at dinner, we'll see which of the angels is around and talk to them about it. I'm all for trying out our skills but I'm not willing to risk the world on it."

"Okay, you win. Now, I think it's my turn to kick your ass."

"You can try," Violet said, with a grin. "Bring it on."

Chapter Fifty-Two

Dinner time came a lot faster than I expected. Now that it was here, I was kind of nervous as to what they were going to say, or which one was going to show up. I decided to go take a shower before I faced the angels. I'm sure they would tell us it was too dangerous and we shouldn't risk it. I kind of agreed, but how are we going to know how to fight them if we didn't ever actually fight them?

As I walked downstairs, I heard Violet and some woman talking. It wasn't her aunt, this woman sounded younger. I got down to the bottom step and stopped in my tracks. There, sitting with Violet, was the most beautiful woman I've ever seen. Her long blonde hair and baby blue eyes drew me in.

"We're not going this long being apart again. I've never been so bored in my life without you there. Even with the hotties keeping me company."

Violet laughed. "It's only been a few days since I went to go see you. You couldn't…"

"Who's the hottie with the grey eyes?"

Violet turned in my direction. "Amy, this is Luca. He is the one who came up with our name Quira."

Amy stood up, came over to me and held out her hand. "It's nice to finally meet you. I was starting to think Violet was keeping you a secret."

I took her hand and kissed the back of it. "The pleasure is all mine."

I didn't know what got into me, but there was something about her that pulled me to her. Like there was a force drawing me to be near her.

Violet cleared her throat to get our attention. We both turned to her. "Now that you guys are well acquainted. Are you ready to ask Davian about your crazy plan?"

The ball of nerves came back. "I guess it's now or never. Right?"

She shook her head and walked past us to go into the kitchen where I assume Davian was. I took a deep breath and started to follow her, but before I could take a step, Amy grabbed on to my arm. "What crazy plan?"

I wanted to run my fingers through her hair. I had to stop myself from doing it. "You're about to find out." I took her hand and led the way into the kitchen. To my surprise, she didn't yank her hand away.

I pulled out a seat for Amy and let her hand go to face Davian. "So, I have a question for you Davian."

Davian smirked before he said, "I'm listening."

I took another deep breath and told him my plan. When I was done, I had to take another breath. He stared at me like I lost my mind, and hey to be fair, some days I felt that way.

"I don't think that's a good Idea until I talk to Aviel and Jodson. They've been the ones overseeing your training."

That was fair. "I understand. I know this sounds crazy, but I strongly feel we need to up our training."

"I agree with you on that, but it's not up to me."

I nodded my head. "In that case what's for dinner?"

Now that I got my nerves under control, I could smell the amazing food in the kitchen. I took a seat next to Amy while Violet took the other side of her. I was just about to ask Amy something when Aviel popped in looking beat.

Violet stood up and went over to him. "You need a break. Have someone else look for a while. I miss you cuddling me at night. That big old bed is lonely," she pouted.

Aviel blinked them out of the room and I was sure I knew what they planned on doing. I brought my attention back to Amy. "So, how long have you known Violet?"

She turned to me. "Ever since freshman year of college."

I smiled at her. "What do you think about all of this… mess?"

She leaned into me and whispered in my ear. "I'm rather fond of it so far."

Was she flirting with me or was this a game? Might as well find out. I leaned back into her. "Now that I've met you, I'm saying the same thing."

She giggled and all of a sudden two plates split us up as they were placed in front of us. I look up to see a smirking Davian. "I think you two need to eat before it gets cold."

I shook my head at his not so subtle way of letting us know to take a breather. "Alright, man, I get it. Thanks for the food." I dug in because let's face it, I was starving.

When we finished eating, I got up and went to the living room. I wasn't tired enough to sleep, so I popped in a random movie to watch, hoping Amy would join me. I didn't want to come off like a creeper.

When she sat down next to me, I had to force myself not to smile. That was harder than one would think.

"What are we watching?"

I looked at her. "I have no clue, I just put one in. I guess we will both be surprised."

She rolled her eyes and got comfy. Just as the movie started, I wanted to groan. It was one of Violet's chick flicks. I couldn't back out of this now.

"You watch chick flicks?"

I rubbed my face with my hands. "To tell you the truth, not really. I didn't know it was a chick film."

She laughed at me. "You never know you might actually like Dirty Dancing. It's Violet's and my favorite movie. She probably had it sitting out for us to watch. There's just one thing missing. Popcorn."

She was about to get up when I stopped her. "I'll go make us some. Do you want anything to drink?"

She looked up at me. "Sure, some wine would be great. Thank you."

I would do anything for her, and I didn't even know why. I felt like I'd known her my whole life and that wasn't even possible, right?

Chapter Fifty-Three

We sat there, watching the movie, only separated by an inch. Even though I just met Amy a couple of hours ago, I couldn't shake the feeling that we were meant to be together.

I noticed the credits start rolling on the TV. Amy was grinning from ear to ear. "I love that ending so much. Even though I've seen it a million times it gets me every time. So, what did you think?"

"To tell you the truth, I have no idea what to think because I wasn't really watching it. Amy, this is going to sound crazy, but I'm just going to say it anyway. We've only known each other for a few hours, but I feel like I've known you forever. It's like I don't want to stop looking at you. I want to touch you, hold your hand and most of all I want to kiss you."

She didn't look at me like I was crazy, instead she moved, so that she was straddling me. "I thought it was just me. I feel like there's this intense connection between us. It doesn't make any logical sense, but I feel it to my core."

"It's because you're soulmates," Aviel said, walking into the living room, followed by Violet.

Amy jumped off me like we were teenagers getting caught by our parents. Aviel and Violet started laughing.

"Relax," Violet said smiling. "We get it."

"Wait," Amy said. "Did you just say that Luca and I are soulmates?"

Aviel nodded. "Yes."

"Soulmates aren't a real thing," I said.

"Of course, they are," he said. "But it's usually two humans or two angels. It's exceedingly rare to mix the two."

"Luca is half-angel, but I'm not an angel, anything," Amy said. "So, doesn't that mean we can't be soulmates?"

"Don't forget Amy," Aviel said, "you were touched by an angel when your grandmother passed away. That changed you forever. It allowed you to be open to anything related to angels."

I looked at Amy and she explained seeing Violet's father take her grandmother's soul to Heaven.

"Wow, that's amazing," I told her. "I've never heard of anyone seeing an angel before this craziness started."

"Come to the kitchen with us," Violet said. "We have to talk."

I had a feeling I knew what it was going to be about. Amy and I got up and followed them.

Aviel started heating up the food they missed out on at dinner. "Davian told me what you want to do, and I think it's a good idea."

"Wait, did I hear you right? You're not telling us no?"

He smiled. "I agree that you're going to have to learn to fight real Dark Angels and their human followers, but there's no way you two are going to do it alone. We'll find them and be there in case anything happens. So be prepared to leave at any time. I have Jodson and Tristian out looking right now."

"Wow, I didn't expect you to agree with me. Thanks, I think." The reality of actually having to fight someone for real suddenly set in.

"Just remember, you won't be alone. You may not be able to see us, but we'll be there."

"We should probably all get some rest," Violet said. "And as for you two," she pointed at me and Amy. "It's going to take some getting used to, the whole soulmates thing I mean. It'll be strange that you'll want to be around each other all the time, but you'll get used to it. Just keep it down, okay?"

Amy and Violet grinned at each other and I was assuming there was something more behind that last comment.

We left Violet and Aviel to finish eating and went to the living room.

"So," I said, "what happens now?"

"With us?" Amy asked.

"Yes."

"I don't really know. I want so badly to go to your room right now and honestly, that's freaking me out a little."

"It's okay, I totally get it. I feel the same and it's a little strange, okay ... a lot strange." I smiled at her. "Do you even have a room here?"

Amy laughed. "I don't know. I was so excited to come and see Violet, I didn't think that far ahead. I didn't bring any clothes, so I guess I should go back to Aviel's place."

"Will I see you tomorrow?" I really hoped she was going to say yes.

"If I have anything to say about it, I'll definitely be back tomorrow."

"Kemuel," she called out.

An angel I hadn't met yet was suddenly in the living room with us. I was as straight as it got but even, I had to admit he was very good looking. He had black hair and bright green eyes that seemed to look right into my soul. I was instantly jealous of Amy going anywhere with him.

"Luca, have you met Kemuel yet?" Amy asked me.

"Can't say that I have."

"He's my Protection Angel."

My jaw automatically clenched when she said "my." And the bastard chuckled.

Amy looked between the two of us. "What am I missing?" She wanted to know.

Kemuel turned his attention to Amy. "Looks like your boy here has a jealous side."

It took her a minute, but she figured it out. "Luca, Kemuel saved me from Lucifer, so sure I'm a little partial to him and he's nice to look at, but that's it. You have nothing to worry about."

"Soulmates?" Kemuel asked.

"Apparently," she told him.

"I leave you alone for a few hours and you go and find your soulmate. What am I going to do with you?"

"Are you teasing me? I didn't think you had it in you," she said to him.

"I don't normally," he admitted. "I guess you're wearing me down."

She laughed. "I'm just going to tell Violet I'm leaving. I'll be right back. Play nice."

Kemuel chuckled again and I glared at him.

"You can calm down," he told me. "I have no interest in Amy, other than to protect her from Lucifer and his followers."

I had never been a jealous man, so this was a new feeling for me, and I didn't think I liked it very much. I took a deep breath. "Sorry. This is new for me."

He nodded but didn't say anything. I was getting the feeling that he wasn't a big talker.

Amy was back a couple of minutes later. "So hopefully, we'll see each other tomorrow. Bye."

I wasn't letting her leave quite yet. I grabbed her hand and pulled her into a hug. "I know it's crazy, but I already miss you."

She giggled. "I feel the same, Luca."

Finally, I let her go. "Take care of her," I told Kemuel.

"I will."

Amy reached out and touched his arm and they were gone. I already felt her loss and I didn't even really know her. This soulmate thing was definitely going to take some getting used to.

Chapter Fifty-Four

I couldn't sleep to save my life. I kept going over everything in my head. From how I have a soulmate, to what if we get our asses handed to us by Dark Angels or the humans. I couldn't get my mind to shut the hell up long enough to even get a few hours of sleep.

Finally, I could see the sun rising. I jumped out of bed and got into the shower. Hopefully, the hot water will wake me up.

After I washed my hair and body, I stood there for a few minutes letting the hot water beat on my skin. It felt so good that I didn't want to get out. I gave myself a few more minutes before getting out. I looked in the mirror and saw I needed to shave. I guess I should have thought about that before I got into the shower.

Deciding against shaving for the day, I got dressed. I was really too tired to even think about shaving. Once I was sure I looked somewhat decent, I headed down to the kitchen. I was hoping Amy was already there. The closer I got; I could hear voices. But the one I wanted to hear was absent.

Walking into the kitchen, I saw another angel I'd never met. I looked over at Aviel who looked to be deep in thought, I thought better than to interrupt him. I went for a plate that was already awaiting and took a seat.

"I'm telling you this Dark Angel is not one you want to mess with. He isn't low in the rankings. He has more power than you think he does," the new angel said.

"That isn't what I was thinking. I'm trying to figure out why he wanted to be seen. I would never let them take on a higher Dark Angel like that. Lucifer is up to something and we need to figure out what it is before it's too late."

"Do you think we should be talking about this in front of him," the guy said, pointing a thumb at me.

Aviel looked over at me. "Yes, they need to know everything we do. Good morning Luca. This is Zayd, Zayd this is Luca. Whatever you think is important you can tell him too. We're not going to keep secrets from the Quira."

"Who is the Quira?"

Both Aviel and I laughed before he answered him. "That is the name they gave themselves. They don't like being called half-angels."

Zayd nods his head. "Cool name. Now can we get back to what Lucifer is doing? I don't like it at all."

"Have Cassandra, Gatlin, and Davian look into it. I need the rest of the Protection Angels where they are. I don't want any gaps for them to slide into."

"What do you want me to do?"

"I need you to find me a Dark Angel that is lower in power. I can't unleash a high power Dark Angel on them. They aren't quite ready for that."

I had to get in on this conversion. "Um, what do you mean we aren't quite ready to take on a higher power Dark Angel? Isn't that what we've been training for?

He gave me a stern look. "Yes, but you aren't there yet. You guys just started training a few weeks ago. I don't think going against Lucifer's fourth in command is the right thing to do."

"Fourth in command. But he can't kill me. Yes, he can hand my ass to me, but he still can't kill me."

"That very well may be true, but if you haven't noticed, I love Violet's ass as you say, just the way it is."

I had to laugh at the man. I don't think I heard him cuss and it sounded strange coming from an angel. "I get where you're going with this and please don't ever cuss. It doesn't sound right coming from you."

He laughed at me. "I'll try to refrain from that, but I can't promise you anything."

I nodded at him. "I'll take it. So, what is on the agenda for today?"

"Today, Violet wants you, Amy and her to spend some time together."

I didn't know if men got butterflies or not, but my stomach did that flip flop thing. "Okay, do you know what they're planning?"

He shrugged his shoulders. "Have no clue. I'll be away looking for the other Quira."

"Still no luck with that huh?"

He let out a frustrated sigh. "It's not easy that's for sure. They have to use their angel side for me to find them."

"How did I use mine? I don't remember using it."

"I have a theory about you. Evangeline caused yours, I'm positive on that. You may have not known she was dark, but your angel side did, and that's when I found you, when she was with you. We can sense an angel when they're near. That's why she was so hell-bent on getting you close. You were the first one they've found.

"That makes sense. So, the female that had a gun to my side was human?"

He nodded his head. "Yes, she could have killed you."

The story of my life it seems. Just when I found my soulmate, things just got more interesting.

Chapter Fifty-Five

I was halfway through eating breakfast when Violet walked into the kitchen, and by the look on her face she was up to something.

"Amy will be here soon," she said with a smile.

At the mention of her name, my heart started beating a little faster. I tried to conceal my smile, but Violet noticed.

"It's okay to be happy that you want to see her," she said. "I get excited every time I see Aviel and I don't see that changing any time soon."

I nodded and stopped hiding the grin that was now there on full display. "Aviel said you have something planned for us today. I'm curious to find out what it is."

"You'll find out when Amy gets here."

"It has to be more exciting than training. I mean, training has been great and all, but honestly it's getting a little boring just being here."

"I totally get it. When was the last time you saw your parents?"

"A few days ago, but that's not really the same thing. I miss walking the streets of Hamburg and people watching on the train. And most of all I miss the food."

"You cook right?" she asked me.

"Yeah."

"Why don't you make dinner tonight? You can have free reign of the kitchen. I'm sure Aunt Milana would like a break."

"You know what, that sounds like a great idea." I got up and started looking in the fridge and freezer to see what we had. It had been a while since I made a meal and I was really looking forward to it. I wondered if Amy liked to cook.

It was as if just thinking her name made her appear. I felt her before she walked into the kitchen and I knew I was grinning like an idiot. When I turned around, I saw the exact same grin on her face.

"Hey," she said.

"Hey back."

"Whatcha doin'?"

"I'm cooking tonight, so right now I'm deciding what to make. Do you like cooking?"

That made both her and Violet laugh, loudly.

"Amy is worse in the kitchen than I am," Violet told me.

"Oh, wow" I said seriously. The other day she burned a pot so badly we had to throw it out.

I looked at Amy. "I was going to ask you to help me but now I'm not sure."

"I can help … I think."

Violet snickered. "Good luck with that."

I started gathering ingredients while Amy and Violet talked for a while. Then Violet announced it was time to do her "thing." Amy reached for my hand and we followed Violet outside. We walked out of the house and into the backyard. We didn't stop and ended up in the woods.

"Is it safe to be out here?" Amy asked, looking around.

"Yes," Violet said. "This property goes way back and the whole thing is protected from Lucifer."

"So, what are we doing out here?" I asked.

"I thought we'd go for a hike."

"A hike?"

"Yeah, you know, get back to nature. We've either been in the house or in the other building training. I thought we could use some fresh air."

"Sounds good to me," I told her.

Amy smiled. "I'm not normally an outdoor kind of girl, but even I'm missing some fresh air. Let's go."

We'd only been hiking for about thirty minutes when Kemuel and Zayd popped in out of nowhere. Amy squealed a little and even Violet jumped.

"I hate it when they do that," I mumbled.

"We found a place for you to test out your skills," Zayd said. "Kemuel is going to take Amy back to the house and you two will come with me. We don't have any time to waste."

The next thing I knew Violet and I were standing in a dark alley. Talk about a cliché.

"Where do you think we are?" I wondered.

"No idea, other than somewhere where night has already fallen."

"So, what are we supposed to do?" I asked Violet.

"We do what we were taught to do. Search for the enemy. We're supposed to be able to feel any Dark Angels, and to a much lesser extent the human followers."

I'd been so anxious to do this the other day, but now I wasn't so sure I was ready. Violet started walking to where the alley met the street. There were a few people walking down the street, but I didn't see anything out of the ordinary.

Violet and I felt it at the same time. Something was to our left. We started moving in that direction. There were only three people in that direction, two men and a woman, and none of them seemed like a Dark Angel.

Glancing at Violet she looked as confused as I did. Not knowing what else to do we walked towards the group on the sidewalk. We passed them and nothing happened. Violet motioned with her head to go to the left. Ducking into a wide doorway, she peeked around the corner to watch.

The feeling was now behind us, so I was pretty sure the people we just walked by weren't actually people but Dark Angels. A loud laugh came out of one of the men and the only way I could describe it was menacing.

"Come out and play," the woman said, in a teasing manner.

"We know you're there," one of the men said.

"I bet they're too scared to face us," the woman taunted.

Violet looked at me. "You ready for this?" she asked.

"As ready as I'm going to get."

"Okay, let's do this."

We walked out of the doorway and faced them. I noticed the trio was about ten feet closer than before. I had no idea what was going to happen. We just kind of stood there, staring at each other. Then all hell broke loose.

The woman ran at Violet and jumped over her, but that was all I was able to see. An energy orb flew past my head and the fight was on. Some kind of instinct must have activated, because my training kicked in and I was able to hit one of them with my own energy ball without hardly a thought. He went down and I moved on to the other one.

He ran at me so fast, I barely had time to react. We collided, but managed to stay standing up. His movements were so quick, I had a hard time keeping up. One thought kept repeating over and over; he can't kill me; he can't kill me.

Suddenly, there were strong arms around me, and I couldn't move. I must have only stunned the other Dark Angel and now he was helping attack me.

The one in front of me laughed at my struggling. That infuriated me and I let the angel side of me completely out. A strength I didn't know I had emerged, and I broke the hold on me. I punched the one I could see in the face. It was hard enough that his head snapped back, and he ended up several feet away from me.

Seizing the opportunity, I used my angel speed and moved far enough away that I could see both of them. Creating a powerful ball of pure energy in each hand I shot them at each of the dark angels. My aim was true and hit both of them right in the chest.

A scream came from each of them then they were suddenly gone. I looked around to see if they'd just transported somewhere else, but I didn't see a thing, but I did hear clapping.

"Well done," Zayd said. "I'm actually impressed."

"Are they really gone?" I asked.

"Yes, they've been eliminated."

"You mean dead."

"Same thing."

"Hey Violet," I said, when she walked over to me. "How did you do?"

"Alright, I guess. I got her in the end, but I'm sure she gave me a black eye. Bitch."

I had to laugh at that.

Zayd looked a little nervous with us standing out in the open. "Time to go," he said, and transported us back to the house.

Chapter Fifty-Six

As soon as we got back Amy rushed over to us. "Are you guys okay? I was so worried about you."

I brought her into my arms and kissed the top of her head. "We're good. More than good. We beat them and there are three less Dark Angels to worry about."

She looked up at me in shock. "You guys killed them?"

I kind of felt guilty about "eliminating" them, but when I really thought about it, they deserved nothing better. "Yes, they hurt people for fun."

She nodded her head in understanding. "Okay, when you put it that way. I just… I didn't know what to expect is all."

I gave her a squeeze and walked her to the kitchen. "I don't know about you, but I'm starving. You still want to help me cook?"

She gave me a sheepish look then nodded. "I'll try, but like Violet said, I suck."

I laughed at that. "I'll have you cooking in no time. Grab me the veggies that are on the plate in the fridge."

I hoped I could have her cooking in no time, but some people were just not meant to cook and that was okay.

It took us longer to make dinner than it should have, but we got it done. I had to say, Amy didn't know her way around a kitchen, at all. I had to explain some of the utensils to her. Once we got dinner on the table, we all sat down to eat. "I can say one thing, I'm good with take out. I don't think I ever want to do that again, that was way too much work," Amy said

I laughed and said. "I'll do all the cooking. I love to cook. Maybe one day you'll change your mind. You never know, baking might be your thing."

She gave me a doubtful look and laughed. "We'll see. Maybe when I'm old and grey."

Violet about choked on her water at that. "Girl no one is getting old and grey around here. I refuse to let it happen."

Amy turns to her best friend. "How are you planning to do that?"

Violet shrugged her shoulders. "I'll figure it out. I'm not living in a world you aren't in. If the theory is correct, we will live a very long time being half-angels. I refused to watch the people I love die because of what I was born to be."

A sadness hit my chest. I didn't think about losing Amy until now. Why would God give her to me just to have her be taken away? It didn't make sense. Maybe it was time to meet my parents and ask them. I didn't want to live without her either.

"Enough with the heavy talk. I still can't believe we took out three Dark Angels in that short of time. It was like my angel side took over and knew what to do."

Violet's eyes got large as she spoke. "I know right, I got pissed off and all of a sudden I had full access to my angel side. It felt amazing. Now if we could only channel that while training, we could really kick some ass."

Amy sat there looking between us like we both lost our minds. "You guys scare me sometimes."

Both Violet and I laughed. Sometimes I scared myself with how we fought and trained. I didn't even know I could do the things I could do now. Until a few hours ago, I didn't think I would be able to take down a Dark Angel, let alone two.

Violet gave her best friend a hug as she got up to refill her glass of water. "There's nothing to be afraid with us. We're the good guys. Have you been doing your self-defense classes?"

Amy nodded her head. "Yep, every day with Becky and Lana. They've been asking about you. I can't make up excuses anymore. You need to come see them soon."

Violet let out a heavy sigh. "I know, I just feel weird being around them now. I can't openly talk about most of this and I don't want to slip up."

"You do know, they know right. You're the one who told them."

"I know, I just wish I didn't tell them. I wish they could go back to being normal."

Amy laughed and shook her head. "There is no going back now, chick. So, suck it up and go see them. Before they have one of the angels bring them here."

"I have to agree with Amy. You brought them into this world, you can't just leave them hanging. That's being a shitty friend. Talking about a shitty friend, I need to go see Erik and Carmen today. It's been a few days. I need to catch them up on things." I looked over at Amy. "Would you like to go with me?"

The smile she gave me almost melted my heart. "I would love to. When do we leave?"

I smiled that stupid smile of mine. "As soon as we get done here and cleaned up."

She bounced out of her chair. "I'm done eating, I'll get stuff put away."

Both Violet and I watched her busy herself with putting the food away and getting the dishes into the dishwasher. I slowly got up and handed her my plate since it seemed like she was in charge of it all.

"I'm going to go change, I will be back down in a few." Kissing the top of her head, I jogged up the stairs two at a time. I was excited for her to meet my best friend and Carmen. My parents on the other hand, I was a little nervous about. I'd only brought one girl home before and it was a disaster. My father disliked her and my mother, well let's just say she never wanted her back in her home ever again.

But Amy was completely different than that other girl, so I was hoping they'd love her. If not it was their loss because she was my soulmate and she wasn't going anywhere.

Getting changed, I rushed back downstairs to find Aviel was there.

"Hey man, how's it going?"

He gave me a smile. "Oh, you know, it's going. I think I may have found the next Quira, but I'm not sure. Hopefully I'll know in the next couple of days. Until then we wait. Nice job on the Aark angels. I knew you guys had it in you. When are you going out again?"

I gave him a confused look. "No one said we were going back out. So, I have no idea."

He nodded. "I'll talk to Jodson and see what the plans are and get back to you on that. I heard you cooked tonight, is there any leftover?"

I smiled and nodded. "It's in the fridge."

Amy came over to me and I tucked her to my side, just like Aviel was doing with Violet. It was a protective gesture, but I didn't care. I'd kill anyone who thought to harm Amy in any way. That was why I thought it was best if I stayed away from their self-defense classes. I'd probably try to kill whoever was teaching them. That wouldn't be a good thing.

Chapter Fifty-Seven

I quickly texted Erik to let him know we were coming. Since he and Carmen were getting closer, I didn't want to pop in on something I really didn't want to see. Amy called for Kemuel and he took us to the house Erik and Carmen were at.

It took no time at all for Amy and Carmen to become friends. They were similar and had a lot of the same interests. When they started talking about shopping, I tuned out their conversation.

"So, soulmates huh? That's … unexpected," Erik said.

I laughed at the look on his face. "Trust me, I wasn't prepared for something like that at all. I mean we only met two days ago, and I don't want to be away from her."

"That's just a little strange you know."

"Oh, I know. It's downright weird, but I wouldn't change it."

"I'm not trying to be a dick about this, but what do you actually know about her?"

I knew he was referring to Evangeline. "Point taken, but she's not a Dark Angel, or even a half-angel, just a human woman. She's Violet's best friend and constantly surrounded by the good angels. She's been well vouched for. Do I know a lot about her? No, but I'm really looking forward to finding out."

"Fair enough, just looking out for you."

"I know, and I appreciate it, brother."

We stayed there for hours and it was late when Kemuel took us back to the house. It was dark and quiet, so I assumed everyone was asleep. I led Amy to my bedroom because there was no way I was letting her sleep another night without me. I opened the bedroom door and stopped without turning on a light. Something wasn't right.

Immediately I pushed Amy behind me. "Stay here," I whispered. Taking another step into the room, I felt movement to my right and automatically ducked. Someone was in here with me and I was going to do everything in my power to protect Amy.

I did a roundhouse and felt my leg connect with something that I hoped was my attacker. Moving in that direction a fist connected with my jaw. I staggered back, but didn't let my guard down. Suddenly, a light came on and I could see. I didn't know the man in my room but that didn't matter. He was going down.

Attacking him, I used everything I'd been learning against him. He fought back. We both landed kicks and punches, but I finally got the upper hand. I pinned him to the ground in a hold I knew he couldn't get out of.

"Who are you?" I demanded. Then I heard clapping coming from the hallway.

"Well done," Aviel said as he walked into the bedroom.

"What the fuck is going on?" I asked.

"You can let him up now Luca. This was a test and you passed with flying colors."

"A test?" I was confused but let the guy go.

"Nice fight," he said, and left the room, limping a little and holding his arm.

"We wanted to know what would happen when you walked into a situation where you didn't know you were going to have to fight someone. How come you didn't use your angel skills?"

"I knew he wasn't a Dark Angel, so that made him human," I told him.

"Very good. I'm impressed."

Violet looked at me with a smile. "Don't feel bad, they did it to me too."

Aviel grinned at her. "And she also did a wonderful job."

"Can you apologize to him again," Violet said. "I didn't mean to break his arm."

Amy's mouth fell open, I smiled and Aviel laughed.

"He knew the risks," Aviel told her.

I looked around the room, it was a disaster. "Is there somewhere else I can stay for the night? I don't feel like cleaning this up right now."

With a wave of his hand, Aviel had the room straightened up in a flash.

"Wow," Amy said in awe. "Can you do that?"

"Afraid not," I told her. "Thanks, Aviel."

Violet took Aviel's hand. "That's our cue to leave. Have a good night you two."

"Are you okay?" I asked Amy.

"Yeah, that was pretty hot by the way."

I chucked. "That's probably the first fight I've been in since elementary school. Do you mind if I take a quick shower?"

"Not at all. I'll just go get my bag if that's okay?"

"Yes. I want you here with me."

She grinned and left the bedroom. I went to the attached bathroom and got into the shower. The hot water felt amazing. I was so focused on the water I didn't hear the bathroom door open and close, so it was a complete surprise when Amy stepped into the shower.

All I could do was stare. This was the first time I was seeing her naked and it was a sight to behold. She had curves in all the right places, and I wanted to touch every single part of her.

She giggled and I realized I was still staring at her. "You're beautiful," I told her. "Come here."

Amy closed the distance between us, and I started kissing her. At first, it was soft and slow, but an urgency took over that I couldn't ignore. Our hands were everywhere and the feel of her pressed against me was something I'd never forget. Shutting off the shower I wrapped her in a towel. She laughed as I picked her up and carried her to the bed.

As she opened her towel, I found myself staring again. I knew right then I would never tire of the sight of her. I crawled onto the bed and moved so that I was over the top of her. Starting with her lips I kissed my way down her body. The sounds she was making were driving me crazy.

"Amy, I want to go slow and take my time, but I don't think I can right now."

She grinned. "I can't either."

Moving faster than a normal human, I got a condom on and was back to her. I watched as her legs fell open and I groaned. Positioning myself at her entrance, I slowly worked my way in. When I was in as far as I could go, I had to take a moment to breathe, but then she wiggled, and I couldn't wait anymore.

Never in my life had I fit so well with a woman. We moved in perfect sync with each other, almost like we knew what the other was thinking. I knew I couldn't last as long as I wanted, but I had a feeling Amy couldn't either. We came at the same time and I'm sure I felt the earth move.

"Wow," Amy said after a few moments. "I can't even describe how incredible that was."

"I know," I said. "It was amazing."

I disposed of the condom and pulled Amy into my chest. I knew in that instant that my life had changed forever, and I was totally okay with it.

Chapter Fifty-Eight

Waking up the next morning with Amy lying on my chest was the best thing ever. I rubbed her back with my thumb enjoying the moment. I didn't want to wake her up, but my body was saying other things.

I rolled over so I was facing her and brought her leg over mine and placed myself at her center. I slowly enter her while kissing her neck. Hearing her groan as she shifted herself to where I was almost all the way inside her. I took that as my permission and began to move inside her. I still couldn't believe how perfect I fit inside her.

"If you go any slower, you'll force me to take matters into my own hands."

I chuckled at her and did as she wished. I went faster and harder. This time I was going to make sure she came more than just once. Last night was too much for the both of us. But today was going to be different.

I knew when she was about to come. Her body arched and tightened around me almost causing me to lose it myself. The sound of Amy screaming my name just made me go harder until she came again. This time I couldn't hold back. I came with her. There was just something about her that made me give her what she wanted.

I held her in my arms not wanting to pull out just yet. If only we could stay this way for the rest of the day, I'd be happy, but training didn't wait for anyone. In order to have a life without danger around every corner, I needed to rid this world of Lucifer. That meant training until that day came to protect Amy and the rest of the people I love.

"As much as I wish we could stay in bed all day, we need to get up before they drag us out of here naked and all," I told her. Even though I said the words my arms refused to remove themselves from her.

She snuggled in closer to me. "Just a few more minutes, please. I don't want to deal with the real world right now."

I brought her in as close as I could and just held her. "Me either." The world could wait a few more minutes. That was, until there was a knock on the door. We both groaned.

"Who is it?"

"We're being summoned to the training room. All of us." We heard Violet say on the other side of the door.

"Give us twenty minutes. We need to shower."

"You've got ten."

Crap. I jumped out of bed, ran to the bathroom, and turned the shower on. I took the fastest shower known to mankind. I knew Amy needed to shower as well and it would be best if we took separate showers if we wanted to make it there on time. As soon as I got out, I called out to Amy. "The shower is all yours love." I grabbed a towel and walked out to find her standing there butt ass naked.

"You didn't wait for me?"

I swallowed hard. "I figured it would be best not to shower together. If we want to make it there in time."

She started to pout. "I see. I'll be out in a few minutes."

As she walked past me, I grabbed her wrist and brought her to me. I kissed her slowly, wrapping my hand into her long blonde hair. When I pulled away, she wasn't pouting anymore. She had that hungry look in her eyes matching my own. I didn't know how we were going to get through this in one piece.

"Go take your shower love, I'll wait for you."

It took everything in me to let her go. I was going to have to talk to Aviel to figure out how to deal with this. There had to be a balance. He and Violet seem to have found it, somehow. Not that I was complaining that I wanted to be with her every second of the day, but the world needed me, too. I couldn't let them both down, I'd rather die than to let that happen.

I heard the water turn off and I realized I hadn't even gotten dressed yet. I went over to the dresser, grabbed a shirt and jeans, and put them on. I didn't even bother with boxers. Grabbing a pair of socks, I walked over to where my shoes were and picked them up.

Amy walked out fully dressed and I was thankful for that. If she would have come out naked, there was no way we were going to remotely be there in time. Putting my shoes on, I got up and picked her up and tossed her over my shoulder using my angel speed to make it there on time. Her laughter only made me laugh too.

We made it there with seconds to spare. I put her down and as I did, I was attacked from behind. It took me a split second to get my bearings back to attack back. This was no human; I could feel she was an angel, one, I had never met before. I gave her all I got. Getting more hits in than I thought I could. I caught her off guard with a lower round kick. She fell flat on her back and I didn't hesitate to put my foot on her neck to stop her. This time there was no clapping.

"No, stop, don't hurt her!" I hear Tristan yell.

I turned in his direction and scowled at him. "She attacked me."

When he got closer, he looked between the both of us. "I'm sure she can explain. Please let her up."

I took my foot off her neck and let her get to her feet. She gave Tristan a sheepish look before she faced me again. "I'm sorry, I thought you were hurting her. I didn't know she was your soulmate until after I attacked you and after that, I was trying to protect myself. Your training is doing you well."

I gave her a look of disbelief. "Why would I be hurting any woman or anyone that didn't deserve it?"

I needed to know what was going on in this woman's head for her to think I would be that kind of man.

"I don't know. I saw her over your shoulder and I just thought she was here against her will."

"We were given a time limit to be here and we were running late."

Amy came over to my side and I tucked her close to me. "I'm sorry, but who are you?" Amy asked.

"I'm Cassandra Daye, I'm Tristan's girlfriend. It's nice to finally meet you, Amy. Tristan has told me so much about you and Violet. I can't wait to meet her."

Amy stared at her before she said, "It's nice to meet you too. We weren't expecting anyone to be here today."

"I asked Tristan to bring me. I wanted to be here when they told you the good news."

Violet and the rest of the angels walked in at that moment. We all turned to them and I was the one to ask. "What is the good news?"

Chapter Fifty-Nine

It was Jodson that spoke. "Since there are still ten Quira we need to find and they'll all have people that'll need protecting, we've been working on a central location that will be safe for everyone. The good news is that it's finally finished. Its state of the art and big enough to hold everyone easily. But most importantly, it's well off the radar from humans and heavily protected from Dark Angels."

"Wow," I said. "Where is it located?"

"In the United States, in the middle of nowhere in Wyoming," Jodson said.

"When do we leave?" Violet asked.

"As soon as possible. We'll get your friends and family, Luca. Violet, your aunt will come with us when you're ready."

"I'm excited to see it," Amy said.

Jodson smiled. "We think you'll like it. I suggest you go pack your things. Just call one of us when you're ready to go."

Every angel except Aviel popped out. The rest of us went back to the house and started packing.

Within the hour we were all ready. Aviel had already taken Aunt Milana and Violet. Finally, he took me and Amy.

I was shocked when we got there. It looked like we were standing in a hotel lobby. There was a TV, coffee bar and several chairs and couches. Amy and Violet were doing the same thing I was, staring.

Violet let out a whistle. "Holy shit. This place is swanky."

Aviel laughed. "Let me show you to our room," he said.

We walked over to an elevator, yes, an elevator. We got in and I saw the buttons said Main, 1, 2, 3.

"The main floor holds the kitchen and dining area. There's the lounging area that we were just in, a pool, a couple of offices and of course the training room. Each upper floor has ten rooms. The first floor is for the Quira and the top two floors are for friends and family."

Violet smacked his arm. "I can't believe you kept this from me."

He chuckled. "We've all kept it a secret until it was ready."

The elevator dinged and we stepped out. It certainly looked like a high-end hotel.

"Violet and I will be in room eleven and you two will be across the hall in room twelve."

I smiled. "And the next Quira we find will be in room thirteen I assume."

"Yes," Aviel said. "Here are a couple of keys." He handed them to Amy. "Go have a look."

She unlocked the door and once again I was shocked. It wasn't just a room but like a small apartment, complete with a living room, bathroom, bedroom, and balcony.

"I could live here forever," Amy said with a grin.

The colors of the room were mostly blue and grey with a few splashes of red. "I agree," I told her.

It didn't take long for Violet to find her way to our room. The girls gushed about how nice everything was. At Violet's insistence, we went to see their room. It was a mirror image of ours except it was mostly green and white.

After that, we had to go check out the main floor. None of us had eaten breakfast yet so we decided to go to the dining area. I was expecting a few tables, but it was more like a restaurant.

Aviel told us to pick a table. I think it was the angel in us that was drawn to the outdoors, so we laughed when Violet and I went straight to a table that was next to the huge picture windows that faced the mountains. Even though it was spring in Wyoming, there was still some snow on the ground. It was beautiful.

"How does this work?" Amy asked Aviel, and gestured to the room. "This looks more like a restaurant than anything else."

"There is someone in the kitchen twenty-four hours a day. They can pretty much make anything you want, but there are specials each day and a set menu as well." He pointed to a place close to what I assumed was the kitchen. "Over there is where we can help ourselves to drinks. They have coffee, juice, and any number of other things like sodas and iced tea. The menus are at each table and the special will be listed there as well. When you know what you want just to enter it on the touch screen station over there. Make sure you put in the table number, so they know who's ordering what. They'll call out the table number when the food is ready."

"Wow," Amy said. "This is so cool."

"And," Aviel said, "anytime you want to cook your own food the kitchen is open to you."

All four of us grabbed a menu and decided on what we wanted. It was pretty simple actually. The ordering system allowed you to add anything you wanted to your food or take out what you didn't want. I ended up with bacon, eggs, and toast, while Amy got waffles with strawberries and whipped cream.

When our food was ready, we picked it up. Everything looked amazing. Twenty minutes later, we were finished and cleared our dishes.

The girls wanted to see the rest of the place, so we started wandering. Aviel had to go to Heaven so that just left the three of us.

The pool was bigger than most hotel pools and even had a hot tub. I loved swimming, so I would definitely be checking that out later.

Next, was the training room. Violet and I both stopped when we walked in. It was huge, at least the size of a high school gym if not bigger. Half of the room was covered in padded mats that would be used for hand-to-hand combat training. There were numerous weight machines as well as treadmills and elliptical trainers.

"This is amazing," Violet said. "I can't wait to get started in here. There's plenty of room for the other ten Quira to train. It's unbelievable how quickly the angels were able to pull this off."

"I have a feeling nothing is off-limits when you can get in and out of Heaven at will."

Since we weren't sure when someone was going to show up for training, we left the training center and headed back up to our rooms.

Amy stopped us before either Violet, or I could open our doors. "So, this place is awesome and all, but what are we supposed to do for the rest of the day? I don't see any of the angels around."

"Aviel said we could take the day off," Violet said. "I think most of them are trying to find the other Quira. I have a feeling things are getting worse in Heaven with Lucifer's followers."

"So, then what are you going to do for the rest of the day?" Amy asked Violet.

"I think I'll hang out with Aunt Milana. We haven't really had a chance to do that and I miss her." Violet grinned. "I already know what you two are going to do. Just keep it confined to your room please."

Amy grinned and I did my best to stifle a laugh. I have to admit that even with seeing this place all I could think about was getting her naked again. I just hoped we weren't interrupted this time.

Chapter Sixty

After Violet took off, I took the opportunity to steal the kiss I'd been dying to give Amy. It had only been a few hours, but those few hours have felt like years. When we pulled away, we were both breathing heavily as I placed my forehead against hers still holding her.

"I'll never stop wanting to do that," I whispered to her.

She unwrapped her arms from around my neck, grabbed my hands and tugged me to the elevator. I was a little confused since I was sure we were headed back to our room.

"Where are we going?"

"I don't know about you, but I want to check out that hot tub," she said, with a wink.

"You naughty, naughty girl." I pulled her to me as the doors opened. We walked in kissing each other. I couldn't keep my hands off of her or my mouth for that matter.

When the doors closed, I picked her up and pushed her up against the elevator wall. If I had my way, I would take her right here, but I would never disrespect her like that. I wasn't that kind of man and never would be.

"If you don't stop, you will force me to do things I've never done before. Like have sex in an elevator," she said breathlessly.

I chuckled at her and let her down even when I didn't want to. I didn't release her though. Just as I was about to say something the doors opened. I tugged on her hand and pulled her down the hall to the pool. I stopped in front of the locker rooms. "Why don't you go change while I go lock the doors, so we aren't interrupted."

She gave me a shy smile before she kissed my cheek and raced into the women's locker room. I made sure the main door was locked and then headed over to the hot tub where I peeled off my clothes. Climbing into the hot water naked was exhilarating. I slowly sank down until my whole body was under the water. I let out a slow sigh. I hadn't realized how wound up I'd been lately.

"If that feels good, I know what will make you feel even better."

I looked up to see Amy standing there on full display and my body responded instantly.

"I think you may be right, but I'd have to find out to be sure."

She quirked her eyebrows at me. "Is that so?" she asked, as she strutted over to me.

I watched her with lust-filled eyes. I'd be lying if I didn't want her to hurry her fine ass up and get in here.

"That's so."

She took her sweet ass time getting into the water and it was killing me. I couldn't take it any longer and went to her. Grabbing her, I brought her to me, and I claimed her lips. I couldn't resist her taste.

She was the one who pulled back and grabbed my manhood in her hands and all I could do was moan. When she went under the water, I knew I was in trouble. The moment I felt her mouth on my cock, my knees almost buckled on me. It took everything in me to keep standing there.

After a few more seconds, I couldn't take any longer, I pulled her up. I moved us over to the edge. I backed her up to it and it was my turn to explore her beautiful body.

Her moans echoed off the walls driving me mad. I knew the moment she couldn't take it anymore. She grabbed my hair and yanked it so I would look at her.

"If you don't take me right now, I swear to you, you're going to regret it."

I knew she was just saying things because I was driving her just as mad as she was me, but I didn't make her wait any longer.

After our skin was wrinkled and looked like raisins, we finally got out.

"Let's go take a shower before we go back to our room."

I still couldn't believe we were actually living together now. It all felt like a dream. One I didn't want to wake up from. Ever.

"Sounds good to me. I wonder if they do room service. I didn't think to ask earlier."

"I guess we will have to find out. When we're done, I'll call down there. If not, we can order and I"ll go get it for us."

"Have I said how perfect you are?"

I blushed at her words. "No, but thank you"

She wrapped her arms around my neck and looked me in the eyes. "You are perfect for me."

I leaned down and captured her lips, holding her close to me. When I pulled away from her I said. "You are beyond perfect for me. I think it's safe to say that I love you."

She sucked in a deep breath through her teeth. I was afraid I scared her. "I didn't want to say it because I thought I would have scared you off. But I love you too. I've never loved anyone before. But with you, I feel like I can be myself and you won't judge me. I love that feeling. I love knowing I'm the only woman for you."

I chuckled. "You are and will always be the only woman for me. God couldn't have paired me up with a better person."

There was a knock on the door and we both looked that way and back to each other. I grabbed a few towels that sat not far from us and I wrapped her up. I wrapped myself up as I walked to go unlock the door.

I didn't expect to see my father when I opened the door.

"Hey, Dad, what's up?"

He chuckled. "I was wondering if you and Amy would join us for dinner tonight. We haven't really got to know her, and we would like to."

I smiled at him. "Sounds good. Let us get showered and dressed."

He nodded his head. "We will see you soon then."

I watch him walk away. As soon as he was out of sight, I closed the door.

"Looks like we are having dinner with my parents. I hope that is okay."

She smiled at me. "Of course. I want to get to know them. I need to know the people who raised an amazing man."

I smiled at her as I walked back to her. "I guess we better hurry then. You want to take a shower down here or up in the room?"

She looked up at me with a serious look. "I think it would be best if we took our own showers if we don't want to keep your parents waiting."

I chuckled at her. "I think you're right. I'll meet you out here in a few minutes then." I placed a kiss on her cheek and went into the men's locker room.

I took a look around and was impressed. There were a dozen showers, with actual doors and not curtains, on one side. Sinks and bathroom stalls on the other side. Everything was in coals and greys. I walked over to one of the showers and to my surprise they had body wash and shampoo in each stall. I was positive I could get used to this.

Chapter Sixty-One

Dinner with my parents went better than expected. Amy seemed to know exactly what to say that had them constantly laughing and smiling. It was a little strange to see my parents like that with my girlfriend, but I was ecstatic that they seemed to love her almost as much as I did.

The next few days were some of the best of my life. We trained hard, but spending the rest of my time with Amy was incredible. We got to know more about each other, and I didn't think there was a single thing about her that I didn't love.

Today our training angel was Kemuel. We didn't get him very often and he was the toughest of the Protection Angels. Both Violet and I were breathing hard and we'd only been training for an hour.

Amy came running in the training room. I smiled as soon as I saw her but the look on her face had me worried.

"What's wrong?" I asked her.

"I don't know. I was just told to come and get all three of you and tell you to go to conference room one."

The four of us raced there and found Aviel, Jodson, and Tristan waiting for us.

"What's happened?" Violet asked.

"Kylen's been spotted," Aviel said.

"Fuck. Where?" she asked.

"About a hundred and fifty miles from here."

"Double fuck."

I was confused. "Who's Kylen?" I asked.

It was Aviel who answered me. "I can't believe we forgot to tell you about him. Anyway, he's a Dark Angel that's way up there in Lucifer's hierarchy. A few weeks ago, he paid a visit to Violet's office, looking for me. We have no idea how he found her, but it was after that encounter that Violet came to stay at my place. He's powerful and bad news."

Violet turned to face Aviel. "So, what are we going to do about it?"

"He's too close to here, so we'll either have to try and take him out or find a way to lead him in another direction. We can't let any of Lucifer's followers get any hint that this place exists."

"I want in," Violet and I said at the same time.

"No," Aviel said. "He's too dangerous."

"I don't care," Violet said.

"I think they should go," Kemuel said.

Aviel whipped his head around to look at Kemuel. "What? Why?"

"Kylen can't kill them and it would be good for them to see what fighting a powerful Dark Angel is like. There's a reason Violet and Luca were the first two half-angels found. They will be the strongest of their kind and the others will look to them for leadership and guidance. They are going to need all the experience they can get before the others arrive."

I looked around the room and everyone looked a little shocked. That was the most I'd ever heard Kemuel say at one time and from everyone's faces, theirs too.

"Kemuel has spoken, so shall it be," Tristan said.

I thought he was joking until I looked at his face, he was completely serious.

Leaning over to Violet I whispered, "What the hell just happened?"

"I have no idea."

"Okay," Aviel said, "Jodson and I will make the arrangements."

Kemuel and Tristan popped out of the room leaving me, Amy and Violet staring at Aviel.

"Care to explain?" Violet said.

Aviel ran his fingers through his hair, it was such a human gesture I almost laughed. "Kemuel is the Head of the Protection Angels. When he makes a decision, we follow it."

"But you're a Warrior Angel," Violet pointed out.

"But I'm not the head Warrior Angel. The only beings who can refuse to follow what a Head Angel says is another Head Angel, and I'm definitely not one of those."

"Interesting," I said. "Did you know this Violet?"

"Nope. I keep learning new things every day," she said, like she was pissed off.

"I think this is our cue to leave Amy. See you two later."

Taking Amy's hand, we left the conference room and went to the dining room. I felt like eating something sweet. That usually happened after training.

"That was a little intense," Amy said, as we got something to drink.

"The Kylen part or the Kemual part?"

"The Violet part. I think she was actually mad at Aviel."

"It's got to be hard sometimes, for the two of them I mean. Aviel has been an angel for over a thousand years and Violet's only twenty-two. Of course, there are going to be things that he knows and won't even think to tell her."

"I hadn't thought about that, but I guess that's true."

I ordered a brownie sundae with extra whipped cream because I knew Amy would steal most of mine. I was right, when I came back to the table with it Amy ate almost all of the whipped cream and all I could do was smile about it.

****

It was two days before Violet, and I was notified that we were going after Kylen. If I was being honest, I was a little bit scared. From everything I'd learned over the past two days, he was as evil as Lucifer. He had no mercy and hated humans. We definitely needed to be on our game when it came to him.

Aviel and Jodson were coming with us. They weren't to interfere unless a human's life was at stake.

"I don't like this," Aviel said, as we waited for Jodson.

"We'll be fine," Violet said.

I sure hoped she was right.

Tristan and Zyad had been keeping tabs on Kylen and he was still close to the Buffalo area of Wyoming. He didn't seem to be trying to hide, and that kind of rang some alarm bells for me.

Finally, Jodson arrived and they transported us to a location that was far enough away from the town, but close enough that he would sense us.

It didn't take long for him to appear.

"Violet," he said, "we meet again."

"Kylen," she said.

"And who might this be?" he said, looking in my direction.

"The name's Luca, and I'm here to send you back to Hell."

Kylen let out a loud belly laugh. "Oh, this is going to be fun."

And before I knew what happened I was suddenly thrown in the air. I landed on my back about twenty feet away. It's a good thing I was half-angel otherwise that could have caused some serious damage. Shaking my head, I got to my feet and saw Violet in a battle with Kylen. I was amazed at how fast she was, but Kylen was faster. He was landing blow after blow on Violet.

Moving as fast as I could I was there to help her. I jumped on Kylen's back and pulled him off Violet. I knew she had to be hurting so it was my turn to take over.

"You two are nothing," Kylen said with a sneer. "If this is all Heaven's got Lucifer will take over in no time."

Suddenly Kylen's wings were out. They were black with red tips and huge. I knew shit was about to get real. Dark energy orbs were being thrown at both me and Violet and it was all we could do to block them. I missed one, it hit me right in the chest and I felt like I couldn't breathe.

Turning my head, I saw Violet on the ground as well. She was on all fours ,but trying to get up. She was hurt but not giving up. At least I could do the same.

Kismet

I made it to my feet and moved over to Violet. Helping her stand we both created an energy ball and threw it at Kylen. He dodged it easily and laughed.

Reaching out I took Violet's hand. "Together," I said, and she nodded.

We pulled energy to us and were able to form an energy ball that felt different somehow. When we threw it, it moved faster than anything we'd been able to do before. Kylen couldn't get out of the way fast enough and it hit him square in the chest.

"Fuck, that hurt. You'll pay for that."

We were suddenly engulfed in dark light and I felt like I was flying, but then I hit the ground. I couldn't move at first, but slowly the feeling was coming back. Finally, I could turn my head enough to see that Violet was out cold beside me. It looked like Kylen had gone and we were alone.

"Jodson," I said, barely above a whisper.

He appeared, standing over me. I'd never been happier to see him. I heard Aviel next to Violet and I was glad he was here for her.

"Let's get you home," Jodson said, and touched my arm.

Chapter Sixty-Two

Getting back to the headquarters was painful. I laid there trying to move to see if I had any broken bones. It felt like all of them were broken, but I knew they weren't.

Amy came racing to my side. When she touched me, I let out a groan of pain. "Oh My God! What happened?" I was in too much pain to answer her.

Aviel spoke from the other side of me holding Violet in his arms. "Kylen is what happened. I said this was a bad idea. No one ever listens to me. He is too strong for them to take on alone."

"If that's what we'll have to deal with when the time comes, we're all screwed. Unless, you have a plan to up our training," I panted.

I'd never felt this kind of pain before. If that was what it felt like to have your bones melt, then I'd pass the next time.

"Why would Kemuel think this was a good idea?" Amy asked, as she took my hand. I tried to hold in the groan as she did.

"Because I wanted them to know what they were really going up against. They need to train harder and faster. I know you just learned you are Quira, but that doesn't mean you get to slack off. From now on I want your full potential. No more babying you."

I tried to move my head to look at him, but all that caused was pain to shoot through my spine. "How do you plan on getting us healed fast enough to get to training."

He stepped in my line of sight and knelt in front of me. "The healers will be here soon. Until then, try to think about something else. I'm sorry you had to get your ass handed to you for you to realize what you were doing wasn't good enough. From now on I will be taking over the training."

He stood and left to go wherever it was he went. I heard Violet moan from my right.

Amy looked over there and I could see the sadness in her eyes.

"Why the hell do I feel like my bones are melted?" Violet groaned.

"I thought it was just me," I said, trying not to laugh but failed causing more pain to rack through me.

"Save your energies. Once the healers get here, you'll need it," Aviel said

"What do you mean by that?"

"As much pain you are in now you will be in more before you're healed. They need to take the dark energy out of your souls."

"Is that what that fucker did to us?"

"That and other things at the same time."

I didn't even want to know at this point. All I knew was I didn't want to be in any more pain than I already was. This fucking sucked ass. I couldn't believe he took us both out like we were flies on a wall. I'd be damned if that would happen again.

Amy leaned down and gently kissed my cheek. "I'll be with you the whole time."

I gave her a small smile. "I know you will be, love. Thank you."

I was about to close my eyes when two new angels popped in. One came over to me and the other to Violet. "We need to move them to their beds." The one in front one me said.

He lifted me up with ease, but the pain that shot through me had me yelling out.

I could hear Amy screaming at the angel to stop hurting me. When the spots finally disappeared from my vision, I was lying on our bed with Amy next to me.

I was sweating and panting from the pain. If I had to go through more pain, I might not make it through.

The angel looked at Amy and said, "I will need you to leave the room. I'm sorry, but I can't have you here as I heal him."

"I'm not going anywhere. I told him I'd be here for him. I don't plan on breaking that."

"It's okay love," I croaked out.

"I don't want to leave you."

"I know, but the faster this is over the faster we can be together." I used the last of my energy speaking to her. I felt my eyelids closing.

The last thing I heard her say was "You better not hurt him on purpose. I may be only human, but I will find a way to hurt you."

The moment he started, I knew there was no way I was going to survive. The pain had me screaming out and cussing. I would rather be in the pain I was in. I knew it had only been a few seconds, but it seemed like years. Just when I was about to tell him to stop, I could feel the pain ease a little bit at a time, or it could be I was getting used to it.

I felt my mind float away as my consciousness drifted into blackness. I felt peace and blissfulness. Something I didn't think I was ever going to feel again.

****

When I woke up it was daylight out. I turned to see the clock to find Amy lying there sleeping next to me. I scooted over to her and brought her into my arms. I didn't care how stiff my body felt. I was just happy the pain was gone.

I gently kissed her forehead, kissing my way down to her cheek. I captured her lips in a long passionate kiss. It didn't take long before she joined in. Her arms and legs went around me. I pulled away from her with a smile.

"That's how I want to wake up every morning."

She chuckled. "You mean, afternoon?"

I looked at the clock and it said three pm. "How long have I been out?"

"Two days. They said your body and mind needed the rest. I wanted to kick him in the balls when I heard you screaming. It sounded like he was killing you."

I let out a sigh remembering the pain. "To tell you the truth, it felt like it. I don't ever want to go through that again, but I have a feeling we will be going through that more times than I want."

"How are you feeling now?"

"I'm a little stiff, but the pain is gone. I could use a run. You want to join me?"

She laughed. "I could give you something better than a run," she winked at me.

I didn't waste any time making her mine for the rest of the afternoon.

Chapter Sixty-Three

It took two more days for me and Violet to fully recover. As soon as we were fully healed, Kemuel re-started our training. I'd thought Kemuel's training had been tough before, but that was nothing compared to what we had to do now.

We were woken up at seven am, eating breakfast by seven fifteen and warmed up and training by eight am. We had a break at ten am, lunch at twelve-thirty, another break at three-thirty, then we we're finally done for the day at six pm. In one word it was grueling.

Three days into the new training schedule and Violet and I were exhausted. Thankfully the new schedule had us training like that for three days and then a day off. By the end of day three, I felt like my legs were made of lead and my arms were limp spaghetti. I went to bed that night right after training and didn't wake up for over twelve hours.

When I finally opened my eyes, I saw the most beautiful sight, a sleeping Amy. Her long blonde hair was spread out over the pillow and she had the peaceful look of sleep on her face.

As much as I wanted to wake her up with a kiss, I needed a shower before I did anything. Moving slowly out of the bed I walked stiffly to the bathroom. Turning the shower as hot as I could stand it, I got in under the spray. Almost immediately, I started to feel like myself again.

I got dressed and slipped out of the room. Going downstairs I got us coffee and breakfast, then brought it back up to Amy. I set everything down and went over to her.

"Wake up sleepyhead," I whispered in her ear, and then kissed her on the forehead.

"Mmm, you smell good," she said, sleepily.

I chuckled. "I showered. And I brought you coffee and breakfast."

"And that's why I love you."

I laughed. "Come on, get up beautiful. We get to spend the whole day together."

That made her smile and get out of bed. She quickly used the bathroom and joined me in the living room. Amy smelled her coffee before she took a drink. I'd quickly learned that she didn't do much until she had her first coffee of the day.

After we ate, she had a shower and got ready. I needed fresh air, so we decided to go for a walk. Violet had told me Amy wasn't the outdoorsy type but so far, she hadn't complained when I needed to get outside.

The Quira headquarters were on hundreds of acres and kind of like a compound with security you couldn't see. I don't know how the angels kept it hidden from Lucifer's followers, but we were told there was no way they'd ever get in.

"It's beautiful here," Amy said. "A little cold, but certainly pretty."

I had to agree. There were mountains in the distance and the sky was clear and blue.

"Just think," I said, "when it warms up, we can bring a blanket and make love out in the open."

She giggled. "We'll see about that. I'm not sure I want to be surrounded by insects while I'm naked."

"Good point. But now all I can think about is you naked. Want to head back?"

"Oh God yes."

We walked back to the main building in half the time it took us to walk out there. I felt like a teenager by the time we got into the elevator. It took me three tries to open the door to our room. As soon as the door was closed, we started losing clothing and for the next hour, I showed her how much I missed her the last three days.

****

The next morning, it was back to the training room. Kemuel was waiting for us and so was an angel I'd never seen before. She looked too beautiful to be fierce, but I knew that Kemuel wouldn't bring anyone who wasn't capable of kicking our asses.

"Violet, Luca, this is Myrna," Kemuel said. "She's an expert in shielding. In other words, stopping the dark energy orbs from hitting you."

I groaned. "I have a feeling this is going to be a painful day."

"Good thing Aviel's in Heaven today," Violet said.

"Let's get started," Kemuel said, leaving no room for argument.

Myrna started by telling us the basics of shielding. The theory was that you draw energy to you and create a "shield" around you. Sounded easy enough, right?

An hour later, Violet and I were both panting. Shielding was way harder than I thought it was going to be. It was ten times harder than creating an energy orb.

We were both exhausted, so Kemuel stopped the training to let us take a break. Someone brought us juice and chocolate. It was surprising how much that helped us to get our energy back. Ten minutes later we were back at it.

By the end of the day, we were both able to create a shield around us but not sustain it when hit with an energy ball. I was never so glad to be done with training as when we walked out of the training room. We went straight to the dining room.

"Fuck," Violet said, "I feel like I've been hit by a truck."

"No shit. That was intense."

"What was intense," Amy asked, joining us at our table.

"We were learning how to shield against the energy that might be thrown at us."

"That doesn't sound so bad," she said.

"I think it's the hardest thing we've had to learn."

"I agree," Violet said. "What did you do today?"

"I've actually started learning how to paint."

"Really?" I said. "I didn't know that."

Amy smiled. "I just started today. It was getting pretty boring just hanging out all day."

"I'm sorry love, I should have thought about that."

"It's no big deal, really. You've kind of been a little preoccupied."

"That's no excuse. Tell me about your painting." I saw Violet smile at us as we listened to Amy tell her hilarious first time attempting to paint.

Chapter Sixty-Four

Two weeks had gone by and both Violet and I had learned how to shield ourselves without thinking. We even got a few hits in on Kemuel, but I think he let us just to make us feel good. We're still getting our asses handed to us, just not as bad.

Amy had finally painted something she was proud of and she'd been spending a lot of time with my parents, Erik and Carmen. I was beyond happy they all loved each other. My mother kept hinting about a wedding. It wasn't that I didn't want one, it was just I didn't know if Amy wanted to get married. She never talked about it. Didn't most girls gush over stuff like that? And technically we'd only known each other a few weeks which seemed way too soon to think about getting married, even for soulmates. I was also too chicken to ask her about it. I didn't want to upset her.

Maybe I'd ask Violet for advice. She would know, wouldn't she? Why are women so complicated to read?

"Hey babe," Amy said. "I was just looking for you. I was wondering if you wanted to hang out with Erik and Carmen tonight since this is your day off."

She walked into my arms and I held her tight. "Only if I get you to myself until then," I said with a growl.

She looked up at me with that smile of hers that made my heart beat faster. "You know it."

I leaned down and kissed her deeply. I'd missed her a lot. As much as I know we need the training, I hated that it took me away from her. I didn't know how Violet and Aviel did it. It was driving me crazy. The only thing that kept me going was that I knew the better I was, the better I could protect her.

I pulled away from her and picked her up. "Do you know how much you drive me insane, woman?"

She kissed me again and laughed. "Just as much as you do me. What do you want to do until we meet up with them?"

"I can think of a few things we can do. All of them involve getting naked."

She laughed my favorite laugh. "I think I like that idea." She hopped down and took my hand.

I led her to the swimming pool. After my workouts, I loved to take a dip. I found out that Amy was a fish as well. She loved the water almost as much as I did.

Opening the door for her, I turned and locked it behind me, so no one would come in. We both love to swim naked, being in a suit constricted us too much.

We didn't even bother changing in the locker rooms anymore. We took our clothes off where we were. Amy folded them and placed them on the chair while I grabbed us some towels. When I got back, she was already swimming laps around in the pool.

I stood there and watched her. She truly looked like a mermaid swimming. Her strokes were perfect along with her timing. "My little mermaid."

She stopped in the middle of the pool and smiled up at me. "Are you going to join me or are you going to tease me?"

I looked down at myself and smiled. "I think I'm going to tease you then please you, if that is alright with you."

She swam to the side of the pool closest to me. "You better be pleasing me a lot sooner than later."

I knelt down in front of her and captured her face in my hand. "Oh love, I will be doing a lot more pleasing sooner rather than later…"

I didn't get to finish my sentence when she yanked me into the pool. I came up from under the water spitting and sputtering. "Oh, you're going to get it now, woman."

She squealed and started to swim away from me. Before she got too far, I grabbed her by the ankle and dragged her back towards me. "Where do you think you're going, love?"

She couldn't stop laughing as I brought her into my arms. I didn't give her time to recover as I slid inside her in one slow movement. She let out a moan that drove me crazy. I moved faster inside her, causing her to moan even louder. I couldn't help it. The sound of her moans did something to me. Like it was filling me somehow. Being with her like this completed me in more ways than one.

****

"I was wondering if you guys were going to show up or not," Carmen said, winking as she opened the door for us a few hours later.

"What can I say, I only get to spend every fourth day with her." I smiled at her

She shook her head at me. "I swear you've become a horn dog since you met her."

I looked at Amy and gave her a goofy smile and wiggled my eyebrows at her. She smacked me in the chest, and I let out a laugh.

"Can we not talk about our sex life please?" she asked, as a blush caressed her face.

I pulled her into my arms and walked us inside. "As you wish my love, as you wish."

"What's the plan tonight?" I asked

Erik came out of the bedroom and patted my shoulder. "Hey man, I thought I heard you two. Carmen asked Tristan to get a game called Battle of the Sexes."

I shook my head at him. "I have a feeling we're going to lose tonight, regardless of whatever we do."

"I get the same feeling man. I think we're both screwed."

"Hey now, I'm standing right here," Amy said

I gave her a squeeze. "I couldn't forget even if I wanted to, love." I kissed the top of her head and smacked her ass as I released her.

She turned to face me and hit me in the chest. "You better stop teasing me if you don't plan on pleasing me," she said, as she walked away to find Carmen.

I stared after her dumbfounded. Wasn't she the one who didn't want to talk about our sex life in front of people?

"Did she just say that?" Erik asked.

I turned to face him and nodded. "Yes, yes she did. Sometimes that woman confuses the hell out of me."

"What do you mean by that?"

"When we got here, she got embarrassed about talking about our sex life, but just then…"

"Women are complicated. I try to just go with the flow. Should we go see what they're up to?"

I nodded and gestured for him to lead the way. "We might as well see what we're going to be doing for the night."

Chapter Sixty-Five

It turned out that Battle of the Sexes was a board game that pitted the men against the women by asking questions the other sex should know. It was hilarious, especially since us guys were winning. Who knew Erik knew so much about the opposite sex?

We were only a couple of questions away from the win when Tristan popped into the room.

"Sorry to interrupt, but Luca is needed."

I nodded as I stood and put my hand on his arm. We were instantly transported to a place I didn't recognize.

"What's going on?" I asked. "And where's Violet?"

"I'm right here," she said from behind me. "There's a semi powerful Dark Angel in that building." She pointed across the street. "You and I are to take care of her."

"Like right now? It's broad daylight. Where are we anyway?"

"Tokyo," Tristan said. "And it's up to you and Violet how you handle her. Just remember, you don't want to cause a scene."

Then he was gone.

"Angels," I muttered. "So, what do we know?"

"Not much," Violet said.

"That's awesome," I said. The sarcasm was clear.

"We're not always going to be able to rely on the angels Luca. You and I need to step up if we're going to lead the Quira."

"You're right. Okay, so we need a plan. They can sense us like we can sense them, so how do we find out what we're dealing with in there?"

"We do exactly what you just said. Remember when we were fighting Kylen at the end and we joined hands." I nodded. "I think we were able to combine our energies a little and create something more powerful than each of us alone. Maybe we should try that and see what we can sense in the building."

"I'm willing to try anything," I told her.

She reached out to me and I took her hand. Last time we were desperate to survive so I didn't really pay attention, but this time as our hands joined, I felt a small spark, like static. Violet looked at me and I could tell she felt the same thing.

Along with shielding, we'd been working on sensing other angels. We both focused on that and directed it towards the industrial-looking building.

Almost immediately, we could sense the Dark Angel we were told was in there, but I felt something else I couldn't really explain.

"What is that?" I asked Violet

"I don't know. I can feel the dark presence is strong, but the other one is different. It's not another Dark Angel and it's like the signal is weak, hard to detect. I don't really know how to explain it."

"I get it because that's what I feel too."

The realization hit us at the same time.

"You don't think it could be a Quira?" Violet asked.

"I think that's exactly what it is, and we can't let the Dark Angels keep them."

Without another thought, we raced towards the building. The door was unlocked so we went in. Sitting in the middle of the room was a woman around our age with blue spikey hair. She was gagged and tied to a chair.

"Took you long enough," a voice said from behind us, and suddenly Violet and I were thrown through the air.

I landed in a way that I kept rolling and popped up onto my feet. Violet did the same thing beside me, but we didn't see the angel.

I looked at Violet. "You go get the girl and I'll keep watch."

She nodded and started slowly walking over to the woman. She was almost to her when she ran into some kind of invisible barrier. As she felt for a way around it, I felt the Dark Angel behind me. I ducked just in time to see an energy orb fly over my head. I shot one back, but she was gone.

"I can't get through this," Violet yelled. I could hear the desperation in her voice. "I'm going to call …"

Her words were cut off as she started dodging energy balls. I looked for the source and saw the Dark Angel on a second-floor walkway. I sent an energy orb in her direction hoping she'd focus on me and not Violet. It worked, a little too well. Now I was the one dodging the dark energy.

"Violet," I yelled. "We need to take her out, like yesterday."

Violet ran for cover and started throwing energy at the Dark Angel, but the angel was fast and was able to avoid everything we threw at her. Then we lost sight of her.

"Fuck!" I yelled. "We need to take out whatever is around the woman and get the fuck out of here. I've never seen an angel move as fast as this one. Keep your eyes open."

Violet nodded and we split up. She went back to the invisible wall and I went in search of the Dark Angel. Neither one of us got far. A bay door opened and about twenty humans ran in and headed straight for us.

They looked like an angry mob. Some had baseball bats and pipes, while a few others had guns. I think I even saw a sword, but there wasn't time to think before the fight was on.

Fighting humans was easier but ten at once was no picnic. I also didn't want to kill any of them so that made it a little harder. I focused on the ones with the guns first. I wasn't sure if our shields would stop a bullet and I didn't want to find out right now.

I took the first three out and the rest seemed a little less eager to fight, but they didn't leave. I sent weak energy orbs at the next two and knocked them unconscious.

I was hit in the side with something heavy from behind. I turned around to see a woman with a baseball bat. She swung at me again and easily took it away from her. I sent her flying across the room just as two more came at me. They were like flies that wouldn't leave you alone. I'd finally had enough and sent a wave of energy out that took care of the remaining humans in front of me. I looked over to see Violet was finishing with the last one that had attacked her.

We both turned around at the same time and saw that the chair was empty. We'd lost the woman. Shit.

Chapter Sixty-Six

I paced the floor of our suite waiting for someone to come up with an answer. There was no way that angel was a lower level Dark Angel. She moved way too damn fast and knew how to get away from us too easily.

"I know you two are upset you lost one of the Quira. We will find her again. It may take me some time to do it, but I promise I will find her," Aviel said, as he was holding an upset Violet.

I stopped my pacing and faced him. "This is my fault. I should have been paying more attention to the Quira."

"If anyone is to blame it's me. I should have known the Quira was in there," Aviel said, shaking his head.

"Okay, enough of this," Amy said as she came over to me. "We're not going to find her by taking blame."

I took her into my arms. I needed her touch more than ever right now. "You're right. What's the plan on getting her back?"

Aviel released Violet and kissed her. "I go to Heaven and track her. Let's hope her angel side has shown enough for me to pinpoint her."

"What do you want us to do?" Violet asked, in a small voice.

"I want you two to stay here and train. Tell Jodson to amp up the training."

Before I could say a word, he was gone.

"I really hate it when he does that," Violet said, with a bite. "He always does that when he doesn't want to argue with me. He knows I'd rather be out looking for her than training."

She came over to us and I placed an arm over her shoulder. "I know the feeling. Most of the time I wish we could do that. It would make fighting so much easier."

Violet let out a laugh. "Can you imagine how much fun that would be?"

I gave her a smile. "Yeah, I can. Even if we had wings, that would be awesome, too."

Being half-angel sometimes sucked. We only get a small part of the angel and not the good parts.

"Let's say we go take a swim. I need to get these knots out of my back before I even think about training." I said, as I started to lead the women to the door.

"You know I'm down for a swim," Amy piped in.

"I don't know. I'm not a water baby like you two. I could use a good soak in the hot tub though."

"Then it's settled. We'll meet you down there. Our suits are already down there."

Violet nodded her head and went to her room across from ours. Amy and I headed to the pool.

Once we got into the elevator, I took Amy into my arms again and kissed her. When I pulled away, I placed my forehead on hers. "I feel like such a failure at every turn."

She pulled away to look at me. "You're not a failure. All of this was thrown in your lap. It's not like you were trained from the time you were born. You both are doing the best you can with what you have. Don't do this to yourself."

I couldn't help the feeling that coursed through me. We let that poor woman get taken away by the Dark Angels. Who knew what the hell they were doing to her.

"I can't help it, love. All I can see is them torturing her."

She wrapped her arms around my waist. "Don't think about that. I think they're keeping her to get to the two of you. They want you two to go after her alone."

"What makes you think that?"

"Think about it. They know the angels are training you and drop you off and are always close by. They also know we are going to do everything in our power to find her. What they want is for you and

Violet to find her yourself. But it would be a suicide mission. I don't want you to do it."

I let her words sink in before I spoke again. "I think you're right. It all makes sense when you put it that way. She was baiting us to follow her this whole time. They know we can sense each other."

"Please tell me you aren't going to go after her alone?"

The doors opened and I stepped out and held out my hand for her to take. "I would never risk my life on purpose. Not if it meant I would lose you. But I am going to come up with a plan that would make those assholes think we're alone. I just need time."

We walked into the pool area and went to the locker rooms to change. The whole time my mind was racing with ideas, but none of them were good enough. What I told Amy was true, I would never do something that would risk my life or Violet's for that matter.

I walked back out to see Amy and Violet already in the hot tub laughing about something.

"Am I privileged enough to know what the two of you were laughing about?"

They both looked up at me with smiles on their faces. "Oh, I don't know. What do you think Amy, is he worthy enough to know?"

"I don't know, I think he has to prove he's worthy enough."

I couldn't help the smile that formed on my face. That was, until Aviel burst through the doors.

"We need to go now! I found her and it doesn't look good. Get dressed and meet me by the front doors."

He left us there, staring at where he'd just been standing. I was the first to start moving. "Come on Violet. We need to get dressed."

I took off to the locker room and yanked off my trunks and got dressed in record time. By the time I got out of the locker room, Violet was hopping out of the locker room trying to put her leg into her pants. I looked the other way until I knew she was fully dressed.

"Alright let's go."

We raced out of the pool and down the hallway. When we got to the main lobby we skidded to a stop in front of the front doors and waited for the plan.

Aviel and Tristan turned in our direction. "This isn't going to be easy. She's surrounded by Dark Angels. I'm calling in everyone to get her. There are humans surrounding the place with high powered weapons. We need to take them out before we can get to her or we won't be able to," Aviel said as he took Violet's hand.

"What about the humans we have? Are they going with us?"

Tristan was the one who answered me. "They're on their way there now to scout things out."

"Let's go get her then. There's no point in waiting around," I said.

Aviel nodded and placed a hand on my shoulder. We ended up in a dark alley in another country, but I couldn't tell you where. At this point I didn't care. I just wanted to get the woman and bring her to safety. That was the only thing on my mind.

I could hear gun fire to my right, and I took off running in that direction with Violet and Aviel on my ass. When I got to the corner, I peeked around it to see if it was clear. There was a man standing there with a gun pointing in the opposite direction. I threw an orb at him to knock him out and took his gun.

Coming back to where Aviel and Violet waited for me, I showed them what I had. "What do we do now? This isn't going to go unnoticed."

"We do what we need to do to get to her," was all Aviel said, before he took off into the mix.

Violet and I followed him without saying a word. I started shooting at anyone who tried to take us out. Violet finally got a gun for herself. We were clearing a path, but it wasn't fast enough.

I looked to my left to see the angels had shown up by the dozens, helping us clear a path faster. Once it was clear, we got to the building and dove in trying to seek shelter from the flying bullets.

I looked down to see I'd been shot in the leg. Violet saw it at the same time, and she rushed over to me. "Oh my God! Is the bullet still in there?"

I looked at the other side and shook my head. "It was a through and through. Find something to stop the bleeding."

If there was any pain, I didn't feel it. Violet was back within seconds and wrapped my leg up. I stood on it and gave her the thumbs up. "Let's go," I whispered.

We both knew to keep our eyes open for anything. There was a door just to the right of us. I nodded to Violet to let her know I was going to open it. When I did, I wasn't expecting to see the woman lying there alone.

I gave Violet a look that said this was a trap and she nodded back to me. I slowly made my way to her with Violet at my back. I kept one eye on the woman and the other on anything that would jump out at us.

We were only a few feet away when ten Dark Angels appeared out of nowhere. I got into my fighting stance with Violet right up against my back. Just as we were about to fight Tristan and Aviel showed up and took us all away.

We found ourselves standing in the Quira compound with the woman lying on the floor.

I spun around looking at the two of them. "What the hell was that?"

"That was getting you three out of dodge to live another day," Tristan said, as he picked up the woman.

"I thought you said it wasn't going to be easy to get her out. Not that I'm saying that wasn't easy because being shot wasn't fun, but that was a lot easier than I thought."

They both look at the blood trailing down my leg. "Shit! We need to get a healer," Aviel said, as he took the makeshift bandage off to look at it.

Now that the adrenaline was over, I felt the pain and it took me to my knees. Before I could say anything, I was picked up by a healer and taken to my room. Amy was already there waiting. When she saw me, she started to freak out. "Amy, love, it's okay. It's not that bad."

"You've been shot. That's bad."

I didn't get to say anything before the healer put me to sleep to heal me. The last thing I thought was why didn't he do this when he was taking the darkness out of me.

To be continued...

Author's Note

Thank you for reading my book. If you enjoyed it, please consider leaving me a review at your favorite retailer. Thank you!
~ Katie Holland & Karen DuBose

About the Author

Hello everyone! I'm so excited to be hanging out with you. Hope you guys are doing great today. First, I wanted to say thank you for having me here. We are going to have some fun today. I hope to get to know you guys as well. Let me tell you a little about myself, so you can get to know me better.

Karen grew up outside of Chicago with her mom, dad and two older brothers. Being the only girl and the baby was hard when your brothers thought it was a good idea to make her the guinea pig. They both were in wrestling and they used her to learn new moves. Fun for them not so much for her. Family means everything to her, and she wouldn't have changed a thing.

She traveled a lot and has finally settled down in a small town in East Tennessee in the mountains. Something about the mountains called to her and still does.

She loves to make her own swag and other gifts. She also loves anything to do with the outdoors.

Her favorite snack is gummy worms and bears. Her favorite drink is a white monster. She says she is a monster before she has one.

Her family is everything to her and they support her 100% with her dream to become a well-known author. She is taking it one step at a time and one book at a time.

She loves to meet her fans at a book signing. To this day she still thinks it's unreal. Like she is going to wake up and the dream will be over.

More books from Karen DuBose

The Elder Series
Black Ruins Forest
Black Ruins Blood
Black Ruins Falls

The Light Realm Series
Untainted Magic
Tainted Magic

The Shady Oaks Series
Wailing Waters
World of Nightmares

****

Where to find Karen DuBose

Fan Page:
https://www.facebook.com/groups/KarensZiloians/
Street Team:
https://www.facebook.com/groups/karensmoonbase/
Amazon:

amazon.com/author/karendubose
Author Page:
https://www.facebook.com/KarenDuBoseAuthor/
Twitter:
https://twitter.com/AuthorKDuBose
Instagram:
https://www.instagram.com/authorkdubose/
BookBub:
https://www.bookbub.com/authors/karen-dubose
MeWe:
https://mewe.com/profile/5ad39562a5f4e53648130b2e
Goodreads:
https://www.goodreads.com/author/show/17000117.Karen_Dubose
Newsletter:
https://mailchi.mp/4222c97d655c/wwwauthorkarendubosecom

About the Author

Katie Holland is the author of Young Adult and Romance novels. If she's not writing you can find her reading, cooking or baking for her family. Her love of writing goes back to elementary school and her love of books goes back even farther than that. She loves seeing new places and enjoying what nature has to offer.

More books from Katie Holland

<u>Young Adult</u>
The Nykara Series
<u>Nykara</u>
<u>Chosen One</u>
<u>Chaos</u>
<u>Believe</u>

Shady Oaks Series
<u>Cursed</u>

<u>Adult Romance</u>
A Slightly Strange Romance
<u>Trapped in a Castle</u>

Bay State University Series
A Mermaid's Kiss
Diving in Deep (Coming Soon

A Coven Queens Novel
Hunting Briar

Children's Stories
The Sneaky Little Kittens

****

Where to find Katie Holland

Facebook Author Page:
https://www.facebook.com/katiehollandbooks/
Facebook Reader Group:
Katie's Books (And Other Awesome Stuff)
https://www.facebook.com/groups/198149120742383/
Instagram:
https://instagram.com/katiehollandauthor/
Twitter:
https://twitter.com/KatieHolland18
Goodreads:
https://www.goodreads.com/author/show/17120174.Katie_Holland
Email:
katiehollandbooks@outlook.com
Amazon Author Page:
https://www.amazon.com/author/katieholland
Website:

https://katiehollandbooks.wixsite.com/website
BookBub:
https://www.bookbub.com/profile/katie-holland
Newsletter:
http://eepurl.com/gOUUkz

About the Publisher

Kingston Publishing offers an affordable way for you to turn your dream into a reality. We offer every service you will ever need to take an idea and publish a story. We are here to help authors make it in the industry. We've been hurt by publishers in the past and we want to provide a positive experience that will keep you coming back to us.

Whether you want a traditional publisher who offers all the amenities a publishing company should or an author who prefers to self-publish, but needs additional help - we are here for you.

Now Accepting Manuscripts!

Please send query letter and manuscript to:

submissions@kingstonpublishing.com

Visit our website at www.kingstonpublishing.com

Lightning Source UK Ltd.
Milton Keynes UK
UKHW050802200820
368544UK00010B/276